My Blood Approves

by
Amanda Hocking

For information:

http://amandahocking.blogspot.com/

My Blood Approves – *Book I*

ISBN 978-1453816721

For Nanny - from whom I learned love and imagination, and who was one of the first people to believe in me

The goose bumps stood all over Jane's shoulder and she stomped her foot, at least partially because of the cold. She'd claim it was only because of her frustration over the line and insist that chain smoking cigarettes kept her warm.

"This is truly infuriating," Jane said, flicking her cigarette to the dampened sidewalk and smashing it with her stilettoed boot.

"Maybe we should just call it a night," I suggested.

Our fake IDs had not been as impressive as Jane's connection had promised, and this would be the third club we'd be turned away from, if we ever managed to make it to the door.

Since we were going out, I had allowed Jane to dress me, so everything was ill-fitting and far too revealing for the Minnesota night. A heavy mist settled over us, but she refused to shiver or admit that any of this fazed her. Her plan was to get crazy drunk and hook up with somebody completely random, and I couldn't reason with her.

"No!" Jane shook her head. "I have a good feeling about this place."

"It's after midnight, Jane." The pair of heels I borrowed from her were damaging my feet, and I shifted my weight to ease the pain.

"I just want to dance and be stupid!" She started whining, making her seem much younger than seventeen so we'd be even less likely to get into the club. "Come on, Alice! This is what being young is all about!"

"I really hope not," I muttered. Waiting in line for hours and getting declined from clubs did not sound like a good time. "We can try again next weekend. I promise. It'll give us more time to find better ID's."

"I don't even have any alcohol." Her expression had gone all pouty, but I knew that she was starting to cave.

"I'm sure we can find some somewhere," I said

Jane could find alcohol the way I found water. She had nothing to complain about. Wherever Jane went, a party was sure to follow.

"Fine." Sighing, she stepped out of line and headed in the direction towards my apartment, away from the bright lights of the clubs and drunken people smoking cigarettes. "But you owe me."

"Why do I owe you?" I demanded.

"For making me leave early."

We'd made it a few feet from the line when I couldn't take it any longer. I stopped and ripped off the borrowed shoes, preferring to walk barefoot on the dirty cement than risk any more blisters. Most likely, I'd get gum or something in a fresh wound and end up with typhoid or rabies, but it still seemed like a better option.

We walked far enough away from the clubs where it started to feel deserted, and two teenage girls walking around in downtown Minneapolis wasn't the safest thing in the world.

"We should get a cab," I suggested.

Jane shook her head, negating cab ideas. We didn't have very much money, so the farther we walked, the shorter the cab ride would be. I lived by Loring Park, which really wasn't that far from where we were, but it still wasn't within walking distance.

A green and white taxi sailed past us, and I gazed longingly after it.

"We need the exercise anyway," Jane said, noticing my expression.

I don't know why I ever agreed to her shenanigans. They were always much more fun for her then they were for me. Being the less sexy sidekick wasn't a very glamorous life.

"But my feet hurt," I said.

"Beauty is-"

"-pain, yeah, yeah, I get it," I grumbled, cutting her off.

Jane lit another cigarette, and we walked in silence. I knew she was sulking about the club and trying to plot some exciting adventure to drag me into, but I wouldn't fall for it this time.

The sound of the traffic from Hennepin Avenue had faded enough where I could hear the footfalls echo behind us. Jane seemed oblivious, but I couldn't shake the feeling we were being followed.

Then the footsteps behind us started to hurry up, becoming heavier and louder, combined with the sound of ragged breathing and hushed male voices.

Jane looked over at me, and the panic in her eyes meant that she heard them too. Out of the two of us, she was braver and stole a look back over her shoulder.

I was about to ask her what she saw when she started sprinting forward, and that was answer enough for me. I tried to catch up to her, but she wasn't about to slow down for me, remaining a few steps ahead.

The street ended with a parking garage. Jane ran into it, and I followed her. There had to be other places with crowds, but her first choice had been a dimly lit underground parking garage.

I allowed myself a look back for the first time. In the darkness, I could see little more than the silhouettes of four large men. When they saw me looking at them, one of them started to cat call.

I ran forward, only to realize Jane wasn't in front of me. I didn't have a very good fight or flight reflex, so I just froze when I didn't see her.

"Over here!" Jane hissed, but the echo in the garage was awful. I couldn't tell where her voice was coming from, so I just stood frozen underneath a flickering yellow light and hoped that my death would be quick and painless.

"Hey little girl," one of the guys purred in a voice that sounded anything but friendly.

I turned to face them. Since I had stopped running, so had they, and they strolled over to me.

"Do you always run from a good time?" another one asked. For some reason, the rest of them thought that was hilarious, and their laughter filled the garage.

The hair on the back of my neck stood up, and I opened my mouth to say something, maybe even scream, but nothing came out. I stood in a pool of cold water and oil, and the light above me decided to go out for good.

Closing my eyes against the dark, I didn't want to risk seeing anything they did to me. They talked amongst themselves, laughing and making perverted jokes, and I knew I was going to die.

Somewhere behind me, I heard the screech of tires, but I just squeezed my eyes shut tighter.

-2-

"Hey! What are you doing?" a voice shouted to the side of me. As soon as I heard him speak, I knew that it didn't belong to the group of guys closing in on me, and I opened my eyes.

"What's it to you?" a large tattooed guy growled, but he started taking a step back. A car had pulled in the parking space to my right, shining the bright headlights past me.

"I think you should just back off," the new voice said.

I peeked over to the side at him, but the shadows from the headlights hid him. It was too dark for me to make anything out, except his pink tee shirt.

He took another step forward, and my would-be-attackers continued taking steps back. They weren't moving fast enough, and then suddenly, the blur of the pink shirt rushed towards them.

The darkness and my fear couldn't let me trust my eyesight anymore. It looked as if the pink shirt was moving faster than humanly possible, and the guys yelled as he shoved them, sending them flying out of the garage.

I blinked my eyes to adjust them better, and then everyone was gone.

Not everyone, exactly. The light above me flickered on again, and the guy in the pink shirt stood next to me. In big black letters across his chest, his shirt read, "Real men wear pink."

He looked older than me, probably in his early twenties, and he wasn't particularly well-built or tall. In fact, he leaned more towards wiry than he did muscular, and I couldn't imagine what had frightened off the other guys.

His face was open and friendly, and he had an easy smile that I couldn't help but respond to, even though I had just been a few moments away from death.

"Are you okay?" he asked, appraising me.

"Yeah," I said in a voice that barely sounded like my own. "You saved my life."

"You shouldn't be out here alone," he replied, completely ignoring the fact that he'd done anything heroic.

"My friend Jane is around here somewhere."

I remembered Jane and looked around for her. Part of me was angry that she had done nothing to save me, but then again, neither had I, and I didn't think that I should hold her to a higher standard than I did myself.

"Two girls?" He raised an eyebrow.

"I think Jane has mace," I added lamely.

"Where is this alleged friend?" He took his turn scanning the parking lot, and then pointed to something by a van parked on the other side. "I think I see her over there."

"Where?" I squinted at where he pointed but couldn't see anything.

"Over there," he repeated, taking a step towards the black Jetta parked next to me. "Come on. We'll go over and pick her up, and then I'll give you guys a ride."

I walked around to the passenger side of the car, and it never occurred to me to say no. Something about him made me trust him.

His car stereo played Weezer, and in the glow of the blue dashboard lights, I got my first real good look at him. His skin looked flawless, but his hair was perfectly disheveled.

He sped off across the parking lot, and I pulled my eyes away from him to look out the window. Jane cowered down behind a white van, and I wondered if she'd bothered to call the police or anything. He stopped the car next to her and rolled down the window so he could lean out.

"Jane?" he said, and she turned to look at him.

I expected her to be afraid, maybe even bolt and run after what had just happened. Instead, she gave him the strangest look. It was almost as if she was in awe.

"Hi," Jane said. It wasn't her normal flirty voice, even though I'm sure that's what she was trying for.

"Jane, he's giving us a ride," I said when it appeared she would just stand there staring at him. "Get in the car."

"Sure." She smiled at him before sliding into the backseat.

"Are you okay?" I looked back at her.

"I'm great," Jane said, still gaping at him. "Who's your friend here?"

"I don't actually know," I admitted, looking over at him.

"I'm Jack," he said, filling in the blank. "And you're Jane." Then he looked over at me. "And you are?"

"Alice."

"Well, I don't know about you guys, but I could really go for a cup of coffee right about now." Jack dropped the car into gear and sped off without waiting for either of us to respond. It wasn't really a question anyway, and neither one of us would've protested.

"This is a really nice car," Jane said, and her voice had fully regained that sickeningly sweet tone. Jack didn't say anything, and the silence started to feel awkward.

"Is this Weezer?" I asked, just to say something.

"Yeah," Jack nodded.

"I like that song 'Pork 'n Beans.'" As soon as I mentioned the song, Jack quickly flipped it to the track.

"I saw them when they were on tour with Motion City Soundtrack," he said.

"Really?" I ignored the annoyed glare Jane gave me and continued. "I really like them. How are they live?"

"Pretty good," Jack shrugged, and turned sharply into the parking lot outside an all night diner.

When we got out of the car, Jane scampered over to him, looping her arm through his. He didn't look pleased by it, but he didn't pull away either.

Outside in the bright glow of the streetlights, I looked him over again. He had on a pair of Dickies shorts, skater socks, and light blue Converse, along with the pink tee shirt. He more closely resembled cotton candy than he did a love interest for Jane.

"Oh crap," I said after I'd gotten out of the car, and looked down at my dirty, bare feet. Blisters and oil covered them, and I couldn't imagine cramming my swollen feet back into Jane's shoes.

"What?" Jack asked, and then followed my gaze down. "Oh. Just don't wear shoes."

"I can't not wear shoes." I didn't see much of another option, but I couldn't go into a restaurant without shoes.

"You can wait in the car," Jane offered up with a smug smile and leaned in closer to Jack, and he pulled his arm free from her and took a step away. She looked a little defeated, but I knew she wouldn't give up that easy.

"No, you'll be fine," Jack insisted. "If they hassle you, I'll take care of them."

"What does that even mean?" I asked, but he'd already convinced me. After all, I'd seen the way he chased off a gang of unruly guys. The graveyard shift at a Denny's rip-off wouldn't stand a chance.

As predicted, nobody noticed my lack of footwear. In fact, nobody noticed me, or even Jane. The waitress kept her eyes completely focused on Jack.

He sat down first, and Jane squished up next to him, so he kept moving over until he was plastered up against the window. I sat down across from them, and Jack rested his arms on the table, leaning towards me.

"What can I get you?" the waitress asked.

"Just coffee," Jack answered. "Or did you guys want something else?"

"Coffee's fine," I said. I was a little hungry, but I felt uncomfortable eating in front of him and Jane.

"Are you sure you're not hungry?" Jane asked, running her fingers on his arm, but this time, he actually recoiled from her touch.

15

"Nope," Jack sighed, then muttered under his breath, "but I wish I was."

"What?" the waitress asked, leaning in closer to hear him.

"Nothing." Jack smiled at her. "Just the coffee."

"Thanks," I told the waitress when she lingered at our table, and she left to get our order.

"Thanks again for saving us." Jane pressed herself against him. "If there's anything I can do to repay you, just let me know." There was definitely something strange going on, but I couldn't put my finger on it.

His skin was beach bum tanned, unnatural for people in Minnesota in March. His eyes were a weird blue-gray color, and there was something tremendously boyish about them, about him really, but otherwise, nothing seemed to stand out as overly attractive.

"Are you famous or something?" I blurted out, and Jane looked embarrassed enough for both of us so I didn't bother blushing.

"What do you mean?" He sounded confused.

"Everyone's staring at us. At you," I corrected myself.

Jack just shrugged and looked down at the table but didn't bother checking to see if I was right.

"I'm not famous," Jack said. He looked like he wanted to explain things more, but then the waitress appeared with three mugs and a pitcher of coffee.

"Is there anything else I can get you?" the waitress asked.

"We're fine, thanks," Jane snapped, putting her hand possessively on Jack's thigh until the waitress left.

"Come on. What's going on?" I rested my arms on the table and leaned in closer to him because I'd lowered my voice.

"I don't have an answer for it." Jack picked up the pot of coffee and poured a cup for himself and me, and then filled Jane's too. "Do you take cream or sugar in yours?"

"Both."

I was perfectly capable of doing it myself, but I think he wanted to occupy himself so I would be less likely to notice him hedging the question. He dumped a creamer and two packets of sugar in my coffee, and stirred a creamer in his, then settled back in the booth.

"I take cream and sugar too," Jane added, and Jack pushed the bowl of creamers and sugar towards her.

"So you're not famous?" I refused to let it go without a direct answer.

"I can assure you that I'm not famous," Jack smiled. This one thing I would say about him; he had to have one of the greatest smiles of all time.

"You just look so familiar to me," I said.

"I know, right?" He gave me a perplexed look that mirrored my own.

"So do I know you from somewhere?" As soon as I said that, I knew that wasn't exactly it either. I could almost guarantee that I'd never seen him before, but there was something undeniably familiar about him.

"That's not possible," he shook his head.

"How is it not possible?" I asked. "Did you just move here or something?"

"It's complicated." He touched his coffee cup and made like he was going to drink it, but he never even lifted it off the table.

Jane resigned herself to drinking her coffee and watching us talk. She finished one cup and poured herself another.

"How is it complicated?"

"It just is." Jack flashed me another one of his amazing smiles.

Somehow, he managed to look very young, like he was fifteen, while simultaneously looking older than me. It was something about his eyes. They were very young and very old, at the same time.

"How old are you?" I asked pointedly.

To my surprise, Jack laughed, and I found something even more incredible than his smile. Easily, he had the greatest laugh in the universe. It sounded so clear and perfect.

"How old are you?" Jack countered, grinning at me.

"I asked you first." I leaned back in my seat, crossing my arms over my chest, and that made him laugh again.

"Why does that even matter?" Jack asked. "You want to know more."

"I'm seventeen," I sighed.

"Twenty-four," Jack said with a wry smirk.

"Don't you feel a little odd running around with two seventeen year old girls?" I asked.

In some part of my mind, it did logically seem wrong for a twenty-four-year-old to be picking up two random teenage girls. But sitting here, in the booth with him, nothing felt more natural or safe.

"I'm mature for my age," Jane interjected.

"As I recall, if I hadn't been around, you would've gotten yourself killed." He rested his arms on the table, leaning more towards me. "What were you doing anyway?"

"We were trying to get into a club, but my feet were killing me and I just wanted to get home," I said. He looked at me for a minute, the serious expression looking out of place on him, and then shook his head and refilled my cup of coffee.

"What club were you trying to get into?" Jack asked, and added cream and sugar to mine. He had yet to touch his own cup, but I decided not to say anything.

"I don't know," I shrugged. I just let Jane drag me wherever she wanted to go and hoped that by the end of the night, I managed to make it home in one piece. "What were you doing downtown? Clubbing it up?"

"Hardly," Jack said. "I was… getting something to eat."

"At midnight?" I raised an eyebrow at him.

"I'm kind of a night owl." Time must've just occurred to him, because he glanced over at a clock hanging on the wall. "It's getting really late. I should probably get you home."

"I'm wide awake," Jane chirped, but unlucky for her, I didn't feel the same way.

Even with the coffee and the adrenaline rush from earlier, I felt very tired. I wanted to continue hanging out with Jack, but my whole body had started to ache, especially my legs and ankles.

"I'm starting to drag." To punctuate the statement, I yawned loudly.

Jack paid for the check, even though I tried to make a play for it. It was only a couple bucks, and I was tired, so I didn't fight that hard.

When I stood up, my legs fought to give out underneath me, but I managed to stay up on my feet. For a second, though, I thought Jack was going to pick me up and carry me out to the car. Jane must've gotten the same idea, because she inserted herself between us.

Almost the instant I sat in his car, I fell asleep. I remember a brief discussion about who he would take home first. I woke up just as Jack pulled up in front of my apartment building. Jane was already gone, so I guess he'd dropped her off. I'm not sure how he knew where I lived, but it didn't seem important then.

I left Jack outside my brownstone and went up to my apartment. Fortunately, my mom wouldn't be home from her shift until after seven a.m., and my younger brother Milo was already asleep in his room.

Painfully, I stripped off the ridiculous get up that Jane had dressed me in and pulled on an oversized tee shirt. I grabbed my cell phone with the full intention of plugging it in, but I collapsed onto my bed with my phone in my hand before I had the chance.

Just as I started passing out, I felt the phone vibrate in my hand, startling me awake.

Sweet dreams :) – Jack

The text message was from Jack, and I felt my heart beat faster. Somehow, when I had been sleeping, Jack had gotten my phone number from my cell and programmed his number into mine.

Under other circumstances, that might have been a little creepy, but in this case, it just made me feel happy and relieved. Clicking off my phone, I set it on my bedside table and promptly fell asleep.

- 3 -

When I woke up, the first thing I noticed, after the painful damage to my feet, were the ten million text messages from Jane. All of them were about Jack, and I felt no urge to reply.

I pulled on sweats, and then stumbled into the bathroom to overdose on painkillers and cover my feet in Neosporin and Band-Aids.

Miraculously, I'd woken up before two o'clock in the afternoon, and that meant that my mom was still asleep. She worked a graveyard shift as a dispatcher in St. Paul, so she usually made it home at an ungodly hour and then slept all day.

My brother Milo was a studious little bastard though, and he'd probably been in bed before midnight and up before nine.

When I made it out to the living room, I found him sitting at the computer, probably researching a paper for school even though we were on Spring Break. He was a sophomore in high school and had the social life of a toddler.

It was a sad, sad thing that I was the cool one in the family.

"What's wrong with you?" Milo asked, glancing up at me.

"What's wrong with you?" I countered, utilizing my quick wit.

I had gone into the small adjoined kitchen and poured myself a bowl of Fruity Pebbles. (Scientists haven't tested this, but I've come to find that a Gatorade, a bowl of Fruity Pebbles, and an Excedrin will cure any hangover.)

"Hung over?" Milo noticed me creating my antidote, and I definitely felt that way.

"Something like that," I said.

With my bowl of cereal and lemon-lime sports drink in hand, I flopped on the couch, determined to find either Looney Tunes or a trashy *Lifetime* movie (the second part of my hang over cure-all).

"What time did you get in last night?" Milo asked with a hint of disapproval in his voice.

He's a year and half younger than me, but he's definitely the parental figure in our relationship. Since Mom's always working, and Dad's been out of the picture since the beginning of time, I guess one of us had to step up and do it.

"I don't know." I tried to think, but I couldn't actually remember.

After we left the diner, I had pretty much been unconscious the entire time. I only vaguely remembered getting the text from Jack, and I guessed it was somewhere around two or three.

"So what did you end up doing last night?" Milo had given up on even the pretense of doing something on the computer and tilted his chair towards me.

His dark brown eyes settled on me with their usual mix of curiosity and concern, as if he always half-expected me to admit to shooting up black tar heroin and having sex for money.

"Nothing," I shrugged.

"Nothing?" He raised an eyebrow, his suspicion making him look older than he really was. Aside from the baby fat that clung to his cheeks, he could actually pass for being older than me.

"We couldn't get in anywhere," I explained through a mouthful of cereal. "So we just wandered around looking for a club until my feet were completely destroyed, and then we came home."

"Jane didn't drag you off to some party?"

"Nope."

"That's very unlike her to end a night without vodka or sex," he commented.

"Life is full of surprises." I had eaten all my cereal, so I drank the rainbowed milk from the bowl and hoped that Milo would let the subject drop. "What are you up to today?"

"This," he shrugged. "You?"

"Same." I set my bowl down on the coffee table and settled back on the couch. "There's a movie about a sex addict on *Lifetime*. Care to watch?"

"Sure." He got up from the kitchen chair that sat in front of the computer desk and planted himself at the end of the couch.

I stretched out, resting my battered feet on his lap. He started to say something about the state of them, but then answered his own question by simply saying Jane. We both agreed that she was the source of all my life's problems.

We spent the rest of the afternoon camped out on the couch watching a *Lifetime* movie marathon. Mom got up, showered, and left for work early, citing overtime, but I was never sure if I believed that or not.

Sometimes I think she just didn't like being in the apartment. At this point, it had become more like Milo and I lived on our own. We even did all the grocery shopping, cooking, cleaning, laundry, etc. (By "we," I mostly mean him. But I did help. Sometimes.)

Around nine, I finally decided that I ought to shower. When I went into my room to gather my clothes, I noticed my cell phone flashing on the table. I had ignored it all day because I had wanted to ignore Jane, but I knew that eventually I'd have to deal with her.

Much to my surprise, buried underneath the mass of texts from her, I found a text message from Jack.

Motion City Soundtrack tomorrow. First Ave. Seven o'clock. I'm buying. You in?

He'd been paying attention last night when I just casually mentioned liking the band Motion City Soundtrack, and he'd invited me to a concert. First Ave. was a rather historic little venue downtown, not far off from where he found us.

I knew that if Milo heard about it, his paranoia would kick in, and he'd do everything but forbid me from going. Despite that, I couldn't feel that way. Sure, Jack was too old for me, but we weren't dating, and I didn't really feel like that would become an issue.

I sighed, then quickly responded with, **That's too much $. I already owe you too much.**

Oh be quiet. Money doesn't matter. Are you in or not? Jack replied within seconds.

Yeah. But don't get in the habit of buying me things. I messaged him back.

Don't get in the habit of protesting when I buy you things. ;)

26

Funny. I replied, hoping it sounded as droll as I wanted it to.

I'll pick you up at six-thirty. Sound good? That was cutting it awfully close to the time the show started, but he was inviting me, so I'd play by his rules.

Yeah. See you then. :)

I decided instantly that I couldn't tell Jane about this. If hanging out with Jack became a regular thing, I knew I'd have to tell her. And Milo.

But for now, I thought it'd be best if I kept it to myself. I couldn't keep anyone's secrets, not even my own, so I couldn't really explain what compelled me to keep this to myself.

I spent the next twenty-four hours avoiding Jane and hedging Milo's questions. He had a sixth sense when something was up with me, and it was nearly impossible to keep anything hidden from him.

When I was getting ready to go out, he knew there was a guy involved. I don't know how. All I had put on was a slim-fitting hoodie and a pair of jeans, so I don't understand what that would give away.

Every time I left Milo home alone at night, I felt terrible. Sure, he was fifteen, and we'd spent most of our lives alone, but it still never felt right to me.

He didn't really want me to go because he didn't know what I was up to, but he assured me that he'd be fine playing *World of Warcraft* on the computer and he'd barely even notice I was gone.

Jack arrived promptly at six-thirty, washing away any feelings of guilt or trepidation. As soon as I saw him, I just felt at ease and vaguely contented.

"Hey," Jack smiled broadly when I hopped into his car.

"Thanks," I said. "For all this."

"All what?" Jack looked confused as we pulled away from my building, speeding towards First Ave.

"The ride, the tickets, saving my life," I elaborated.

"Oh, that," he laughed. "It's really not a problem. Trust me."

"Just because it wasn't a problem for you doesn't mean that I'm not grateful," I pointed out.

"Fair enough," he allowed. "Well, you're welcome then."

Parking downtown should've been impossible, but he managed to find a spot half a block away. It was obvious that he could walk much faster than I could, but he kept his pace to match mine, making me feel guilty for holding him up.

It was almost seven when we reached the door, and I knew part of the problem was because I slowed us down. I started to apologize, but he wouldn't hear of it.

By the time I saw all the kids inside, I had already resigned myself to standing in the back, unable to catch sight of the band onstage. Jack took my hand to weave us through the crowd, and there was something very odd about his touch.

His skin was neither hot nor cold. It just felt… temperature-less. Although his skin was tremendously soft, it reminded me of a lizard. The way they can't regulate their temperature at all, so they're always whatever temperature the room is or whatever's touching them.

We made our way up close to the stage, but thanks to my height, it did me little good. When the band came out and the crowd rushed forward, I ended up with my head smooshed into the back of the guy in front of me.

Jack managed to stand his ground, creating a little pocket of unmashedness. He noticed my predicament, and rather deftly, he scooped me up and dropped me on his shoulders, so my legs were straddling his neck.

I became very conscious of the fact that I weighed something over a hundred pounds (the exact amount is irrelevant) and that had to be heavy. Hell, fifty pounds sounded heavy when it's sitting on your shoulders.

"Let me know if I get too heavy," I shouted over the music.

"You won't!" Jack yelled back. I didn't believe it, but I knew he wouldn't tell me if I did.

Throughout the entire show (which was spectacular), he never faltered or even hinted at putting me down. When the crowd started to disperse, I was still on his shoulders, and I thought he might carry me out. Instead, he lifted me up off his shoulders and set me on the ground.

"Holy cow!" I said after he'd put me down. "You must eat like a double dose of Wheaties every day!"

"What are you talking about?" Jack asked, looking at me like I was insane.

"You're super strong!" Without thinking, I reached out and grabbed his bicep, trying to feel some massive amounts of hidden muscle, but honestly, it felt pretty ordinary.

"You're just really light." Jack started walking away, attempting to end that line of conversation, but I hurried after him.

"What's your angle?" I asked, trying to sound more playful than demanding.

"Isosceles," Jack quipped.

"What?" If Milo had been there, he probably would've understood the reference, but geometry wasn't my thing.

"You asked me what my angle was, so I said isosceles," Jack explained, looking down at me to make sure that he wasn't losing me in the crowd. "It's a type of a triangle with two equal sides. I suppose that's not really an angle, and I would've said something like acute or obtuse, but I thought that would either sound like I was hitting on you or calling you stupid. I should've said oblique. That would've been good. Damn! I'm gonna remember that for next time."

"You're the most cryptic person I've ever met," I sighed.

We stepped outside into the night air, and I pulled my sweatshirt tighter to me, flipping the hood up over my head. Normally, the night air felt refreshing after being all sweaty and crammed with other people on the floor, but since I'd been on Jack's shoulders, I hadn't gotten hot at all.

He didn't look sweaty from fighting off the mosh pit, and the cold didn't seem to affect him either. I was tempted to reach out and take his hand to see what the temperature felt like, but it felt too awkward.

"So, did you have fun?" Jack asked me as we strolled to his car.

"I did," I smiled at him. "Did you?"

"Of course."

There was always this wonderful rush after a good concert, like adrenaline but less panicky. So when they let out, I usually talked a mile a minute about the show, the people, just anything, and everything.

Tonight, though, I fell silent. There were millions of things running through my mind that I wanted to talk about, but very little had to do with the performance I had seen, so I kept my mouth shut.

"I don't mean to be cryptic," Jack said at length.

We were almost to his car, but he stopped walking and kept his gaze focused on some point straight ahead. His hands were shoved deep in the pocket of his Dickies shorts, and he sighed.

"I don't have an angle. Just..." He looked over at me, as if to make sure that I was still listening. I peered up at him from underneath my hood, and he smirked a little. "You're cold. We should get in the car."

"No! Tell me what you were going to say first!" I demanded, sounding more forceful than I meant to, but Jack only laughed. Then he went back to staring straight ahead, and his expression went somber.

"I don't want you to think that I'm completely egotistical, cause I'm not. I'm just realistic."

"You're talking about the way all the girls look at you?" I asked. Jane and the waitress had gawked at him the night we met, and I'd noticed a lot of other girls eyeing him up during the concert.

"Yeah," Jack said sheepishly. "Everyone kind of... *reacts* to me a certain way. And you don't. It's refreshing. So that's what I'm doing here. With you."

"Wait, wait, wait." I waved my hands at him, feeling a wave of disappointment. "What about the way other people react to you? Why do they do that?"

"I don't know." Jack shifted slightly, and I knew he was lying. He knew exactly what was going on, but he wasn't going to tell me.

"That's not fair!"

"See?" Jack smiled. "This is refreshing. Do you know how many other people argue with me, about anything?"

"If you think this is refreshing, just wait." I tried to glower at him, but his smile was just too damn infectious.

"Come on," Jack started walking towards the car again. "You're gonna freeze to death."

"Jack!" I protested but hurried after him. "What is it? Is it something in the way you smell that I'm just not getting?" He got a look of total surprise and made a clicking sound with his tongue. "What?"

"Well, yeah, that's actually pretty much it," Jack admitted. He unlocked his car and then walked around to the other side, still looking a little stunned. I hopped into the car and he continued, "It's a pheromone or something like that."

"So, wait. Is that a medical condition or something?"

"Yeah, I guess." He nodded, as if that answer was sufficient.

"What kind of medical condition?" I pressed, oblivious to the fact that that kind of information was really personal. Something about Jack made me lose any sense of formality.

"A rare one," he replied flippantly and started the car.

"Well, why don't I react to it?"

I started to wonder if maybe there was something very wrong with me. Everyone reacted to him, except for me. Maybe I had a seriously botched sense of smell or a brain tumor or something equally horrible.

"That is a very good question." He pulled out of the parking lot, slipping easily into an opening in the traffic.

"You don't actually know why, do you?" I asked. "You don't know why I'm different then everyone else."

"I do not," Jack admitted, then looked over at me. "But look, Alice, I don't want you to get hung up on this thing. It's too hard to explain and… for our purposes, it doesn't even matter at all."

"What purposes?" I narrowed my eyes at him.

"In order for this friendship to work, you're just going to have to accept that there are certain things that I'm not gonna tell you," Jack said firmly. "I'm not trying to be a dick about this but that's just the way it is."

"And what if I can't accept that?"

"Then we can't hang out anymore." He tried to sound matter-of-fact about it, but I could hear the sadness in his voice.

"This doesn't make any sense," I said, but I was already relenting. "Why can't you just tell me things?"

"I can't tell you why I can't tell!" He said it like it meant something, like I would go, oh yeah, I get it now.

"This is gonna frustrate me to no end." I was sulking, but that only made him smile.

"I know." He was still smiling, but he sounded apologetic. "I'll drop you off and then you can take some time to think about things and decide if hanging out with me seems worth it. And then, if you still wanna hang out, you can text me. Okay?"

"Okay." I tried to sound as dejected and pouty as possible, hoping that would change his mind somehow and he would divulge all his classified information to me.

He only laughed again as we pulled up in front of my apartment building. I told him I'd talk to him later as I got out of the car, but he only waved, and I went inside.

After a brief interrogation from Milo, I laid awake in my bed for hours, running a million different theories about Jack. Weird government experiment? CIA? Werewolf? Nothing really seemed to fit.

My most promising one was that he was a celebrity of some kind pulling some ridiculous *Hannah Montana* lifestyle. That would explain why everyone noticed him. And if he was going for some kind of secret hidden identity, then he couldn't tell me.

That still didn't explain why everyone else would recognize him but me, or why he'd want to live incognito. But at least it was a theory.

Since I had been up until the wee hours of the morning trying to figure Jack out, and I didn't have school, I fully intended to spend the entire day sleeping, curled up in the soft comfort of my down blankets.

Unfortunately, my Jane embargo fell through. Or rather, burst through my bedroom door, destroying any chance of sleep.

"What the hell is going on?" Jane hissed after she'd thrown open my bedroom door so hard that the knob left a mark in the plaster.

I jumped up, tangled up in a mass of blankets and sleep induced confusion. I could barely focus my eyes on the blurry vision of Jane, standing in my doorway, with her hands on her hips glaring down at me.

Milo cowered behind her, muttering things about how she needed to keep it down or Mom would completely freak out. Whenever Jane was around, he acted like a puppy about to pee on the floor, and it drove me nuts.

"What are you talking about?" I asked groggily. I flopped back down in bed, trying to remember the dream Jane had ripped me from.

"You know what." Her lips curled back into some kind of sneer and she stepped her Jimmy Choos over my dirty clothes strewn about my room.

Out of the corner of my eye, I could see the alarm clock telling me it was 11:13 am, and I grimaced. It wasn't even noon yet, and Jane was in heels and red lipstick.

"I really don't," I yawned and pulled the covers up over me more.

"Why haven't you answered my zillions of text messages or phone calls?" Jane yanked my covers off me, forcing me to talk to her.

"Because there were zillions of them," I said and grudgingly sat up.

"Ugh," Jane groaned. She sat down next to me in a terrific huff. "There wouldn't have been so many if you just answered me."

"Sorry."

"Well?" Jane looked at me.

Her expression had softened, so she'd apparently forgiven me, which was pretty amazing. Jane's one Cardinal Sin was ignoring her, and I had managed to for almost two days.

"What?" I didn't really know what she was trying to get at. Was I supposed to thank her or something?

"Have you talked to *him*?" she asked, and I rolled my eyes.

"Him who?" Milo visibly puffed up at the mention of a guy, preparing himself to defend my honor.

Milo was the kid at school that got shoved into lockers, and he was younger than me. I don't know who exactly he could protect me from, but it would be a pretty sorry excuse for a guy.

"Jack!" Jane answered him like it should be completely obvious. When she realized that Milo had no idea who she was talking about, her mouth fell open. "Oh my god, Alice! You didn't tell him about Jack?"

"I have not, no," I shook my head. In fact, I hadn't planned to tell Milo about Jack until I had things sorted out better, but thanks to Jane, that would no longer be an option.

"How could you not tell him?" This fact just flabbergasted her. She couldn't grasp a world where one didn't incessantly talk about Jack.

"I don't know, Jane," I sighed. "It just didn't come up."

To be honest, her instant obsession with Jack was the first thing about him that truly made me nervous. If he had this affect on her, what was he doing to other people? And why wasn't I the same way?

"Wait," Milo said as it dawned on him, and I would've cut off my leg to keep him from completing his thought. "Is Jack the guy you went out with last night?"

"You went out with him?" Jane gasped.

"We just went to a concert. It was no big deal." I kept my tone casual and nonchalant, but I heard her sharp intake of breath.

"Who is this guy?" Milo demanded. Jane's reaction made him nervous, and he did his best to look as threatening as he could.

"Jack is just like the most amazing guy ever," Jane said eloquently.

"He's just a guy," I continued with my ultra-casual voice, and even added a shoulder shrug for good measure.

"How can you even say that?" Jane asked. In her mind, he'd been stacked up with the gods and should only be gushed about in revered tones normally reserved for shoes and hand bags.

"You know what, I just don't get it." I turned to her. "What is it about him that you like so much?"

"You've got to be kidding."

"I'm not."

"But you've met him!" Jane insisted.

"I know that. I still don't get it. You're crazy about him. You've got to be able to articulate what it is that you're attracted to."

"He's just…" Jane fumbled for words. He'd been the only thing on her mind, so why couldn't she explain him? "It's like… There's just something about him. It's completely indescribable. I just want him. More than I've ever wanted anything."

"Huh." That was all I could think to say.

"You're telling me that you don't want him?" Jane asked me in total disbelief.

"No, I don't," I said honestly.

I liked Jack in a really weird way, but not like Jane. It was much simpler and less carnal. Or at least that's what I gathered from the way she talked and acted.

"Did he say anything about me?" Jane returned to the only topic that truly mattered to her – herself.

"Nope." I stood up and started going through my dresser drawers for clothes. The whole conversation had run its course with me, and I was moving on to take a shower and start my day.

"Not a thing?" Her voice sounded so small and sad, but I ignored it.

"Nope," I repeated. "But, look, I'm gonna hop in the shower. And you've probably got better things to do than wait around for me."

"I guess," Jane mumbled.

She looked totally dejected, but I figured that in a few short hours, she'd probably be drunk and dancing topless on some poor guy's table. It was kinda hard to feel sorry for her.

After she finally pulled herself together and left, Milo questioned me about Jack. It took a little while, but I managed to convince him that everything was okay. Reluctantly, he dropped the subject and allowed me to take a shower.

The hot water felt good on my skin, and I let my thoughts wander to where I had left off last night. Something Jane said, about how in love she was with Jack even though she couldn't think of a single reason why, stuck in my head.

That's when it hit me. Jack, the way I saw Jack — attractive with a boyish charm — that's who he really was. What everyone else saw, like Jane and the waitress at the diner, they were just responding to something that wasn't real. The pheromones or whatever created some kind of illusion.

But maybe I wasn't immune. Maybe there was nothing spectacular about Jack at all, but I was just responding to it on a smaller scale. Maybe I was falling for the same trap Jane was.

- 4 -

The television channel TNT, in its infinite wisdom, had a John Hughes marathon running on all day. Milo, who had never understood the appeal of Molly Ringwald, watched them with me. He tried to convince me to watch something else, but I was stronger than him and manhandled the remote.

We started onto our second viewing of *Pretty in Pink* when my cell phone started to jingle. It was going on midnight and I assumed it was Jane calling for some kind of sober cab service (even though I did not possess a car), but I picked up my phone off the coffee table anyway.

Instead, I found a text message from Jack.

So. You haven't texted me.

You're very observant. I responded.

My plan was to try to be indifferent. I didn't appreciate the idea that I had probably fallen victim to some kind of spell or hormonal manipulation.

Does that mean you don't want to be friends?

He actually typed that, like a note I'd get in the first grade. Something about that completely endeared him to me, and since I couldn't smell or see him, I decided that must mean that I actually liked him.

No. I do. Definitely.

"Who is that?" Milo asked with an edge to his voice. He was sitting at the other end of the couch from me, and he leaned over so he could look at my phone, but I turned it away from him. "It's that Jack guy, right?"

"You do realize it's perfectly legal for me to text members of the opposite sex." I gave Milo a hard look and he just shook his head.

"Whatever," Milo said and turned his attention back to the movie. My phone rang again, and Milo made a humph sound.

Excellent. Wanna do something? Jack messaged.

What did you have in mind?

Anything. Everything. The city is our oyster! Jack texted back.

That sounds pretty ambitious. I replied, but it did sound exciting.

It is. So can you be ready in like fifteen minutes? Jack asked.

Sure. Meet you outside.

In a flash, I touched up my makeup and slid on shoes. Before rushing out the door, I promised Milo that I wouldn't be home too late and that I had my phone if he needed me. He grunted at me, and then I dashed out to meet Jack.

He was already waiting outside, this time in a bright red sports car that looked like it cost more than a house. He grinned wildly when I opened the car door and jumped inside.

"So, this is nice," I said, referring to his overly flashy car.

"It's more than nice. It's a Lamborghini Gallardo," Jack explained with that foolish grin plastered on his face. "There are only six thousand of these in existence."

"Is it new?"

"Nah, it's my brother's," Jack said.

Before I could say anything more, he put the car in gear and it thrust itself into the street. I had thought we had gone fast in the Jetta, but it had nothing on this.

"Your brother must be loaded." The car gracefully slid around a corner and weaved in between cars. Quickly, he turned it onto I-35, presumably so we could get the full effect of it going top speed on the open road.

"He kind of is," Jack shrugged. "I don't really worry about money, I guess." It was the casual way someone talked when they never had to struggle for anything, and I wondered if Jack was wealthy and where he came from.

"It must be nice," I muttered.

We were pretty poor, but not quite so poor that I felt like I had to get a job and bring in my own money. Just enough where I felt it.

"There are plenty of other things to worry about," Jack replied seriously. "Believe me."

"Like what?" I looked over at him, instead of the blur of the scenery flying past us. He smirked at me and shook his head. So that was another thing he wouldn't talk to me about. "So you have a brother?"

"Two, actually," Jack said. "And a sister. Well, she's actually my sister-in-law, but she feels like a sister."

"So is she married to your brother, or are you married?" I asked tentatively.

"No, I'm not married," Jack laughed. "She's my brother's wife."

"What are their names?" With the endless amount of things I wanted to know about him, I was stuck asking safe questions.

"Peter, and then Ezra is married to Mae. Ezra is the oldest."

"What about your parents?" I turned towards him and rested my head against the seat. The rush of the world around us had made me a little dizzy.

"Dead." His voice was emotionless, but his eyes got hard, which didn't look right at all.

"Sorry," I offered lamely.

"Nah, it was like fifteen years ago." He shook his head, trying to brush me off, and then he turned to me, his face brightening again. "What about you? You have family?"

"My mom, and a younger brother," I answered. "But he's more like an older brother sometimes." Jack laughed loudly at that, his wonderful laughter echoing throughout the car and sending waves of warmth over me.

"Yeah, I can completely relate," he grinned.

"Really?" I had always thought of Milo as an oddity, but it was nice to know that there was someone out there like him.

"Yeah, but Peter's something else," Jack said. "Really. I doubt you'll ever meet anyone like him."

"Well, I'd have to meet him first," I pointed out.

"Maybe someday." He sounded weirdly far off, almost apprehensive.

"You're not married, but does that mean you're single?" I asked.

"Uh, yeah." Then, before I could ask him more about that, he turned the tables on me. "What about you? Are you seeing anyone?"

"Hardly," I snorted. Other than a few drunken make out sessions at a couple parties, I had nothing to show for a love life.

"Why not?" Jack pressed.

"You saw my friend Jane," I said dully. "She has this way of completely stealing all the light in the room."

"Oh, she does not."

"Why don't you have a girlfriend? The ladies obviously like you." I changed the subject back to him.

"That's actually part of the reason why. Everyone likes me without ever knowing me. It makes it hard to have a real relationship with somebody."

"So... what's the other part?" I asked, and he didn't answer. "You're not going to tell me."

"I think there's a midnight show of *Rocky Horror Picture Show* in Lakeville," Jack announced randomly. "Are you up for it?"

"Sure." I glanced out the window, watching the car glide through traffic. "So, why didn't you drive your car tonight?"

"That's not really my car, either." He didn't really answer my question, but I was starting to get used to that. "It's my sister Mae's."

I noticed that he called her his sister, not his sister-in-law, and I wondered if that was simply an oversight. His insistence on being so mysterious was making me overanalyze everything.

"Do you even own a car?"

"Yeah, a jeep. I just haven't felt like driving it lately." Then he flashed a sly smile and looked over at me. "Besides, this is so much faster."

"That doesn't seem fair at all," I said tiredly after riding in silence for a minute. My mind had been trying to figure out all the things he wouldn't tell me. "You won't tell me anything about yourself."

"Hey, I'll tell you almost anything about me." He kept his tone light, but he looked a little wounded. For the first time, I realized that he not telling me bothered him just as much as it did me.

"My favorite color is chartreuse. I love the Ramones and the Cure. My bedroom walls are painted dark blue. I had my first kiss when I was fourteen while listening to 'Rock Lobster' cause she really, really liked B-52's. I should've taken that as warning sign that it would never work, but I was awfully young and stupid."

"Chartreuse?" I questioned, skipping over the remainder of his confession. "I don't even know what that is."

"It's sorta like a bright olive," Jack explained. "It's the color most visible to the human eye because of where it sits in the light spectrum."

"You're incredibly random." We turned into the parking lot of the multiplex, and I realized he had managed to avoid really telling me anything. When he pulled into park, I looked at him seriously. "So why can't you tell me things?"

"Why do you think?" Jack asked, not unkindly.

"Witness protection." It was an idea I had actually considered but quickly crossed off because it didn't really explain anything. And just as I suspected, Jack laughed.

"Okay, that's not it." Still smiling and shaking his head, he hopped out of the car, and I quickly followed him.

"Hey, does that mean you'll actually tell me if I guess right?" The movie had probably already started, so Jack was walking rather fast towards the theater, and I chased after him as swiftly as my short legs would carry me.

"I don't see why not," Jack said, and that perplexed me even further.

"If I can guess it then why can't you just come right out and tell me?"

"It's just the way it is." He opened the big glass doors of the theater for me, and I walked inside, furrowing my brow.

When he went up to the cashier to buy tickets, I started rummaging in my pockets for my own money, but he just waved me off and paid for my ticket. If I hadn't been so preoccupied by this new development, I probably would've protested further.

"So, are you Rumpelstiltskin?" I asked him, leaning up against the counter as he got our tickets.

He laughed loudly, and the cashier blushed at the sound. He was completely oblivious to it, and I hoped that I would hurry up and feel the same way. I hadn't really staked a claim on him, but it was still irritating to notice girls drooling all over him, especially when I was visibly with him.

"That's awesome!" He handed me my ticket, and while I did feel overly happy about his minor compliment, I only let the frustration show on my face. He walked to the theater, slowing enough so I could keep up with him. "Rumpelstiltskin. That's really awesome. I'm gonna tell Ezra that."

"Why? Are you guys like a family of goblins or something?"

Jack laughed, shaking his head, and then pushed open the door to the movie before I could question him further.

45

The movie had already started playing but just the very beginning. Many people were dressed up in costumes from the movie and throwing popcorn at the screen, so for once nobody noticed us sneaking into the back row.

Rocky Horror Picture Show was a pretty good movie and I did rather enjoy it, but either Jack had ADD or he had being evasive down to an art form.

Deciding to make the best of the situation, I followed suit and watched the movie. Jack was a borderline fanatic. He hadn't dressed up in a black corset or anything like that, but he shouted right along with all the lines.

When "Time Warp" came on, I thought he might get up and dance, and he probably would've if there'd been enough room in the aisle.

Towards the end of the movie, I had settled back in my seat, and even his enthusiasm had faded a bit. My arm casually brushed against his, and I felt struck by his odd skin temperature again. His skin was soft and warm, but it felt more like touching fabric than it did like touching a person.

It was such an odd sensation that I felt like I had to get more of it. I pushed my arm over on the shared arm rest, very deliberately pressing my bare skin against his. The back of his hand felt impossibly soft.

He hadn't pulled his arm away, but I felt his gaze so I looked up at him, finding a very perplexed expression on his face.

"Are you trying to hold my hand?" Jack asked, as if the idea were completely alien.

I was not trying to hold his hand, but I didn't appreciate the way it seemed so offensive to him. What would be wrong with that?

"What if I am?" I stuck out my chin, ready to hold my ground and find out what would be so bad about hitting on me.

Without hesitation, Jack called my bluff and took my hand in his. It definitely felt like I was holding hands with doll or something other than another person, but then it started to warm up, his skin heating up unnaturally, and I pulled my hand from his.

"Okay. That's just weird," I whispered.

In response, he just shrugged, apparently deciding against explaining his abrupt temperature change.

We watched the rest of the movie in silence (or at least I did – he continued shouting lines and singing). By the time it ended, I had started yawning, and I knew that I'd have to call it a night pretty soon.

Not that I wanted to. Bizarre handholding and classified information aside, I really enjoyed spending time with Jack and I didn't want it to stop. Not ever.

"I hope you had fun tonight," Jack said when he pulled up in front of my place.

"I did," I nodded. Only he could make frustration so much fun. "So… we'll hang out again?"

"Of course," he smiled, holding his hand towards me. "Let me see your phone."

"Why?" I asked, but I was already pulling it out of my pocket and handing it to him.

"One second." Taking my phone, he started scrolling through it and doing things that I couldn't see from my angle. A minute later, he handed my phone back to me, looking rather mischievous.

"What'd you do?" I flipped it open and started looking through it, trying to see what he could've done.

"You'll see," he smiled.

"Oh, you are trouble." Shaking my head, I shoved my phone back in my pocket, and he laughed.

"You have no idea."

When I got out of the car, he was still laughing. Being with him was strangely exhilarating, but it also ended up a little tiring. Even when he wasn't moving, he had so much energy about him, and it seemed to take so much energy just being around him.

I'd barely made it inside the apartment when I saw Milo looking sheepishly at me, and I knew there was trouble afoot. He leaned against the kitchen counter, all decked out in pajamas since it was past his bedtime.

I was about to ask what was going on when I heard the rather shrill voice of my mother, and looked over to see her sitting in the tattered easy chair in the living room.

"Glad to see you finally made it home," Mom said.

Her graying hair was a frayed mess spreading out from her bun. Her eyes were unusually large, a feature that both Milo and I had inherited, making us appear much younger than we were. She lit another cigarette as she cast a cold glance at me.

"Why aren't you at work?" I asked.

"They had a bomb threat to the building so they shut it down for the night," Mom said. "They're diverting all the calls to Edina's station."

"Oh." I stood awkwardly in between the kitchen and the living room, waiting for someone to tell me what was going on.

"What were you doing out so late?" Her voice lilted at the end, taunting me.

"I don't have school, and I don't have a curfew," I answered cautiously.

In theory, I might've had a curfew, but we'd never even talked about it and she always worked nights. On weeknights, I tried to be in by midnight, mostly because Milo would freak out on me.

The only thing Mom really kept track of was whether or not we went to school and passed all our classes. As long as I did that, everything else seemed fine with her.

"So, you weren't out with a guy?" Mom asked pointedly, and I saw Milo looking ashamed out of the corner of my eye.

"Well, yeah, I was." I drew my shoulders back a bit, telling myself that I hadn't done anything wrong, no matter what my mother's angry glare said. "Is that a problem?"

"Who is he?" She flicked an ash off the arm of the chair, looking down instead of at me.

"His name is Jack." I shifted uneasily, and stole a glance at Milo.

I felt very sorry for him. I had no idea how long he'd been forced to stand here with my mother, and I couldn't imagine the kind of interrogation she had put him through.

Let me be clear: she wasn't a bad mother. She was just a tired, lonely woman that worked seventy hours a week and hardly ever saw her kids. She barely had time to try to convince us not to make the same mistakes she had.

"I see." Abruptly, my mother put her cigarette out and exhaled deeply. When she spoke again, her voice was sweet, much too sweet, and my skin wanted to crawl. "I think I should meet this boy."

"How? When? You work all the time."

"Well, he seems to be a night owl, much like yourself." She looked up at me, batting her eyes exaggeratedly. "I'm sure that you could find a time within the next two days."

A million different arguments ran through my head, but I didn't want to set her off further. I just nodded instead.

"Okay. I'll figure it out."

"You better." She sounded a little surprised that I had complied so easily, and I wondered if I spent a lot of my time arguing with her just for the sake of arguing. I was probably a very bad daughter. Maybe even a very bad person. "And if I decide that I don't want you to see this boy anymore, then that's it. Do you understand?"

"Completely," I nodded again. Of course I would see him anyway, but that wasn't something I would tell her.

"Good." Mom got up, grabbing her purse off the table. "I'm going to go to the casino now. I'll see you sometime tomorrow."

She was apparently satisfied with the conversation, and she hadn't even really screamed at me. It was actually a pretty good talk, as far as our talks go.

Mom brushed past me on her way to the door, smelling thickly of cigarettes and cheap brandy, but she paused at the door, turning slightly towards me. "I am glad that you're home safe."

"Thanks," I said, unsure of how else to respond. Then she nodded once and walked out the door.

Milo apologized as soon as she left, but I assured him he had nothing to apologize for. He always looked out for my best interest, and I knew that. Besides, I was too tired to worry about anything else.

I decided to get it over with and text Jack to ask if he could meet my mother. When he messaged me back a few seconds later, I realized what exactly he'd done with my phone. He had bought the song "Time Warp" and set it as his ringtone, so when I got a text message or call from him, that's the song I would hear.

Thankfully, he agreed to come over for supper the next night at 8 p.m. sharp, and I tried not to think about how terrifying that prospect was.

First thing when I got up, I briefed Milo on Jack's arrival, but Mom was still asleep. For some reason, Milo had been gifted with everything domestic, meaning he was the cook in the family. I let him make supper, but scurried about trying to help him and straighten up the apartment.

We actually had a nice apartment; it was just very small. It was important to me that we impressed Jack with where we lived, and I didn't know why.

I didn't know why I felt anything I did about him, but I pushed that out of my mind. That wasn't tonight's problem.

Then the unthinkable happened. Jack arrived *early*.

"Jack," I said breathlessly when I opened the door. He had found my place without me telling him the apartment number, but I couldn't mention that in front of Milo.

"Hi," Jack beamed at me. He wore a simple tee shirt with Dickies, but it was the first time I'd seen him in pants. I suspected that this was his attempt at dressing up, and it made me smile.

"You're early," I told him. I held the door open, but I hadn't let him inside yet, so he stood in the hallway, giving me an odd look. Milo had been behind me in the kitchen, noisily preparing something, but he hadn't made a sound since we'd heard the knock at the door.

"Is that a bad thing?" Jack asked.

"No, not really," I admitted, and finally took a step back so he could come inside. He smiled at my brother and his eyes quickly scanned the apartment. "My mom's just not awake yet."

"Oh." He glanced at the clock on the wall, noting that it was after seven. "When does she get up?"

"I'll go get her now," Milo offered, wiping his hands on his jeans and stepping away from a pan.

"Oh, sorry," I fumbled, realizing that I hadn't introduced them. "Jack, this is my brother Milo. Milo, this is Jack."

"Nice to meet you." Milo did a little half wave/half nod combo, and then darted off to get my mom.

"I think I make him nervous," Jack told me quietly.

"Everyone makes him nervous."

We stood rather awkwardly in the kitchen, although I did feel slightly better now that he was around. He had a kind of calming effect on me, but I didn't know if that was good or bad.

My mother squawked things rather loudly at Milo, so I decided to make conversation to drown out the sound of her.

"So, are you hungry?" I gestured to the pans of some kind of Italian creation Milo had been making on the stove. "Milo's making something delicious. He's a really good cook."

"Actually, I just ate." Jack smiled sheepishly and put his hand on his stomach. "Sorry. I figured that since we were meeting so late, you'd probably already have eaten. And Mae insisted on feeding me."

"Oh, that's okay." But I felt more nervous.

I wasn't that hungry and I could really care less if he ate or not. Without the distraction of eating, a conversation with my mother would be much less pleasant.

Then a tantalizing idea occurred to me. Maybe we could just turn this into more of a meet-and-greet kind of thing, where Jack could say hello to my mother and then just sweep me away.

"So… do you wanna go someplace or something?" I asked.

"I thought I was meeting your mother." Jack looked confused and pointed to my mother's closed bedroom door, where Milo was trying to convince her to put on some pants to see Jack.

"I mean, after that," I clarified. "Since you're not eating. It would be silly to sit around here and watch them eat."

"Aren't you hungry?"

"I'll live." There were like ten million places to eat in the Twin Cities, and this was the only one that included strained dinner conversation with my mother.

"Alright," he shrugged and leaned back against the kitchen counter. "What did you have in mind?"

"Pretty much anything, as long as it's not here."

"I'm up!" Mom shouted, and a few seconds later, Milo rushed out of her room, looking rather frazzled.

"She'll be right out," Milo said.

He went back over to the stove and stirred something simmering in a pan, looking relieved to be back cooking instead of with Mom.

"Do you need help with anything?" I offered.

Freshly washed vegetables sat in the sink, and he had two pans on the stove boiling with food, not to mention the oven was preheating for something.

I felt guilty about him making this massive feast on my behalf, and I wasn't even going to eat it. Well, later on tonight, I'd dig into the cold leftovers and watch cartoons, but that wasn't the same as sitting down to it.

"You can slice some of the vegetables if you want," Milo glanced back at me.

"What are they for?" I pulled out the cutting board and a knife, setting them on the counter next to where Jack leaned. Grabbing a tomato and green pepper from the sink, I repeated the question to Milo, who'd become distracted by seasoning a red sauce bubbling in a frying pan. "What am I cutting the vegetables for?"

"The salad." He tasted the sauce, which must've satisfied him, because he flipped off the stove, and pulled out a cake pan.

I think he was making some kind of special lasagna with all types of homemade everything, but I couldn't be sure because when he explained things to me, he always used culinary terms that I didn't understand.

"Everything smells fantastic," Jack complimented him.

Milo had his back to us, but I could see his cheeks reddening a little as he laid out noodles in the pan. Maybe Milo wasn't completely immune to Jack's allure either.

"I have bad news though." I lowered my voice, afraid my mother might hear me. She had yet to emerge from her bedroom, but I decided that was a good thing. Carefully slicing a green pepper, I saw Milo's shoulders tense up and he looked hesitatingly at me. "We're not actually gonna eat here." His face fell, but he quickly looked away, trying to hide it.

"It's my fault really," Jack said. As he talked, his voice worked its magic on Milo, and he relaxed a little. "I didn't realize I was supposed to eat here, so I went ahead and ate at home. And then I made plans for us in a little bit. I'm really sorry, though. I can tell I'm missing a fantastic meal."

"Its fine," Milo said, and he sounded almost like he meant it.

He put the pan in the oven, and he'd already set the table, so he went over to clear the extra two places for Jack and me.

"Milo-" I turned to apologize to him further.

He had this way of looking like a little boy when he was sad, and it just broke my heart. Unfortunately, I decided keep cutting the green pepper as I turned, and that wasn't the smartest move ever. The knife sliced sharply into the index finger of my left hand, and I yelped painfully.

"What?" Milo instantly stopped what he was doing and rushed over to me. He'd spent enough time with me in the kitchen to know that I usually ended up with cuts or burns. "What'd you cut?"

"I just got my finger," I winced, squeezing my fingers around it to stop the bleeding. Milo, being the smart one, grabbed a washcloth to put on it.

"Maybe you should run that under water," Jack interjected, his voice sounding oddly stiff.

Milo turned on the water, yanking my hand under it, but I looked over at Jack. He had taken a few steps away from me, and he'd gone pale. I guess the sight of blood didn't agree with him.

Milo examined my finger under the water, but I kept my eyes fixed on Jack. He had looked away from me and taken another step back. The sight of the blood, even the small amount that it was, had really affected him, so I hurried to clean it up.

"It's not that bad," Milo said. "I'll get you a Band-Aid."

He darted off to the bathroom to retrieve a Boba Fett Band-Aid from the medicine cabinet. I left my finger running under the water, even though I think it had stopped bleeding.

With my other hand, I used the washcloth to wipe off the cutting bored, pushing bloodied slices of green pepper into the sink and down the drain.

"What's going on?" Mom always had the best timing and chose just then to come out of the bedroom. Her hair was its usually frizzy mess, but she'd put on worn out jeans and an over sized sweatshirt.

"I just cut my finger." I held up my injured appendage.

Milo came out of the bathroom and jogged over to me. As if I were a complete invalid, he started drying my finger with a paper towel before putting on the Band-Aid.

"Milo, you know better than to let her help you in the kitchen," Mom said.

She went over to the coffee table to grab an ashtray, and then lit a cigarette as she walked back into the kitchen. Her eyes scanned over Jack, but she didn't say anything to him. Instead, she just set the ashtray on the kitchen table and sat down.

"Sorry," Jack mumbled once my finger was sufficiently bandaged. Whatever had gotten into him seemed to be dissipating and the color in his cheeks returned.

"I'm the one that cut my finger. There's no reason for you to be sorry." I looked over at him, and he smiled at me, but it wasn't his usual cheerful grin.

"We don't really need a salad anyway," Milo decided.

He pushed past me, collecting the vegetables that I'd cut and tossing them in the garbage. They all hadn't been tainted with my blood, but enough of them had where it didn't seem worth it.

"So…" Mom blew out a smoke ring and gazed intently at Jack. Her features still had that same worn look they always did, but there was something extra in her voice. "You must be Jack."

When she accented his name, that's when I realized what it was. She wasn't as overt as Jane had been, but the look in her eyes and the tone to her voice... it was definitely seductive. My stomach twisted nauseously.

"And you must be Alice's mom," Jack grinned at her, authentically this time. He leaned back against the counter and crossed one foot over his ankle, bouncing the toe of his blue Converse on the tile.

"Anna." This time, my mother actually did a "casual" lick of her lips when she looked at him.

I rolled my eyes, and then looked to Milo to see if he noticed her being so ridiculous, but he was no help. He just stood in the middle of the kitchen with his arms crossed over his chest, staring at Jack.

"Anna." Jack repeated, and my mother looked down, flicking her cigarette in the ashtray.

"So tell me about yourself." Her eyes went back up to him, and they had never looked so young before.

My mother was only thirty-four, but she usually looked much older than that. But when she looked at Jack, this girliness underneath came through. I could see how beautiful and radiant she must've been when she was young, before she had me.

"What do you want to know?" Jack tilted his head at her.

"Everything," she asked, coy.

"Well, that's an awful lot to tell. Where would you like me to start?"

"What do you do with yourself?" Her eyes had gone sultry, and I had to fight the urge to vomit or take Jack's hand or something.

Milo pulled up a chair next to Mom, but he didn't look even slightly disturbed by her behavior. He had become too enamored by Jack and just listened for his answer.

"Not a lot really," Jack admitted.

"You don't work?" Mom pressed.

"Nope." He shrugged, and this time I felt irritated that he didn't have to work and didn't think anything of it. Mom should've felt the same way, but she didn't. "I mean, I've done a lot of odd jobs over the years. Like I tried some bartending for awhile and once I was tour guide for Niagara Cave down in Harmony, but that was too far away so I quit. I don't know. Nothing's just really stuck, I guess."

"How do you support yourself?" It was a logical question, so it kinda surprised me that Mom had even bothered asking it.

"Well…" Jack laughed a little, and both her and Milo closed their eyes, as if the sound was just too pleasurable for them to handle. "I guess I don't really. I live with my family, and… they kind of take care of me. I guess."

"But you're twenty-four," I interjected.

Really, if his family was loaded and wanted to take care of him, then I'd say, more power to you. But if Mom wasn't going to ask the tough questions, then I was.

"I know." Jack didn't look ashamed at all, though, like I probably would if somebody called me out on being in my mid-twenties, unemployed, and living at home. "It just makes sense for us. I don't know a better way of explaining it."

"So you live with your parents?" Mom took a drag on her cigarette, keeping her eyes locked on him.

"No, they're dead." He said it with the same flat tone that he had before, and there was something off with it. "I live with my brothers and, uh, my sister-in-law."

"Oh?" Mom raised an eyebrow, and she was probably excited of the prospect of their being even more guys like him. "How old are they?"

"Ezra's twenty... six, and Mae is like twenty-eight or something, and Peter is nineteen," Jack answered.

"Hmm," Mom purred. This was so disturbing, and I was so glad that I had never seen my mom date anyone ever. "So, um, what about college?"

"I went for awhile, but I dropped out." Jack shrugged again. "It just wasn't my thing."

"What is your thing exactly?" I asked.

As far as I could tell, working, school, having a relationship, doing anything that required any amount of responsibility just wasn't his thing. What was my attraction to him?

Then he laughed, reminding me exactly what attracted me to him.

"I'm still figuring it out."

"You're still young," Mom added quickly, trying to pull his attention back to her. "You have plenty of time to figure things out."

"That's what I think," Jack agreed, and when he looked back at her, she let out a moan of some kind, and that was it for me. I'd let her stare at him enough.

"Well, we really should get going," I announced abruptly.

"What?" Mom looked sharply at me, her face getting this stricken expression. "Aren't you staying for dinner?"

"I misunderstood what Alice meant," Jack explained, his voice getting overly soothing, but I decided that whatever would get us out of here without a fight was fine by me. "I already ate, and then I made plans for us. We really do have to be going."

My mother tried to think of things to keep him trapped in the apartment with her, but I stuck to my guns. I escaped into the hall while they finished saying their good-byes, but I could still hear the unusually sweet tone to my mother's voice as she cooed all sorts of things to him.

Once Jack finally made it out to the hall and shut the door behind him, I shivered visibly, trying to shake off what I had just witnessed.

"What?" Jack laughed, looking at me as I pushed the button for the elevator.

"Oh my god, that was so disgusting!"

"I thought that went very well, actually," Jack smirked. "Your mom seemed to like me."

"Ugh, she wanted to jump your bones," I groaned. The elevator doors dinged open and we stepped in. Leaning back against the wall, I shook my head. "It was so disturbing."

"It's not my fault everybody wants me." Jack laughed again and pushed the button for the lobby, and I knew he was only half-teasing.

"I don't want you," I crossed my arms over my chest.

"Yeah, I know." Jack got quiet and thoughtful for the rest of the elevator ride, but I wasn't sure if it was because he was disappointed that I didn't want him or he just didn't understand it. He tried to change the subject as the elevator doors opened into the lobby. "So, your brother's gay?"

"He is not gay." I bristled and stepped out of the elevator.

It wouldn't really bother me if Milo was gay, but he wasn't. I mean, I would know if he was.

"Oh, so he hasn't told you yet." Jack shoved his hands in his pockets, following me as I hurried out into the cold night air.

Once we got outside, I realized that I didn't know where he'd parked or even what car he'd driven, so I stopped and waited for him.

"There's nothing to tell," I insisted. He turned to the left, walking a little ways down the block, when I saw his Jetta.

"Oh, come on," Jack scoffed. "You had to have noticed the way he looked at me."

"Everyone looks at you that way." I tried to think back and I couldn't remember if the guys had been doing it too.

Everyone reacted to him in a very friendly fashion, but I was pretty sure that guys hadn't given him that particular look, not the ones like my mom or Jane.

"No, everyone does not." Jack played with the keyless entry, and the Jetta beeped loudly, announcing that it was unlocked.

"So how does that work?" I asked, opening the car door. "Your pheromones only react to people that would be sexually attracted to you anyway? How can they possibly know that?"

Jack stood outside until I could finish my question, then he just got in the car, and I knew that was his official answer to that.

"You probably shouldn't say anything to you brother," Jack said once I'd gotten in the car. He started it, revving the engine for a second, and then pulled away from the curb. "If he hasn't told you yet, then he's probably not ready for you to know."

"He isn't gay," I repeated firmly. "He's only fifteen."

"Oh, right, cause when you were fifteen you didn't know you were straight." Jack rolled his eyes.

"How do you know I'm straight?" I countered. I mean, I am straight, but he didn't know that. "That would explain why I'm not attracted to you."

"You are attracted to me." He kept his eyes straight ahead, and adjusted the stereo, so Joy Division played softly out of the speakers. "Otherwise you wouldn't be in the car with me. It's just not the same as it is with them."

"Whatever." I crossed my arms again. Then I softened a little as I thought about Milo, and all the weird little things he did that I had always just chocked up to him being younger than me and more responsible. "So… you really think Milo's gay?"

"Yeah, he's gay," Jack replied definitively. "And before you ask, yeah, it's something I know. I can't explain it, but I just know. Like the way a lion always knows the weakest zebra in the pack."

"Are you comparing being gay to being weak?"

I was just coming to terms with the probability of my brother's homosexuality, but already I felt defensive about it. Milo was my little brother and probably the only person in the whole world that really cared about me.

"No, I'm comparing my uncanny ability to detect things to that of a lion," Jack clarified.

I was still kind of sulking, reeling from the fact that both my mother and my newly discovered gay brother wanted to do things to Jack, but Jack made it hard to mope.

"Hey, you know what would cheer you up?"

"I can only imagine," I said dryly.

"Playing *Dance Dance Revolution* at the arcade." Without warning, he flipped the car into a u-turn across three lanes of traffic.

"That doesn't sound that great." It didn't really, but Jack thought it was the greatest idea ever, and that managed to convince me somehow.

I was starting to realize that my feelings seemed to be mimicking his, and that should alarm me, but he wasn't alarmed, so I was incapable of it.

I got home very late from hanging out with Jack, as per usual. After the arcade had closed, we had loitered at a Blockbuster, before deciding that neither of us wanted to rent anything, and then drove around for awhile before Jack finally dropped me off at home.

Mom was gone at work, and Milo had gone to bed, so there was nothing said about Jack's visit.

When I finally roused the next day, I immediately went to talk to Milo about Jack. I hadn't expected him to expound very much, but his very clipped, "He seems nice" did not do the night justice.

The fact that Milo was apparently hiding something so important from me made me feel uncomfortable. A part of me wanted to just bring it out in the open and demand that he tell me, but it was his thing and he had to come to terms with it on his own time.

Because of my unease, I decided to camp out in bed all day, reading and listening to Death Cab for Cutie. When Mom got up, I went out to get a soda and find out her thoughts on Jack, but disappointingly, they just mirrored Milo's sentiments.

It wasn't that I wanted her to gush about Jack until I threw up, but their hesitance to say anything real about him disturbed me. I knew that they'd probably been embarrassed about the way they had acted but still.

Once Mom confirmed that it was acceptable for me to continue seeing Jack, I gave up on it. At least she liked him, and I could do what I wanted.

I went back into my room to figure out why it was so important to me that I kept seeing him. I hadn't fallen under his spell the same way most people did, but that didn't mean I wasn't under one. As he had pointed out, I was attracted to him, otherwise I wouldn't be there.

I sprawled out in bed and wondered if it was something like that bad *Love Potion No. 9* movie with Sandra Bullock. They drank this potion, and suddenly, everybody wanted them. Maybe Jack had done that too, in some kind of weird government experiment.

But we lived in Minnesota. Why would the government experiment here? Were there even like CIA or FBI headquarters here?

That would be a really stupid test anyway. What would the practical applications of such a potion be? And does anyone really make potions anymore?

Milo sat on the computer the entire day and barely said a word to me. I couldn't tell if he was mad at me for ditching him last night, or just going through his own conflicted deal about his sexuality.

Either way, I didn't push him on it, so I ate quickly, and then spent the rest of the night in my room. I went to bed that night, feeling a little surprised that Jack hadn't talked to me at all.

Since it was my last day of Spring Break, I decided to make the most of it by sleeping the entire day away. I knew that it would only make it harder when I tried to go to bed at a decent time or get up for school the next morning, but I didn't care.

When I finally rolled out of bed, I showered and got ready for the day. I still felt like avoiding Milo, so I text messaged Jack.

What are you up to today? I sat on my bedroom floor, painting my toenails dark blue.

Just woke up. He texted me back promptly.

Sorry. Did I wake you? It was after six o'clock, but from what little time I'd spent with Jack, I had a feeling he never went to bed before dawn.

Kinda. But it's ok. I needed to get up anyway.

So, did you want to do something today? Fanning my freshly painted nails so they'd dry, I stared at my phone expectantly.

Yeah. When?

Probably sooner rather than later. I have school tomorrow.

Ridiculous! :(Ok. Let me shower and I'll pick you up in an hour. Cool? Jack responded, making me laugh. The fact that I was going to school would impede his life in some way, and it made me feel a little special.

Cool. See you soon.

Once my toenails dried, I finished getting ready. I slipped on a pair of skimmer shoes, which completely covered up the polishing I had just done, but it was still too cold for anything open-toed.

Milo was staked out on the computer when I went out into the living room. I'd just put on a tee shirt and jeans, so I slipped on my white zippered Famous Stars and Straps hoodie over it. Even with that, I'd still probably freeze my butt off outside, but I thought my jackets were gross, so this was the better option.

"Going out?" Milo didn't look away from the computer screen, and his voice was too flat for me to decipher.

"Yep." I nodded. I really didn't appreciate the lack of communication between us, but I didn't know how to fix it. "With Jack. I won't be out too late. Cause of school in the morning."

"Whatever," Milo said noncommittally. There was no lecture or disapproval, and I sighed.

"Okay. I guess I'll see you later." I started walking towards the door, but he didn't say anything, so I waited to leave until he responded. He grunted something that sounded vaguely like "bye," but I figured that was the best I would get, and I headed outside.

Jack had driven the Jetta again, and I wondered how he decided which car to take. He was singing along very merrily with Kanye West to "Stronger," and he barely seemed to notice me when I hopped into the car. We sat outside the apartment building until the song finished, and then he turned down the radio and grinned at me.

"So, I was thinking we would take a walk tonight," Jack said brightly.

"Okay. Where?" The night was a bit chilly, but it wouldn't be unbearable. He wore a hoodie and pants today, forgoing his normal tee shirt and shorts combo that seemed highly inappropriate for March.

"Loring Park." He had started pulling away as soon as he said it.

The park was only about half a mile from where I lived, but because it was on the other side of the highway, it made it almost a necessity to drive to it. I-94 had split it in half. It used to be connected to the Minneapolis Sculpture Garden, where they had that giant spoon with the cherry (*Spoonbridge and Cherry*) along with lots of other fancy little sculptures.

We ended up going to the actual Loring Park, without all the sculptures but with lots of paths and trees.

After he parked, I got out of the car and admired the stars shining brightly above us. They were usually hard to see, thanks to the city lights, but the cold, spring air made them stand out sharply.

I looked around for Orion, the only constellation I really knew, but Jack started walking down a trail, so I followed him, vowing to search the skies later on.

"So you really have school tomorrow?" Jack asked grumpily once I caught up with him. He shoved his hands in his pockets and stared down at his Converse as he walked, while I tended to admire the scenery and the stars.

"Yeah," I grimaced.

I had a whole paper due on the War of 1812, and I hadn't done anything. In fact, the only thing I knew about the war was that it had happened in 1812. If Milo and I had been on better speaking terms, I'd probably go home and bug him about it until he just gave in and did it for me.

"So what time do you have to be home?" He kicked a stone with his foot, reminding me very much of a little boy who had just been told he'd have to go to bed early because he'd been bad.

"I don't know. Before midnight, I guess." That really wasn't that much earlier than when I normally went home, but Jack sighed and grumbled something unintelligible. "What?"

"Nothing," he mumbled, still looking at the ground.

"Did you have some big plans for tonight?" I asked, trying to figure out what had him so depressed. I was the one that had to get up at seven in the morning, not him.

"No. I just don't like it when things are finite." He sighed again, and then looked up at the sky.

"That's kind of weird," I said. Milo had a phobia of wet sand, and Jane hated the word kumquat (it sounded too perverse, even for her), but it was pretty strange to dislike anything that had a definite ending. "Everything ends."

"I know. I mean, we don't hang out forever anyway. It's just..." He shook his head, and then stared off at the Basilica of St. Mary. It was this huge, beautiful cathedral, and we could just see the top of it, arched out into the sky above the trees. "Mae wanted to get married there."

"What?" I asked, confused by his sudden topic change.

"My brother's wife." He nodded at the church. "But Ezra didn't want to."

"Why not?" It was a stunning piece of architecture, so I understood the urge to marry there. I personally wouldn't want to, but most of the time, I wasn't even sure if I wanted to get married.

"They're not Catholic, for one thing." There was more to the story, but Jack seemed hesitant to tell me about it. Finally, he continued, "It just didn't seem right. It was Mae's second marriage. So they found something else, and it worked out better anyway."

"How long have they been married?"

"I'm not really sure," he shrugged.

Pulling my hoodie tighter around me, I shivered. Jack glanced over at me, and he didn't seem even slightly bothered by the cold. Nothing really seemed to bother him, except my bedtime.

"Do you want my sweatshirt?" He started pulling on his sleeve, like he was going to take it off, but I held up my hand to stop him.

"No, I'm okay." Since he had actually bothered to put on something warmer today, I wasn't about to take it from him because I thought my jacket was ugly.

"Are you sure?"

"Yeah, I'm fine," I insisted. Flipping up the hood over my head, I smiled up at him. "See? Fine."

"If you say so." Jack pulled on his sleeve, adjusting it back to normal. "Let me know if you change your mind."

"I won't."

"I know," Jack said, sounding a little exasperated. "You never change your mind about anything."

"You haven't known me for that long," I scoffed. "How can you be so sure?"

"I'm just very certain of things," he replied simply.

That was true enough. He didn't always have an answer for everything, but the things he knew, he really knew. I was about to ask him what the deal was with his sixth sense about everything, but then his head shot up sharply.

"Watch out."

"Watch out for what?" I tried to keep my voice even, but the instant he got nervous, I was terrified.

He stepped in front of me to shield from me something, but I peered around him, looking into the dark for some lurking danger.

- 6 -

At first, I thought it was a giant grizzly bear barreling towards us. Then it ran underneath a lamp on the path, and I saw it was just a massive brown dog. There was a dog park on the other side of the park, so I wouldn't have thought anything of it if Jack hadn't been on such high alert.

"It's just a dog," I told him, hoping that would somehow relax him.

"I know what it is." He seemed to be debating something, probably whether he should run or stay put, but the dog was approaching quickly, making his decision for him. "Ah, hell."

The dog snarled at us, but it never even slowed down. Drool and slobber spewed from its mouth, and its eyes had a crazed, intense look I had never seen on an animal before.

Without any provocation, it suddenly lunged at Jack. He held one arm behind him, trying to protect me more from the dog, and he held his other arm in front of him, using his forearm to block the attack.

The dog latched on it with a loud crunching sound that made my blood curdle, and I screamed. With one swift movement, Jack whipped his hand around, grabbing the dog by the back of the neck.

"Go back to the car!" Jack shouted.

He had pinned the dog to the ground by kneeling on its back and wrapping his hands around its neck. There was blood streaming down his arm, and all the while, the dog was snapping and growling viciously.

But I stayed frozen, gaping at Jack and the dog.

"Alice! Go back to the car!"

"Why?" I felt nauseous, but I didn't want to leave Jack. If I did, I knew that something bad would happen, although I didn't even know what that meant.

"Alice! Just do it!" Jack growled.

Adrenaline surged through my body, and my feet were happy to comply when I started running back to the car.

Before I had even made it there, I heard the dog yelp, and my stomach dropped. My heart pounded erratically in my chest, and I wanted to throw up.

I made it to the car, and I fought the urge to just keep running. I collapsed on the pavement next to it, gasping for breath.

When I saw Jack walking towards me, I stood up and hurried towards him, but I stopped sharply before I met him.

Part of me really wanted to hug him, but another part of me knew what he had done, and it scared the hell out of me. Irrational tears streamed down my cheeks, but I tried to ignore them.

"Jack, what did you do?" I wiped at my eyes to erase the tears. "What'd you do with the dog?"

"Alice…" He closed his eyes, as if it would hurt him too much to watch me react. "I didn't have any choice. You saw him. He was going to kill somebody! What if you had been here by yourself or with Milo?"

Everything he was saying was true. The dog had looked insane and probably rabid, and even before I left him, I knew that Jack would kill the dog. But it didn't change anything.

Hurting any animal for any reason would always reduce me to tears, especially when I had been some part of it. He had killed that dog to protect me.

"I don't care!" I cried harder, and I wished I would just stop.

It seemed unfair to me that I would be angry with Jack for saving my life, but I couldn't help it. He moved awkwardly, as if he wanted to hug me, but he knew that I would push him away if he tried.

"Alice," Jack breathed deeply, looking away from me. He had this agonized expression on his face, and he took a small step back from me. "Everything just got so much more complicated."

"What are you talking about?"

I felt something shift, and a whole new fear ran through me. As upset as I had been over the dog, I hadn't hated Jack, or even really been mad at him.

"This!" Jack shook his head and walked past me. "Everything! This is so stupid. I am so stupid."

"What are you talking about?" I ran after him, wondering what I had done that had been so terrible. I reached out for him, but he pulled his arm away before I even got close to it.

"I'm taking you home." We had reached the car, but he stood outside of it, waiting for me to get in. I had stopped in front of it and refused to go any further.

"No!" I insisted. "Why?"

"Why?" He laughed, but it was humorless and sent nervous shivers all over me. Then he reeled on me, his face stone cold, and his voice harsher than I had ever imagined it could be. "I killed a dog – to save your life – and you look at me like I'm a monster!"

He rubbed his temple, and I saw blood covering his hand. Somehow, I'd managed to forget that the dog had bitten him.

"Jack, I don't think that you're a monster," I explained softly. "I just don't like it when things die."

"Nobody does, Alice," Jack replied icily. He bit his lip and shook his head, then mumbled, "The damn thing was probably rabid. It was gonna die anyway."

"I know that," I swallowed hard. "I don't know what I did that upset you so much, but I'm sorry. I never wanted to offend you. And I don't think it's fair that you're going to cut me out of your life because I cried over a dog."

"It's not because you cried." He softened a little, but he still wouldn't look at me. "It was the way you looked at me."

"I'm sorry!" I insisted. "I was in shock! The dog just charged at us and attacked you and then... I don't know. I'm sorry. It was just because it was a dog. Remember when you beat up those people in the parking garage? I didn't cry then."

"No, you didn't," Jack agreed, and he finally seemed to be relenting. I took a step closer to him, eyeing up the ragged holes in his sweatshirt and the blood on his hand.

"We should go the hospital," I said.

"Why?" Jack looked up at me, his eyes terrified. "Did he get you? I thought I blocked him-"

"No, I'm fine," I cut him off, and he relaxed again. "I was talking about you. The dog bit you."

"No, that's fine." He waved his arm absently and moved closer to the car, like he would escape into the car and away from my prying eyes. "It's not a big deal."

"Yeah, it is," I continued towards him. "Your shirts all torn up and I can see the blood. Plus, like you said, the dog's probably rabid. You're going to need a rabies shot."

"I'll go tomorrow. It's not that bad." Jack had stepped so far back that he pressed up against the door. I reached for his arm, and he pulled it back from me, but I wouldn't have any of it.

"Jack!" I said firmly, and he let out an exasperated sigh.

"It's really not that bad," he repeated, but he let me take his arm.

The hoodie was soaked with blood that covered his hand, so I doubted his claims. Very carefully, I pulled up the sleeve of his shirt and gasped.

There were three little teeth holes in arms. That was all. They were slightly red and raised, but they were smaller than a pencil. On top of that, they weren't even bleeding.

Blood covered his arm, but the trails seemed to connect just outside of where the teeth marks were. He had blood, but almost no wound.

"I told you it wasn't bad." Jack yanked his arm back from me and pulled down his sleeve.

"How?" I stared up at him.

"I bleed easy. I'm a hemophiliac," Jack replied, and for some reason, that answer made him smirk.

"No, it's not possible," I shook my head. "I heard the dog crunching into your bone. There's no way that wounds that shallow would hit bone."

"It all happened so fast. You can't be sure of what you heard," he attempted to explain it all away.

"I know what I heard!" I said it with more conviction than I actually had. "You should have massive bite marks and maybe even a broken arm. And how did you even get that dog down?"

"You saw me do that." He looked at me skeptically, but there was something brewing in his eyes that I couldn't read.

"That dog was huge and crazy!" I remembered the way that Jack had stopped it with one hand before he threw it the ground. It easily weighed over a hundred pounds, and it had clamped onto his arm. "It's not even humanly possible for you to be able to stop a dog like that, not without a massive fight, and you have one barely-there bite mark! If he could be taken down that easily, then…"

"What exactly are you saying?" Jack narrowed his eyes at me, but there was a brightness to them. He was hoping I would figure it out.

"You were bit, but there's hardly a wound, and…and you have like super human strength and… everything in the whole world wants to have sex with you and… you don't have a temperature!" I spouted.

Biting my lip, I didn't look at him. I tried to figure it all out, but none of it made sense. I could feel him looking at me, but I just couldn't put the puzzle together.

"So?" Jack asked encouragingly.

"So…" I threw my arms up in the air, feeling completely exasperated. "I don't know! You're a werewolf!" Jack scoffed and looked disappointed.

"There's no such thing as werewolves," he rolled his eyes and opened the car door.

"Well, what else is there?" I whined, but he shut the door instead of answering me. I ran around to the other side of the car and jumped in. "What's going on, Jack?"

"I bleed a lot, you're confused cause you got caught up in the emotion, my adrenaline gave me the power to take down the dog, and I am just stunningly attractive," he explained, but his tone was teasing, especially on the part about him being attractive. "Oh, and I do to have a temperature. Everything has a temperature."

"Okay, yeah, but you don't have a normal human temperature."

"Are you like a walking thermometer?" Jack started the car and looked over at me.

"Where are we going?" I asked, ignoring his question.

"I'm taking you home," he said, then added, "Just for the night. I'll see you tomorrow. But you've had a long enough night, and you have school in the morning."

"You still need to go to the hospital," I pointed out. "The bite broke the skin. You need a rabies shot."

"I do not." He started to pull out of the parking lot and turned on the stereo, but kept it low so we could talk.

"Look, I know the wounds aren't very big, but if any of his saliva mixes with your blood, you can get rabies," I said. "I read this book by

Chuck Palahniuk all about rabies, so I'm almost nearly an expert. It's even sexually transmitted."

"Well, luckily for you-" (at that point he stopped to wink at me, but I just rolled my eyes) "-I do not have rabies."

"You don't know that," I said. "It wouldn't hurt you just to get a stupid shot."

"No, Alice, I don't need a shot." He looked at me, completely serious, and then it finally dawned on me.

"You can't get rabies." I sighed and leaned my head back against the seat. "That really blows my whole werewolf theory."

"I already told you they aren't real."

"So is it just rabies or is it any communicable disease?" I asked it even though I wasn't sure he would answer. "Oh my god. It's any disease, isn't it? Any form of illness?"

"You've had a very long night," he said quietly. "Maybe we should drop it for tonight."

"But-" I started to protest but I couldn't think of a single argument for it. All of this was getting maddening, but for whatever reason, he couldn't tell me what was going on. So all I could do was get more and more frustrated and perplexed. "You're okay, aren't you?"

"What do you mean?"

"Like... you got injured tonight for me, and I just want to know that you're okay." That might be the only information I'd get, and it had to be enough for me to settle with that.

"Yeah, I'm fine," Jack smiled at me. We had stopped in front of my building, but I was reluctant to get out.

"Ugh, this is so unfair," I groaned, opening the car door to get out.

"You know what you're problem might be?" Jack asked, giving me an odd look. "You worry too much."

"Yeah. That's my problem," I grumbled getting out of the car.

Jack was still laughing when he pulled away, and I stood on the curb for a minute, trying to put everything into perspective. Sure, he had killed a rabid dog and then magically healed from the attack, but he had saved my life. Again.

There isn't a single sound in the world that's worse than an alarm going off. After Jack had dropped me off last night, it had been all but impossible to fall asleep. Between lingering adrenaline from the near-death experience, and Jack's increasingly cryptic responses and bizarre behavior, I had too much on my mind.

Once the warm water of the morning shower splashed my face, it all seemed even more ridiculous. I lived in Minneapolis, not Gotham City, or whatever other bogus city that stuff happened.

Here, in the real world, there were no super powers or werewolves or unicorns. Everything in life had an explanation, and Jack's probably had more to do with cocaine or mescaline than it did magic.

People addicted to speed were known to exhibit superhuman strength, and combine that with some kind of chemical imbalance that made him smell irresistible to women, and there it was. Problem solved. And he was just kind of a jackass and didn't want to let on that he had a drug problem.

I spent too much time in the shower, and I almost missed the bus to school. Milo sat next to me, but he didn't seem to be in a talking mood, so I put in my ear buds and decided to pass the time listening to Rogue Wave on my iPod. Resting my forehead against the glass of the window, I watched my breath fog it up.

Milo kept giving me the cold shoulder even though I hadn't done anything wrong, and this guy that I barely knew but really liked had fought off a rabid dog last night. What exactly had happened to my life over Spring Break?

School passed more slowly than it ever had before. I slept all through my second hour, but I managed to sneak my iPod into my other classes. I just stared out the window, at the chilly rain falling down, and tried not to think about Jack. By the end of fifth hour, I had completely exhausted myself not thinking about him.

When I stopped at my locker between classes, I managed to drop my History book on the ground. I bent down to pick it up, and when I stood back up, Milo was standing right next to me, scaring the crap out of me. He admired the clutter that occupied my locker, including the obligatory collage mess of magazine cut outs lining the inside of the door.

"God, you scared me," I grumbled, shoving my History book into my book bag.

"So are you gonna be at home tonight or not?" He had one of his hands on my locker door, and he swung it back and forth, just enough to make it squeak.

"Of course I'm gonna be there. I live there." I continued fiddling around with something in my bag, but mostly I was trying to look busy.

"I meant, are you gonna hang out with Jack?" His tone was icy, and I didn't understand what he found so offensive about me being with Jack. Even if he was having some kind of jealousy, shouldn't he be trying to cover it up better?

"Yeah, probably," I shrugged.

We hadn't actually talked yet, but Jack had said that he would see me today, and I didn't have any reason to doubt him. Well, except for the fact that he was hiding something major.

"So are you guys like dating or what?" Milo asked, dripping with angry sarcasm.

"No. It's not like that." I slung my bag over my shoulder, and he just narrowed his eyes at me.

Suddenly, it pissed me off that I had to explain myself to him. We weren't dating, but it shouldn't matter to him anyway. It wasn't my fault that Jack's abnormal attractiveness had made his sexual orientation even more confusing. If he had told me he was having issues with it, I wouldn't have brought Jack around.

"Whatever," Milo muttered.

"What exactly are you accusing me of?" I slammed my locker door shut. He let his hands fall to the sides, looking startled. "Even if I am dating Jack, so what? I can do that. There's nothing wrong with being friends with him or dating him or whatever it is I decide to do with him. He's a nice guy and it's a perfectly reasonable thing to do."

"Whatever you say," Milo said, but he wasn't as confident or angry.

"Milo, this is stupid." I readjusted the strap over my shoulder and looked at him softly. "I get it, okay? I saw the way that you looked at Jack."

"I don't know what you're talking about." He flushed and averted his eyes, shifting uncomfortably.

Outing him in the middle of the hall at school probably wasn't the best idea, but I just couldn't take his indifference to me anymore. He normally told me everything, and it looked like he wasn't going to talk to me about this unless I got the ball rolling.

"It's okay." I lowered my voice so other people wouldn't overhear. "If you're gay. It's okay. I understand."

"You don't understand anything!" Milo shouted.

When he looked up at me, tears filled his eyes, and I realized that I had made a terrible mistake. I couldn't force him to come to terms with anything, and if he wasn't ready to talk about it with me, I should've respected that.

"Milo-" I started to say something, but I didn't really have anything to follow it up.

He didn't wait around for it anyway. He just turned and stormed off down the hall, leaving me alone to think about what an ass I was.

When I got on the bus after school, he made sure to sit on the opposite side. On the way to our house from the bus stop, he jogged on ahead of me. I tried to hurry and catch up, but by the time I made it inside, he'd already slammed the door to his bedroom.

He must've been really upset if he risked the wrath of our mother just to show me how angry he was. I sighed and flopped on the couch, wondering how he had managed to put up with me for so long.

I had made it through two full episodes of *Judge Judy* while lying sprawled out on the couch without any word from Jack or Milo, and I was starting to think that maybe the whole world had ostracized me. The only time that Jane had talked to me all day was during lunch, and then it was just a list of how much she drank and who she had sex with over the break.

I just wanted to curl up on the couch and completely give up on life, but then I heard the familiar ring of "Time Warp" and I quickly snatched up my phone.

Are you done with school yet? Jack text messaged, making me wonder how long it had been since he went to school.

Yeah. I've been done for like two hours. Why? I replied.

Good. Ready to hang out? He hadn't really answered my question, but hey, what's new?

Yeah. Sure. What did you have in mind? I messaged him.

I'll pick you up in 15.

And that was that. My clothes from school were fine (I'd gone with jeans, a long shirt, and a cute little black vest), but most of my makeup had worn off, so I rushed to the bathroom to reapply and run a brush through my hair.

I started heading towards the front door, but decided against it. Exhaling nervously, I knocked on Milo's door.

"Milo?" I said cautiously. He didn't respond, but I continued anyway. "I know you're mad at me, and I don't blame you. I did a stupid, stupid thing. But um…" I sighed, and tried to figure out what I wanted to say. "You can talk to me if you want to. But I just thought I'd let you know that I'm going to go hang out with Jack. But you can call me if you want to. Okay?"

He still didn't answer, but I waited a minute just to be sure. Then since I'd already spent too much time getting ready, I hurried out to meet Jack.

I stepped outside, feeling like the worst sister in the world, just in time to see Jack pull up. I trudged over to the red Lamborghini and fell into the seat heavily.

The Ramones blared out the speakers, and he turned them down quickly, looking at me with a mischievous grin. Even though my sour mood had to be obvious, he was oblivious to it, so it soon faded away.

"What?" I asked. He bit his lip, as if he couldn't decide whether to tell me or not. "What's going on?"

"I think that its time you met my family." He sounded wildly excited by the idea, but also a tad nervous. Whatever made him nervous tended to terrify me, so I gulped. "No, it's a good thing. Yeah." Then he nodded, more to himself than me. "Yeah. It's good."

He had thrown the car into gear, and we were flying down the street and turning on the highway before I could even really protest, not that I would've anyway. Meeting families was usually my least favorite thing in the world, but a family that spawned Jack intrigued me.

"After what happened last night, I think it's time," Jack explained, but I had no idea what his family could possibly have to do with a rabid dog. Unless his family were dog breeders or something.

Then I remembered what happened and looked over at Jack's arm, which was bare thanks to his return to his tee shirt uniform. (He wore one today that read "Frankie Says Relax.")

I leaned in closer to inspect both his arms, thinking I must've looked at the wrong one. But neither one of them had a scratch or a mark or even a scar.

He noticed me looking and immediately chastised me. "No. Don't even think about it."

"What?" I leaned back in my seat, still staring at his arms. "You mean asking how you magically got rid of any trace of the dog bite so quickly?"

"Precisely. Don't ask any questions about anything like that, not about me, not about anyone else," Jack warned me.

"They're like you, aren't they?" By now, nothing should come as a shock, but I still looked at him in disbelief. Every time I thought things couldn't get any weirder, they did.

"I want you to meet them, but you can't be like this. You have to act completely oblivious." His tone was light, but he was being firm. "I mean it, Alice. My family. My rules."

"Yeah, yeah, I get it." I rolled my eyes and turned my attention to the world speeding past us out the window. "Where do you live anyway?"

"In St. Louis Park, by a lake," he said. "It's not that far."

I didn't know a lot about that area, but what I had heard is that there were lots of nice, expensive homes. So it would make sense that Jack lived there, since we were cruising down the highway in a bright red Lamborghini.

"Don't worry," he attempted to reassure me. "They'll like you. I think. Well, Ezra isn't there. So it's just Mae and Peter. That should make it easier."

"Where's Ezra?"

For some reason, knowing one of his brothers would be gone made me more nervous. Maybe Jack knew Ezra wouldn't like me, and that's why he was bringing me over when he wasn't around.

"Business thing," Jack shrugged. "He's gone a lot with stuff."

"Well, the Lamborghini doesn't pay for itself."

"Yeah, I guess that's true." He looked over at me, and then laughed at my nervous fidgeting. I had started chewing on my nails, which was an awful habit that I kept vowing to quit. "Seriously, you'll be fine. They'll like you. I mean, I like you so… they'll like you."

"Yeah, cause everything in life is really that simple," I sighed.

"This one thing might actually be," he smiled confidently.

The car started slowing down, and he turned off the road, meaning we were getting closer, and my heart thudded painfully. When he pulled up to his house, I cringed.

Incredibly beautiful and massive, it was more of a mansion or a castle than a house. There was a five stall garage at the end of a short, winding driveway. The whole place had been done in some kind of pale sandstone.

The front door entered right into a rounded tower. There was a large rectangular window above it, covered in wrought-iron bars. The tower flowed into what would otherwise be a rather conventional square house, if not for the gorgeous black iron balcony coming out of a second story window underneath a weeping willow.

"Oh my gosh," I gasped as we pulled into the garage. "You live here?"

"Yeah." He heard the awed tone in my voice and chuckled. "It's just a house."

"Nothing is 'just' anything with you," I said under my breath.

He laughed harder and started getting out of the car, and I followed suit, but much slower. I had never felt so intimidated in my entire life. Everything about me suddenly seemed plain and dreary, and I felt totally ashamed that I had let him see the inside of my disgustingly tiny apartment.

"You know I didn't buy this, right?" Jack turned to look back at me as we walked past the four other vehicles in the garage (Mae's black Jetta, a green Jeep Wrangler with a canvas top, a black Lexus LS, and a shiny silver Audi TT Roadster). Then he gestured to the impressive collection of cars. "I didn't buy any of this. None of it's really mine."

"Then who did buy it?"

"Ezra, mostly. And Peter." We had reached the huge wooden door that presumably led into the house, and he turned back to grin at me. "Mae and I are just eye candy."

Jack threw open the door, shouting hello. I had barely crept in the house behind him when a giant mass of white fur flung itself at him.

It caused a mild flashback to the night before and I almost yelped, but Jack was scratching the dog and telling her how pretty she was, and I realized that it was just his gigantic Great Pyrenees.

"Matilda!" A warm voice with a soft, British accent filtered through the house, and then I saw her rushing in to greet us.

She was beautiful, probably in an unconventional sense, but that almost made her more stunning. Her long, light brown waves of hair had been clipped back to keep it out of her honey colored eyes. Her skin looked like white porcelain, but warmth came off her in comforting waves.

She went over to the dog, pushing her down off of Jack with ease, and in a slightly scolding tone, she said, "Oh, Matilda, do be a good girl. Please."

"Ah, she's alright." Jack crouched down to continue scratching the dog's head. Watching him play with her, I realized for the first time how hard it must've been for him to kill that dog last night.

"I'm so sorry," she apologized breathlessly, putting her hand over her heart to show how sincere she was. She looked at me for the first time and smiled. "Matilda's still a puppy."

"Mattie's always a good girl, aren't you?" Jack's voice was verging on baby-talk, and Matilda licked his face appreciatively.

"Well, look at you!" Her smile grew broader and warmer. "You're lovely!"

"Thanks," I mumbled, feeling my cheeks burn with embarrassment. She was far more beautiful than I could ever hope to be, and I didn't know really how to respond to her open affection.

"Oh, sorry." Jack gave the dog one final pat before standing up. "Alice, this is Mae. Mae, this is Alice."

"It's a pleasure to meet you," I floundered.

Something about her made me feel safe and oddly loved, but it was so unexpected that I didn't really have time to collect my thoughts and respond.

"The pleasure is all mine!" Mae gushed, placing her hand over her heart again. "You really have no idea."

"What have you been saying about me?" I gave Jack a sidelong glance, wondering what he possibly could've said to get her so excited over me. He was the one with all the magical powers. I just argued with him and got myself in ridiculous situations.

"Not that much," Jack shrugged, but he didn't seem embarrassed or surprised by Mae at all.

"Shall I give you the grand tour?" Mae asked, looping her arm through mine. Then she looked over at Jack. "Would that be alright with you?"

"Yeah, go ahead." He had already started playing with the dog again, seemingly contented to let Mae kidnap me and do as she pleased.

"This is the entryway, obviously," Mae gestured to the vaulted ceilings and marble floors around us, and the rings on her fingers flashed in the light.

Then she started to lead me into an adjoining room, which appeared to be some kind of expansive living room. The rest of the house had dark golden oak wood floors and cream colored walls. Somehow, it managed to combine a warm modern motif with touches of a castle. It was beautiful and perfect and really, so utterly Mae.

"Here's the living room. Windows, fireplace, etc." Before I could even really take it all in, she started leading me into the kitchen. The tiles were granite in natural neutral colors and the cupboards matched the hardwood floors.

Off the back of the kitchen, giant windows and glass French doors revealed a beautiful view of the lake. A massive stone patio sat right outside the doors, leading down to the lake.

"This is the kitchen, and the view."

"That is truly breathtaking." I pulled away from her just enough so I could peer out the window. It was dark out, so I couldn't fully appreciate it, but several large lights lit the backyard and I got a glimpse of it.

"That's why Ezra chose this place." Mae put her hand on my arm when she returned to my side, and I noticed that her skin felt the same as Jack's — silky soft, but completely temperatureless, like touching a doll. "This land, anyway. He built the house."

"He designed it and everything?" I know I sounded surprised, which made me feel embarrassed.

Of course her husband had built this amazing piece of architecture. They were obviously superior to everyone in every way, and I'd better start getting used to it.

"Well, I helped, a little." Mae smiled modestly at me, and I realized that I was already falling in love with her. Not sexually or anything lesbian like that, but they were just so inviting and charismatic, I couldn't help it.

That's when I realized that I was a little bit in love with Jack. He was impossibly wonderful, and I couldn't stand to be away from him. I had started craning my head to look around for him when Mae pulled me onto the next room.

"This is a really fast tour you're giving me," I commented as she went through the grand dining room connected to the kitchen. We had just started down a hall and she laughed.

"Well, you'll see the house enough, I'm sure." Her eyes sparkled at me, and I knew that she was implying that I'd be hanging out there more, which suited me just fine. "I really just wanted a chance to get acquainted with you, and this seemed like the perfect way."

"Oh." I nodded as if I really understood.

"There's the lou if you need it," Mae gestured to a gorgeous bathroom, and then vaguely pointed to two rooms at the end of the hall. "That's Ezra's office at the end, and our bedroom next to it. They're not that exciting, really."

"Somehow, I doubt that," I said, but I let her pull me onward and up the stairs. She claimed that she wanted to get acquainted with me, but I didn't understand how she really meant to do that when she was rushing me through the house.

"Here's Jack's room," Mae pointed to an open door at the top of the stairs, and I took a moment to peek in.

The walls were dark blue, as he had told me they were, and the bed was massive and laid out in black silk blankets. A giant flat screen television hung on the wall, and tons of gaming gear and videogames filling the built-in entertainment center in the wall. Some clothes were strewn about the room, but really, it was exactly as I expected it would be.

"There's a guest room, with another bathroom, at the end of the hall," Mae explained, then looked a little perplexed. "I don't know why there's another bathroom up here. Each bedroom has its own attached bathroom, and its own fireplace. I think someone must've suggested it to Ezra that it was a good resale point."

"This house is all bathrooms and fireplaces," a velvety voice grumbled, and my heart stopped at the sound. It was coming from the bedroom across the hall from Jack's room, and completely unabashed, I took a step towards it.

This room had been styled much closer to the rest of the house, with wood floors, and a four-poster bed made with white linens. There was a large white rug in the center of the room, and the French doors leading out to the balcony were open, letting the cool breeze ruffle the thick curtains.

Books lined the walls, and someone sat in the white chair in the corner. An aged copy of a German book covered his face from me, but just the sound of his voice had already mesmerized me. He wore faded jeans and a close fitting sweater.

His slender fingers were deeply tanned, but they seemed to be gripping the book unnaturally tight. I wondered if I was irritating him in some way, so I took a step back, trying to sneak out of his room, but I bumped right into Mae.

"Alice, this is Peter. Peter, this is Alice," Mae introduced us. Maybe it was just my imagination, but her voice seemed to have filled with a sense of self-satisfaction. He grunted something but didn't lower the book. "Jack told you that she'd be coming over tonight."

"I remember." Peter definitely sounded annoyed, so I tried to edge my way out of the room, but Mae, who either chose to ignore or didn't notice his growing irritation, blocked my path.

"You could at least say hi to our guest." Mae reprimanded him, but her tone was playful. "It's the polite thing to do."

"Hello," Peter sighed and finally lowered his book.

At first, I could only see his eyes. They were an intoxicating shade of green and captivated me. His thick, chestnut hair landed just above his shoulders, and he tucked it behind his ears. His jaw had tightened.

He breathed in sharply, and his lips parted. It wasn't his intention, but there was something so seductive about that. He was stunningly perfect in a way that made him almost painful to look at.

"Aha!" Mae exclaimed quietly behind me, but I was too preoccupied with Peter to figure out what she meant.

"Shouldn't you continue your little tour?" Peter asked icily, and his eyes dropped from mine.

I suddenly remembered to breathe and tried not to gulp down air the way my lungs requested. My heart pounded wildly, and I felt the blood burning my cheeks.

"I think we've seen all the main points," Mae looped her arm through mine, and the combination of her soft voice and reassuring touch calmed me down. "Would you care to join us, Peter?"

"I've seen the house." He lifted the book again, hiding his exquisite features from me.

"Peter's always a grump," Mae explained, but she sounded a tad disappointed when she started leading me away from Peter's room. "Come on, love. There's still more for you to see."

"Well?" Jack appeared at the bottom stairs, looking up expectantly at us. There was something anxious and almost protective about him. Mae and I walked slowly down towards him, and I couldn't meet his gaze, afraid he would see what a fool I had made of myself over his brother.

"Well what?" I asked, feeling dazed.

"What do you think?" He waited until I was at the bottom of the stairs, then I felt him inspecting me. The dog came over and licked my hand, and I absently started petting her.

"The house is amazing." I tried to force a smile to prove how spectacular I thought everything was, and I hated that that sudden random confrontation with his brother had distracted me from all my other pleasant feelings about the house and Mae.

"Peter's upstairs being a crab," Mae told Jack dramatically.

"Oh," Jack replied knowingly and exchanged a look with Mae that I couldn't read. "Peter is such a jackass."

"Oh, he is not," Mae said, and she'd taken to stroking my hair gently, and that alleviated some of my tension and shame.

"Peter!" Jack shouted up at the stairs at him.

"I am reading a book!" Peter growled down.

"Peter!" Jack shouted again, growing more irritated.

"I am reading, Jack!" Peter responded, and I winced at the anger in his words.

"Jack." Mae shot him a look. "Let him be."

"Whatever." He relented, but he didn't look happy about it. Then he turned his attention to me and smiled. "So, Alice, wanna have some fun?"

"Sure?" I replied hesitantly. His eyes had a mischievous glint, and I hadn't decided whether or not I should trust it.

"Hot tub!"

"I don't have a suit." This was true, but I was sure they would have a solution for it. I had a feeling that Mae and Jack would have a solution for nearly everything.

"Oh, I have the perfect one for you!" Mae smiled, her earlier excitement returning.

She ushered me down the hall towards her room. We went into Mae's room, where Jack proceeded to flop back on the overstuffed bed. She opened the doors to her closet, and it was larger than my entire bedroom. She started searching through her multitudes of bathing suits, making me nervous.

Once she found one she liked (a pale blue two piece with a ruffled skirt around the bottoms), she insisted that I go into their adjoining bathroom to try it on. It fit, and it was more flattering then I had expected it to be, but it also felt incredibly revealing.

When I came out, she gushed over how amazing I looked. I might've believed her if she hadn't already changed into her own bikini in the closest, and I looked like nothing compared to her. Jack didn't say anything, but the approving way he looked at me made me blush.

Jack was a typical guy and decided that wearing just his black boxers would suffice. I took a moment to admire the perfection of Jack shirtless, but I did it as discreetly as possible.

We went outside through the French doors, and the cold stung. Mae and Jack didn't appear to notice it, but that didn't surprise me.

I climbed into the hot tub. The way it instantly warmed my entire body reminded me of the way that I had felt when I looked at Peter. Then I remembered the ice in his voice and tried to push thoughts of him out of my mind.

We spent quite a bit of time in the hot tub, and when I finally let myself relax and enjoy it, I did. Matilda lay sprawled on the patio next to us, and Jack tried to splash her until Mae made him stop.

I just sunk in the water, trying to forget all the stuff about Jack that didn't make sense, and the fact that my brother hated me, and Peter's piercing green eyes.

"It's getting late," Mae announced and looked sadly at me. "I really enjoyed having you over, and I do hope you come again. But you probably should get home before it's too late."

"It's never too late," Jack grumbled, dipping his head back under the water as if that could block out the truth in her statement.

"No, she's right." Using most of my strength, I pushed myself from the warm, comfort of the tub and felt the frigid air on my skin. "Oh my gosh, it's freezing!"

"I brought out towels," Mae gestured to a pile of plush white towels lying on a nearby chair, and I rushed over to them.

When I picked up a towel, I happened to glance up, and I saw Peter standing inside the kitchen, staring through the French doors at me. The towel had unrolled in front of me, but I just stood there, holding it, unable to actually start drying myself. The cold was painful, but Peter had captivated me.

One of his arms folded across his chest, while his hand rested on his chin. His brilliant green eyes were giving me a look that could kill, and my heart felt eager to please, so it completely stopped beating. It might have stopped forever if Mae hadn't interrupted and pulled me from the trance he'd put me in.

"Peter! Would you care to join us?" Mae called at him. Still glaring at me, he shook his head, then turned on his heels and stalked off. "Don't mind him, Alice. He's really not so bad."

"It's okay," I lied, then suddenly started feeling the cold again and wrapped the towel around myself.

"You make him nervous," Jack whispered, suddenly standing directly behind me.

"Why?" I asked numbly.

It didn't make any sense that I could make someone as composed and perfect as Peter nervous. I was inconsequential in every way. Naturally, Jack didn't answer me. He just shrugged and walked into the house.

"Hurry up before you freeze to death!" Jack yelled, and I rushed in after him.

By the time I had gotten dressed, Jack was waiting by the door for me. He twirled the car keys on his hands and whistled a song that sounded suspiciously like "Walking on Sunshine."

At the door, Mae hugged me tightly and reminded me that I had to come visit her soon. Looking rather pained, she apologized for Peter's behavior, and I wondered what he had done that had offended them so much.

"Which car are we taking?" I had followed Jack out into the garage, but he looked like he was walking all the way down to the other end, so I already knew what it was.

"The Lamborghini, of course."

"How do you decide which car you're going to take?" Now, with a million other questions burning in my mind, this was the only question I wasn't afraid to ask.

"I only take this when Ezra's gone," he explained sheepishly as he hopped in the driver's seat. When I got in, he started it and adjusted the stereo. "He thinks it's too flashy. And my Jeep is fun but it's not as fast, so I usually just take Mae's Jetta. The Lexus is Ezra's 'every day' car and the Audi is Peter's."

"If you like the car so much, why didn't you just get one?" I asked as Jack backed out of the garage.

"Ezra says we don't need to stand out that much."

"Well, then why did he even bother buying this car? And you live in a house shaped like a castle and he drives a Lexus. How is any of that inconspicuous?" I looked at him skeptically, and he grinned at me.

"Exactly!" He pulled out of the driveway and sped down the road. I leaned back in the seat and closed my eyes, trying to take in everything that had happened. When Jack spoke again, his tone had gotten somber. "So, what did you think of my family?"

"I liked them. Mae is very nice, and your house is stunning." I kept my eyes closed and listened to the Joy Division cover playing on the radio. It reminded me of Gary Jules, but I knew that wasn't it. "Who is this?"

"Honeyroot doing 'Love Will Tear Us Apart,'" Jack answered, and without missing a beat, returned to the topic. "So you had a good time then?"

"I did." Mostly. Except for the parts when Peter sucked all the air from my lungs and I wanted to die.

"You're awfully quiet. I'd been expecting a million questions from you."

"Oh, I have them," I reassured him. "Is Mae from England?" Jack laughed, and I turned to look at him. "What? Was I way off?"

"No, it's just… that's the question you ask?" He shook his head, smiling. "That's like the most normal thing you could possibly ask. I just wasn't expecting it."

"What were you expecting me to ask?" I raised an eyebrow, trying to figure out what part of the night he thought I'd find the most odd.

"Yeah, she's from England." He once again hedged my question.

"They're like you, aren't they?" I asked, watching him carefully.

"Nobody's like me," Jack replied flippantly. "I'm a one in a million, baby!"

"Jack, you know what I mean."

"I do," he sighed. His expression got pained, and he was almost pleading with me. "You liked them and you had a good time. Can't we just leave it at that?"

"Why did you want me to meet them?"

Meeting them had made him more vulnerable and more susceptible to my questions. I don't know how it benefited him. Mae had wanted to meet me, I'm sure, but he could've put that off.

"That is way too complicated for me to answer right now," Jack said simply.

"When will things stop being so complicated?" I had started whining a little, but I'd had a long day, so I thought I had earned the right to whine just a bit.

"That's probably the best question you've ever asked me." Jack sounded very far away and rather sad, so I knew the answer wouldn't be anything I'd want to hear anyway. For once, I was grateful for his silence. After a very pregnant pause, he exhaled deeply. "I feel drawn to you."

"That's why things are complicated?" I sat up straighter in my seat, eager to hear what sounded like a legitimate answer.

"No. Well, kinda, but that's not what I meant." He glanced over at me, and then returned his gaze to the road. "That's why I wanted you to meet my family."

"So was that like me meeting your parents?" I crinkled my nose. "Like we're dating?"

"No, it's not like that. You know what I mean. You feel it too, right?" His eyes flitted back over to me, then quickly away again. "Like you feel drawn to me. You enjoy me and everything, but you feel kind of compelled to be around me."

"I guess," I said noncommittally. He'd actually hit the nail on the head, but I didn't want to admit to that.

"Well, that's how I feel." He had put himself out there for a minute, and he shifted uncomfortably. I felt bad for not being more honest with him.

"But... what does that have to do with your family?"

"That's the complicated part," he smirked.

"You can't tell me anything?" I asked. I knew that if I were smarter, I'd probably have everything pieced together already. Jack was probably growing frustrated with me failing to follow his little half clues.

"They like you," he offered helpfully.

"Yeah, I could tell that Peter's a real big fan," I scoffed, and he just pursed his lips grimly.

"It's really, really complicated, Alice. But..." He sighed again. "Okay. That's all I can say."

"Why?" I demanded. We had already pulled up in front of my house, making the trek home in record time. He looked over at me, his expression grave but affectionate. "Why can't you tell me more?"

"Honestly?" Jack bit his lip, and I could see the internal debate raging. "I like you too much."

"That doesn't make any sense! If you like me, you should just be open and honest with me. That's what people do. That's how it works," I said. His eyes looked conflicted and pained, and I thought I almost had him, but then he looked down at his hands and shook his head.

"I saw your face yesterday." His voice clogged painfully. "I don't want you to ever look at me that way again."

"I won't!" I insisted, but we both know that I couldn't be sure of that. I had no idea what he wasn't telling me, so I couldn't promise my reaction to it.

"It's late."

"Fine, be that way." I threw open the car door. "I had a really lovely time tonight and I hope we can do it again real soon."

"Sweet dreams," Jack smiled at me, and I smiled back, despite my frustration.

"Yeah, you too."

By the time I made it up to my apartment, I was struggling not to cry. All Peter had really done was look at me, and it was somehow devastating. An unfailing insistence inside me wanted him, but I refused to listen to it.

Jack and Mae liked me, probably more than they should, and I really liked them, definitely more than I should, and that was enough. That was more than enough! Why did I have to be so greedy?

"Alice?" Milo said timidly, startling me from my thoughts. The apartment was mostly dark, and I hadn't seen him sitting on the couch, waiting up for me. I had just been leaning against the front door. "Are you okay?"

"Yeah, I'm just peachy." I swallowed hard and walked over to the couch.

Milo was talking to me, and that was pretty damn exciting. I pushed Peter and Jack from my thoughts and sat down next to him.

"Did you have a nice time tonight?" Milo asked, and I nodded quickly.

"Yeah. I did. What about you?"

"It was okay," he shrugged.

"I'm sorry. For the things I said today." I wasn't sure if that was the right thing to say, or if it made me sound like I was sorry he was gay or something. But it was too late, and I would just deal with how he reacted.

"No, don't be." He ran a hand through his brown hair and looked away from me. "When I asked if you were gonna be home tonight, I was upset. But it was because you've been gone so much lately, and the other night, when I thought you were going to stay home and eat with me, you left. I just haven't seen you very much. I kind of missed you."

"Oh, Milo, I am sorry!" My eyes filled with tears.

He had just missed me, and then I had been so horrible to him. I had been gone a lot lately, thanks to Jack, and I hadn't even really considered how Milo felt about it. No, scratch that. I did consider it - I just didn't care. I had to be the worst sister in the world. Really.

"Let me finish," Milo interjected quietly. "But... you were right. I am attracted to Jack. And guys in general. I just didn't know how to tell you, or even how to tell myself, I guess. So that's why I've been so distant lately."

"You know I love you no matter what, right?" I threw my arms around him. He squirmed a little but let me hug him. "I am so sorry I haven't been around! I promise I'll spend more time with you!"

"You don't have to." He pulled back from my grip but stayed close to me.

"I know that! I want to! I've missed you too. And I'm just so sorry for everything."

"You can quit apologizing," Milo said, not unkindly. "You didn't really do that much wrong."

"I still feel horrible."

"Yeah, I get that." He smiled, and I laughed a little.

"We'll hang out tomorrow. I promise."

"Okay," Milo yawned. "I really need to get to bed, though. It's way past my bedtime." He got up and started walking to his bedroom.

"Okay," I nodded, feeling genuinely sad to see him go. "Hey, Milo? I love you."

"I know." Then he disappeared into the darkness of his room. I went into my room and changed into my pajamas.

I curled up underneath my covers, and for the first time in a long time, I cried myself to sleep.

- 8 -

At school, Jane poked and prodded me, then repeatedly told me that I looked like hell. I'm sure it had to do with how terrible I slept, and all the strange dreams I couldn't quite remember. They were mostly a blur of images that I couldn't decipher, except for one clear image: Peter's eyes burning through me.

Of course, I couldn't explain any of this to Jane. It still was a struggle for her not to mention Jack, so I couldn't either.

Milo had seemed to return to his normal self, much to my relief. When we got home, he started talking rapidly about a new recipe he wanted to try out.

Last night, I'd managed to forget to eat anything, and at lunch, I had still felt too tired and out-of-it to eat. But once I was in the safety of my apartment listening to Milo rattle of a list of tasty ingredients, my appetite came back full swing.

We went to the grocery store to get his recommended supplies, but I was too hungry to wait, so I ate a pear in the store. Milo looked embarrassed, even though I insisted that I'd pay for it (and I did).

Taking the groceries home was always a project because we had to take the bus with arm loads of bags. I wished Mom would spring and buy a car, but it didn't seem like it was in the cards.

Jack hadn't text messaged me yet, and I tried to pretend like that didn't bother me. All through supper, while I attempted to help Milo cook, I had to constantly fight the urge to check my cell phone in my pocket to make sure it was on or I hadn't missed a message.

After my finger cutting incident (which apparently hadn't been that minor since I still required a Boba Fett Band-Aid), Milo left me with all the easy jobs, like washing vegetables, measuring ingredients, and buttering bread.

His supper was ridiculously good. We sat at the table, where I promptly devoured everything.

Mom woke up, and we offered her a plate, but she just shook her head and hurried out the door. We'd seen her for a total of ten minutes that day, but I imagined that if we were to add it up, we saw her an average of an hour a week.

"You should really go to culinary school," I told Milo. "You're amazing. This is definitely something you should do for a living."

We were still sitting at the table, and I had one knee pulled up to my chest, which was getting more uncomfortable the more I ate. I had already cleaned one plate and had started on a second, but my eyes were larger than my stomach.

"I've kind of looked into it." He shrugged modestly. Milo never believed he was good at anything, no matter what I told him. "I don't know."

"Well, you still have a few years to think about it, but you're too good to keep this hidden from the world." I took another bite, but my stomach screamed in protest. I forced myself to push my plate away, knowing that I would explode if I continued eating.

"What about you? You're graduating before I am. What did you have in mind?" Milo turned the tables on me, and I squirmed a little.

He knew my grades at school, and he was constantly trying to talk to me about my future, but I avoided it as much as possible.

"I don't know." Lately, with everything that had been going on with Jack, I had a new found appreciation for paranormal studies and biology. "Maybe I'll go to med school." I had meant it as a joke, but Milo just nodded, like it would make sense.

"I could see you as a psychiatrist," Milo said. "I mean, not anything that had to do with blood or surgery."

"No, that would definitely be out," I agreed readily. When I saw all the blood on Jack's nonexistent wound, I had to fight the urge to vomit. "But I can't imagine me being a psychiatrist."

"Really?" He raised an eyebrow, as if it seemed like an obvious choice to him. "You're a pretty good listener, and you love figuring people out. Everyone is like a puzzle to you, and you're trying to put all the pieces together."

"I guess that is true." Essentially, that's all I'd been doing for the last few weeks, but until Milo had said it like that, I didn't realize that's what I did.

"I mean, you figured out that I was gay." Milo spoke quietly and kept his eyes down, so I knew it was still something that was uncomfortable for him to talk about.

"When did you know?" I pulled my plate back over to me, but I just pushed the food around. I was too full to eat, but when I felt awkward, I wanted to keep my hands busy with something, and this was better than biting my nails.

"I don't know." He sighed a little, and I wondered if I should change the subject, but then he went on. "I suspected for... ever, I guess. I mean, as soon as I learned what gay was, I thought, 'maybe.' But really, it was when I met Jack." He blushed deeply, keeping his eyes fixed on the floor. "I'd just never been so attracted to anyone like that before."

"Yeah, Jack does that." I had meant to comfort him with that statement, but I ended up sounding exasperated.

"But you're not attracted to him." Milo looked up at me, looking both confused and disbelieving. "How is that even possible?"

"I'm attracted to him, definitely," I explained the best I could. "I just don't want to have sex with him." Then I remembered what he looked like last night, sliding shirtless into the hot tub.

"But…" Milo shifted uncomfortably, and he sounded unsure of himself. "I don't mean to sound gross, but that was all I could think about."

"That's not gross," I replied quickly, but then recanted. "Okay. It's a little gross, but only cause you're my little brother. Not cause of the whole gay thing."

"Even Jane went crazy about him, and she's never crazy about anyone, except for herself." He was waiting for an explanation, but I didn't have one.

"I don't get it either," I told him finally. "I don't see what you guys see in him, even. I mean, he's attractive and funny and everything…" I trailed off, realizing that maybe I did feel the way they did about Jack, then suddenly, I remembered Peter. "I met his brother last night."

"And?" Milo leaned in closer to me, his eyes shining brightly.

"And nothing. He's gorgeous, like unbelievably so, but he hates me." I shrugged, trying to make it look like it didn't bother me as much as it did, and went back to picking at my plate of food.

"He hates you? Why?" At least he was incredulous at the idea of anyone hating me. Maybe I was more likable than I gave myself credit for.

"I honestly couldn't tell you." It physically hurt just thinking about the way that Peter had glared at me when I was by the hot tub. I would gladly throw myself under a bus than endure another look like that. "I don't think I even spoke to him."

"Then how do you know he hates you?"

"If you had seen the way he looked at me..." I shuddered at the thought of it and decided that that was enough of talking about Peter and Jack. I stood up and started to clear off the table.

"I don't get you, Alice," Milo muttered when I took his plate.

"There's nothing to get," I replied glibly.

Since he had cooked, that usually meant that I would do the dishes, but he helped me out tonight. He had just started doing his homework when I decided that a nice long, hot shower was in order. But when I went into the bathroom, the hamper was overflowing, and we were completely out of clean towels.

Milo had tons of homework, and he actually planned to do it, so I offered to go to the laundromat. I loaded up as many clothes as I could into three massive laundry bags, and then made the excruciating trek the block and a half down to the laundromat. The superintendent kept promising he'd put one in the basement of the building, but he'd yet to follow through.

I filled four washers with clothes (the maximum amount allotted to one person), then settled back in the hard plastic chairs to watch clothes spin around for an hour. I had just started doing a quiz in *Cosmo* ("Are You Pleasing Your Man in Bed?" – the perfect quiz for a single virgin) when my pocket started to ring.

What are you doing? Jack text messaged me.

Laundry.

Wanna do something? Jack replied.

I wore a pair of drawstring sweats, a faded *Darkwing Duck* tee shirt with an unzipped navy blue hoodie, my makeup had completely worn off, and my hair was pulled back in a pony tail. Of course he'd want to see me when I looked like that.

I'm already doing something. Laundry at the laundromat. And I will be until the end of time. I text messaged him back.

Luckily for you, I have that long. Care if I join you?

Sure, why not? As I'd fervently pointed out to Milo, I wasn't sexually attracted to Jack, so what did I care if he saw me looking like this?

Cool. I'll be there in a few.

Do you even know where it's at? I waited ten minutes for him to reply to that, but then I realized that he was already on his way.

Somehow, he'd know where I was at, just like he knew my apartment number without me telling him. He just knew everything, and it was flipping' irritating.

The bell chimed above the laundromat door a few minutes later, and I didn't even have to look up to know it was Jack. There was an

Indian girl a few seats down from me, and she gasped when he came in.

"Hey, there." Jack plopped on the seat next to me, wearing a Space Invaders hoodie and a pair of Dickies shorts. His sandy hair looked crazier than normal, and he smiled brightly at me.

"How did you know where I was at?" My tone had long since stopped being accusatory. When I asked him things, I was just curious and mildly amused, and always expecting no answer.

"You told me where you were." He looked at me like I was an idiot, which was somehow flattering.

"No, I didn't. I said I was at a laundromat. There's like a million in this city," I explained.

"This one is the closest to your house, and you don't drive." His response surprised me because it actually made sense. There was nothing odd or vaguely psychic about it. He turned to watch the washing machines and crossed his legs underneath him, apparently settling in for the long haul. "You know we have washers and dryers at my house."

"I'm not at your house," I said, instead of commenting on his plural use of washer and dryer. Knowing them, they probably had one for every room, like the bathrooms and fireplaces and balconies.

"You could've asked to come over and do laundry," Jack said. "Mae was really taken with you."

"I really enjoyed her, too." That was all I was going to say on that subject. The last thing I wanted to do was talk to Jack about Peter. It felt wrong somehow to admit any attraction to him to Jack. "That doesn't explain how you knew where my house was."

"Why would it? Mae liking you has nothing to do with where you live."

"No, I mean, do you always know where I'm at?" I looked up at him, and he shook his head.

"I'm not psychic."

"What about when you took me home that first night? I was sleeping in the car. How did you know where I lived?"

"Jane told me." He kept looking straight ahead, and I wondered when he would grow tired of my constant stream of questions.

I knew that normal friends didn't just continuously interrogate each other like this, but normal friends didn't act like Jack.

"Why would she tell you that?"

"I asked her," Jack said, again looking at me like I was an idiot.

"If I called and asked her that, is that what she would tell me?" I challenged him, and even pulled out my phone to prove I would call her. (I really wouldn't, because I was avoiding talking to her about Jack, or anything, really.)

"I don't know what she'd say, but it's the truth." That felt very true. Jack may not tell me things, but he didn't lie to me.

"So, how did you know which apartment was mine that night you came over for supper?" I asked.

"See my answer to the last question."

"She told you my apartment number and everything?" I asked skeptically. That seemed like an awful lot of information for her to give out to a complete stranger about her unconscious best friend, but then again, she was completely in love with him at the time.

"Sure did." Jack shrugged. "You were passed out. I thought I might have to carry you up."

"You would've carried me into my apartment and put me in my bed and everything?" I furrowed my brows at him. When I said it aloud, it sounded terribly creepy, which is why I had said it aloud. I wanted it to feel as creepy as it sounded, but it didn't. It felt oddly natural. "You just met me."

"Would it have bothered you if I had?" Jack asked me honestly.

"That's still a peculiar thing to do." I purposely didn't answer his question. "And you have an awful lot of secrets for someone that knows so much about me."

"I guess I do," he laughed, and then turned to me. "So when are you coming over again?"

"I don't know," I said hesitantly. He must've noticed my reluctance because he bumped my shoulder with his. "I can't tonight. I'm doing this and then I have school tomorrow."

"Tomorrow then, after school." It wasn't exactly an order, but it wasn't really a question either. "Ezra will be home."

Everything about me tensed up. After reacting the way I had to Peter, I was terrified to find out how I'd react to his other brother. Maybe it would be worse, and even if it wasn't, it wasn't worth the risk of lusting after Mae's husband. That would be embarrassing and it'd feel like a betrayal.

"He'll like you. Trust me." Then he softened and lowered his voice, leaning in closer to me. "It won't be like with Peter."

"How do you know?" I asked stiffly, and even I wasn't sure if I was asking how he knew what it was like with Peter, or how he knew that this time would be different.

"I just do." Then he bumped into me again, teasing. "You know that I know. I don't know why you always have to argue."

"It's just in my nature, I guess."

"What's that?" He noticed the *Cosmo* on my lap, and before I could stop him, he snatched it up. Embarrassingly, I had left it open to the quiz I had been taking.

"What man are you pleasing in bed? And question four, you really do that?" Jack asked with a laugh. He gave me a look that was both appalled and admiring, and I tried to take the magazine back from him, but he moved too quickly for me. "I had no idea you were that kind of girl, Alice! I mean, this completely changes my opinion of you!"

"I was bored!" I finally managed to grab it from him. He laughed freely at my humiliation, and I just shook my head. "Ha ha. Very funny."

"Yeah, it kind of is," Jack said when his laughter died down. He leaned back and spread out his arms on the back of the chairs, so one of his arms was behind me. "The truth is, though, that I know exactly what kind of girl you are."

"Oh yeah?" I asked, intrigued. "And what kind of girl is that?"

"Oh, you'll see," Jack smiled at his cryptic answer.

"You say stuff like that just to drive me nuts, don't you?" I shot him a look, and he just laughed, confirming my suspicions.

Jack waited with me until all the laundry finished. To pass the time, we did a few *Cosmo* quizzes (although I refused to answer any

116

about sex) and a crossword puzzle in the newspaper, which he was amazing at. He had to be the smartest person I had ever met, but he did a pretty good job of keeping it secret.

When the laundry was done, he carried all three massive bags out to his Jeep. He offered to take them up to my apartment, but I thought it would be better for Milo if he didn't see him. Jack's effect on people tended to wear off the longer they went without contact.

Before I went into the building, he reminded me that he was picking me up tomorrow at six, and whether I liked it or not, I was spending the evening with his family.

- 9 -

Jane had always been much more clothes obsessed, but suddenly, there were not enough clothes in my closet. It actually wasn't the amount of clothes so much as the fact that they were all terrible. I'd even done laundry, so everything I owned was clean and neatly folded or hanging up, but none of it was good enough. I must've changed my outfit like fifty times before my phone rang.

"I know, I know," I answered the phone breathlessly.

"I just wanted to make sure you didn't chicken out," Jack said. Fortunately, he sounded more bemused than he did angry. "I'm outside waiting."

"I'll be out in a minute." I flipped my phone shut and rushed over to the mirror to inspect myself. Milo, who had been my wardrobe supervisor, sat on my bed amidst discarded outfits.

"Jack?" Milo asked, trying to sound offhand.

"Uh huh," I mumbled absently and tried to smooth out the hem.

I wore a dark blue tunic dress that fell just above my knees. I'd gone with opaque tights underneath and a pair of skimmers. I wasn't sure if I'd gone casual enough or too casual or what, but either way, I felt stupid and I wanted to change again.

"This is horrible!"

"You look great," Milo admonished me. I'm sure he'd grown tired of listening to me whine and change for the past three hours, but

I really wanted to make a good impression. "And Jack is waiting. You don't really have a choice anymore."

"Promise?" I asked, looking over at him.

"Yes. They'll love you. And even if they don't, I do. Now go!" Milo stood up and started shooing me out of my room.

"Okay, okay." I groaned, but Milo just kept pushing until I was out the front door.

I ran out to Jack's car before I could change my mind. He had taken the Jeep again, and I was glad for a slower ride.

"You look great," Jack grinned when I hopped in.

"Whatever." I flipped down the visor so I could investigate myself in the mirror. My eyeliner was thicker than I ordinarily wore it, but it made me look more dramatic and mature so I liked it.

"Fine, you look terrible," Jack laughed and sped off down the road.

"Can you slow down?" My nerves made my stomach flip out, and I knew I could feign carsickness since it would almost be the truth. I just didn't like the idea of us getting there in like ten seconds.

"You're really that nervous?" Jack was growing concerned, and he slowed down a little.

"No," I lied.

I flipped the visor back up and sunk in the seat. I was completely dreading meeting Ezra, and seeing Peter again, while simultaneously being really excited to see him. I hated my body for its ability to have contradictory emotions.

"It's really not that bad. Ezra will like you."

"Will you stop trying to convince me that everyone likes me?" I snapped. "You're making me paranoid."

"That doesn't make any sense," Jack looked over at me, sitting next to him being petrified, and he sighed. "You know, Peter really didn't mean anything."

"I don't wanna talk about Peter," I replied through gritted teeth, but that wasn't it exactly. I couldn't talk about him. Just thinking about him made my heart race out of control. There didn't seem to be enough oxygen in the Jeep.

He knew that I was inclined to silence, so he turned up the stereo. Today it was the Smashing Pumpkins, singing about a bullet with butterfly wings.

Even though he had slowed down, the drive to his house still went by much too fast. By the time we had pulled into the garage, my heart was beating so fast that I was sure I was going to die. I thought about telling Jack this, but by the grim look on his face, he already knew.

"You've got to calm down, Alice." He touched my hand to reassure me, and amazingly, it worked.

"Is that another one of your superpowers?" I asked when my heart stopped feeling like it would explode.

"What?" Jack kept his tone sober, but I could see the corners of his mouth creeping up at my use of the word "superpowers."

"Calming me down or making me feel whatever it is you feel." I had expected him to avoid the question or shrug me off, but instead he got serious and his forehead creased.

"You feel what I feel?" He cocked his head to the side a little bit, looking at me curiously.

There was a good chance that I was blowing everything out of proportion. He was charismatic and excitable, so his emotions had a way of dominating situations. That didn't mean that I actually felt what he felt.

"Not literally, I'm sure. It's just like when you want me to calm down, I usually do. Or when you were nervous about the dog, I felt you tense up so I got freaked. But it's probably nothing more than what normal people feel."

"Hmm." He didn't look convinced, but he pulled his hand back from mine and opened the door to the Jeep. "You must be feeling pretty calm and happy right about now, so let's go inside before it wears off."

"That's actually a good idea," I agreed and got out of the Jeep.

"You mean it does actually wear off?" He hurried around to meet me, and it felt weird for me to be on the other side of the question-and-answer game we always played. I wrapped my arms around myself and shrugged. "No, seriously. I don't understand how this works."

"I don't know either. I just assumed you'd know what I was talking about." We had reached the door into the house, but he paused, staring off into space.

"Unless..."

"Unless what?" I asked.

"Nothing." He shook his head, shaking off whatever thought he had.

"Jack!" I protested, and he smirked at me.

"I'll tell you later." He'd never said that me before, and it surprised me.

"Really?" I asked hopefully.

"No. Come on." Before I could argue more, he opened the door and walked into the house. "Hi, honey, we're home!"

"Peter, hold Matilda!" Mae shouted from another room, and I cringed, knowing that Peter was just a room away. Then Mae raced into the entryway, her arms already open to hug me. "Alice!" She threw her arms around me, holding me tightly to her. "I'm so glad you're here!"

"Me too," I told her, and I was surprised to find I actually meant it.

"You know, I'm here too," Jack pointed out when she released me. He had only meant it as a joke, but she turned and hugged him anyway. "Thanks."

"You know we're always glad you're here," Mae smiled at him.

"I know you're glad that I'm here," Jack corrected her, and a new fear gripped me. Maybe both Peter and Ezra didn't like him, meaning that I wouldn't even stand a chance.

Suddenly Matilda came bursting into the room, but Jack intercepted her, and she jumped happily into his arms. This is a hundred pound dog, and he caught her in his arms with ease. I knew that eventually I'd have to stop being so amazed by Jack.

"Peter!" Mae shouted towards the other room, where Peter remained hidden.

"She got away from me!" Peter said, his silken voice shooting through my body. If he had even half the strength that Jack had, hanging onto Matilda wouldn't be a problem. He'd let her go to spite us in some way.

"Peter," another voice boomed. His voice was deeper than Jack's or Peter's, and it resonated in a way that made me flush warmly. He was disapproving, and I knew that if I had been on the receiving end of his disproval, I'd probably faint.

"Sorry," Peter grumbled.

"That's Ezra," Mae told me, smiling proudly just at the mention of her husband.

Jack finally put down Matilda, who had completely saturated his face in slobber, and she bounded away. Mae looped her arm in mine, and I knew she would revel introducing me to Ezra, so I let her lead me into the next room.

"He's really not scary at all," Jack reassured me as he wiped dog slobber of his face with the back of his arm.

Then we walked into the living room, and as soon as I saw him, all my fears melted away. My very first thought was that he looked like an angel. He was taller than Jack and Peter, but he didn't seem to tower over anyone.

As I had suspected, he was gorgeous, and he wore a white dress shirt with the sleeves rolled up and collar unbuttoned, revealing a tantalizing hint of his chest. His eyes were deep mahogany and infinitely warm. His skin was the same tanned color as Peter's, but his hair had sun kissed streaks through it.

He was in his mid-twenties, and he looked amazing, but he also looked… old somehow. Around his eyes, I could tell that he was much wiser than his age belied.

"And you must be Alice," his deep voice rolled warmly towards me, sending pleasurable chills coursing through me.

There was something about his voice, I'd heard it when he said Peter's name, but I couldn't quite place it until he spoke more. He had a faded accent, maybe Irish or Australian, but I couldn't be sure since it was so soft. He stepped closer to shake my hand, and that's when it finally dawned on me.

Ezra had an accent, but Peter and Jack didn't, and maybe Ezra being born in another country while the other boys were too young to pick up an accent could explain that.

But their eye colors were all so distinct and completely different. Ezra had deep brown, Peter's were shocking green, and Jack's were a soft blue. There was no way they were brothers.

"And you must be Ezra," I said.

He held my hand in both of his, and he smiled so warmly at me, I thought I would melt. Out of the corner of my eye, I could see Peter standing in the corner, casting an odd look at us, but I tried to ignore it.

"I've heard so much about you." He let go of my hand and took a step back so he was at a polite distance. Mae stayed planted at my side, and she had started stroking my hair again. I realized belatedly that she was showing me off.

"All of it good, I hope," I said quietly. It was an incredibly cheesy thing to say, but I couldn't think of anything better.

With Ezra stepping back, he didn't quite eclipse my view the way he had before, and I couldn't help but sneak a glance at Peter, who was staring straight back at me. He leaned his shoulder against a wall with his arms crossed over his chest. Wearing tight fitting jeans and a black tee shirt, he was so amazingly gorgeous that I had to pull my eyes away to look back at Ezra, who suddenly didn't seem quite as astonishing in comparison.

"Isn't she lovely?" Mae gushed, putting her arm around me. All the attention was flattering, but very odd. Mae treated me as if I had cured cancer or walked on water, and all I had done was show up.

"She is something," Ezra said, and I felt him appraising me, so I straightened my back slightly. "But you knew she would be."

I didn't know what that meant, and I wanted terribly to ask, but I knew it would have to wait until we left and I was safely in the car with Jack.

"She's just a girl," Peter scoffed, making me crumble inside.

My body slouched automatically, but I fought to keep my facial expression even. Ezra turned to shoot a glance at Peter, who just looked away and shifted his weight.

"Peter." Ezra wasn't disapproving this time. He just sounded like he didn't understand him at all.

"Well, you don't need to put her on display," Peter muttered. He refused to look at me, but he snuck glances at Ezra. "She's here. I get it."

"I was just introducing her to Ezra," Mae told him, but there was a protective edge to her voice.

"I'm sorry about Peter," Ezra turned back to me, smiling apologetically. "He seems to have completely lost his mind."

Peter rolled his eyes at that, and I wondered what it was about me that bothered him so much. I'd barely said anything around him. In fact, I'd mostly just stood there and stared dumbly. How could that be so offensive to anyone?

"You know what would be fun?" Jack asked. He'd been standing off to the side of me, crouched down on the floor so he could pet Matilda, who had rolled over on her back so he could rub her belly.

"Nobody wants to play *Guitar Hero*." Mae sounded exasperated when she turned to give him a look.

"But you can play the Beatles! You loved the Beatles!"

"He's back on that again?" Ezra asked, looking a little disappointed.

"He bought a new system or something," Mac said wearily. "I don't know. It's just been the past couple days."

"Well, maybe we should let the kids play, and you can fill me in on what else I've missed while I was gone," Ezra suggested.

Mae took a step away from me, and he slid his arm around her slender waist. They really looked perfect together, and something about them made me incredibly jealous. Not because I really wanted to be with Ezra (although, there were much worse things I could do) but because of how obviously they were made for each other. I wanted to be made for somebody like that.

"Have you played *Guitar Hero*?" Jack asked suddenly. I'm assuming he was asking me, but he was already hurrying over to the giant plasma television hanging on the wall and hooking up the gaming system.

"Let me know if you need anything," Mae gently touched my arm. "And don't be afraid to tell him when you've had enough. He can play that game for hours, so you're gonna have to be the one to stop him."

When they walked out of the room, Mae rested her head on Ezra's shoulder, and I couldn't help but feel sad to see them go. Peter, strangely enough, didn't take this as his cue to exit, and stood where he was, glowering at everyone and everything.

"So have you?" Jack looked back over his shoulder at me.

Matilda had followed him over to where he sat crouched on the floor, putting the game in the player and hooking up the wireless guitar controllers. She shoved her nose right in his hair, drooling over it, but he didn't seem to really mind or notice.

"Like once, at a friend's house," I said. Jane had been making out with a guy the entire time, while I sat downstairs in the living room and played *Guitar Hero* with his nine-year-old brother. It had been a hoot.

"It's really awesome," Jack said.

"I don't know why you're making the poor girl play with you," Peter said. For once, he didn't sound angry or irritated, and I think he was almost coming to my defense. "You're going to completely slaughter her."

"I am the greatest *Guitar Hero* player of all time." Jack was insanely proud of this accomplishment, and why wouldn't he be? He had amazing talents that he downplayed constantly, but he was really, really good at a video game. He had his priorities in order.

"Of course you are." I took the plastic guitar from him and dropped the strap over my shoulders.

"What song do you want?" He started scrolling through the song list so fast I could hardly even read it, but I caught a few that I liked.

"Um… how about Interpol?"

"Good choice," Jack commended me.

I was acutely aware of the fact that Peter was staring at me, and it made me extremely self-conscious. His gaze didn't feel quite as hateful as it had before, but that didn't change the effect he had on me. Ezra had been able to calm him down somewhat, and for that, I would be forever grateful. I couldn't bare him hating me.

A few strums on the guitar switch later, and the game started rolling. The object was to hit the colored buttons on the arm of the guitar in time with the same colored buttons flashing on the screen, but it was much harder than it sounded.

Jack had put me on the easy skill level, but he was on expert and flying through it. Peter had been right. There was no contest between the two of us. I could barely even finish the song.

"Oh, that was brutal," Peter said when we had finished playing.

He left his place on the wall and walked over to me, making my heart pound so loudly I could barely hear myself think. He was careful not to look me in the eyes, and I could tell that was a very deliberate decision. Then he held his hand out towards me, and at first, I didn't understand.

"Give me the guitar. Jack needs a good ass kicking."

"You need it more than I do," Jack scoffed.

I started to pull the strap off over my head, but it tangled in the length of my hair. Peter reached out to help me, and for a second, his hand was over mine.

His skin felt much different from everyone else's. It was just as baby soft, but it was burning hot. It reminded me of when I accidentally touched an electric fence when I was a kid, except this was pleasurable. It actually sent a jolt through me, and I saw his eyes flash up, meeting mine for just a second, so I knew he felt it too.

Then he quickly untangled the guitar and took it from me, without saying a word or looking at me again.

"What song?" Jack asked Peter, with a strange edge to his voice.

"Your choice," Peter said. He sounded perfectly even, but when he looked at me out of the corner of his eye, I could tell that he was a little startled by our moment.

Feeling weak and shaky, I walked back and collapsed on the overstuffed plush couch. Matilda decided that I needed company and climbed next to me, resting her enormous head on my lap.

I stroked her ears and watched Peter and Jack play the game. They were playing so fast it didn't seem humanly possible, but then I remembered that they probably weren't humanly possible.

My whole body still felt electrified from the touch, and I tried to decide whether or not I should ask Jack about it. It still felt weird to me to talk to him about his brother, even though it wasn't as if Jack and I were dating or anything.

Peter beat Jack the first round, so Jack demanded a rematch. They played on for awhile, and Jack kept looking back at me, to make sure I was still there.

Peter did, too, but always quickly looked away. Every time he glanced back, my heart would flutter, and I swear every time that my heart beat sped up, Peter and Jack would tense up.

"You're not even letting her play?" Mae appeared in the door with her hands on her hips, sounding appalled. Ezra stood behind her, but he just chuckled at the boys, as if he hadn't expected any different from them.

"She played," Jack said defensively. "She just, you know, wasn't very good."

"I had to put Jack in his place," Peter said.

"Well, that's enough of that," Mae informed them. She walked over to the couch, pushing Matilda onto the floor and sitting next to me. "She's probably bored out of her mind."

"I'm okay," I smiled at her. Truthfully, I hadn't had a chance to be bored. Watching Peter do anything was intoxicating.

"Turn that off anyway," Mae gestured to the game.

Jack grumbled, but he complied. Peter took off his guitar and set it down in front of the entertainment center, and then he sat in the chair on the exact opposite side of the room from where I was sitting.

"It's a fun game," Jack complained to no one in particular, then sat down on the floor in front of me. Matilda grabbed a thick rope chew toy and brought it over to him. He started yanking on the rope, and she growled happily and wagged her tail.

"So, Alice, are you still in high school?" Ezra asked. He'd been standing in the doorway, but somehow, he'd moved into the chair closest to me without me noticing.

Mae was running her fingers through my long hair, and I thought about how weird it was. If any other person had been doing that, I would've pushed them off and thought they were insane. But with her, it felt perfectly natural and comforting.

"Uh, yeah, eleventh grade," I answered.

Ezra looked at me as if I was fascinating, but I couldn't imagine anything about me would interest a person like him. It reminded me of what Peter had said, about them putting me on display, and it did kind of feel like that. Not that that made any sense.

"Are you doing well in school?" Ezra asked.

"Not really," I admitted. I knew that I could lie to him, and part of me wanted to in a desperate attempt to impress him, but I also knew that I wouldn't lie to them. It just didn't feel right.

"Are you planning on continuing your education?" Ezra leaned back in his chair, but there was nothing disapproving about him at all. He was merely taking it all in and trying to find out more about me. No matter what I had to say, it wouldn't upset him, because it was part of me, and for whatever reason, he approved of me.

"Maybe." I felt sheepish, but decided to continue anyway. "I was thinking about being a doctor."

Peter chuckled, and then shook his head. "Of course she is."

"I was thinking of psychiatry, actually." I started blushing when Peter laughed. I hurried to explain myself, so they wouldn't all think I was a total fool.

"I can see that," Ezra nodded, looking intently at me. "You have insight."

"How can you even say that with a straight face?" Peter asked Ezra incredulously, who just turned and looked at him sharply.

"She's only seventeen," Ezra reasoned. "You don't think she has insight for being that age? And she must have an incredibly high tolerance since she hasn't yet killed either you or Jack. That's patience and wisdom brewing."

I blushed even more deeply at his compliments and dropped my eyes to the floor. Nobody had ever talked about me like that.

"Don't." Peter's voice had gone hard again, and he gave Ezra a look, which he returned evenly. Then Peter shook his head. "She's too young! And she's too…" He decided against finishing his sentence, and then got up suddenly and stormed out.

"Peter!" Jack groaned, then got up and went after him.

"Jack, leave him," Ezra called after him, but Jack just shook his head and kept going.

"He can't keep getting away with this," Jack said and disappeared out of the room after him.

"You just have to ignore him," Mae purred warmly in my ear. She began braiding my hair, something my own mother had never done, and tried to comfort me. "He's just that way."

"I just don't understand." Confused, hurt tears were stinging my eyes, and I wished they would go away. I thought about wiping at them, but Ezra was staring at me, and it would only make my crying more obvious.

"What, love?" Mae asked softly, pushing stray strands of hair out of my face.

"Why he hates me so much," I mumbled.

"He doesn't hate you," Ezra said. "He just wishes he did."

I know that was meant to comfort me, but I don't really know how that made things better. Wanting to hate me felt almost worse. It was a choice he was trying to make.

"I need to use the restroom," I announced. I wouldn't be able to fight the tears much longer, and if I cried, I'd rather do it in the privacy of the bathroom. I stood up, and Mae's hands reluctantly fell away.

"Do you remember where it's at?" Mae started rising to show me where it was at, but I nodded first.

"I'll be right back." I dashed out of the room as fast as I could without making it obvious that I was running away to cry.

On my way to the bathroom, I had to go past the stairs, but that was as far as I made it. Peter's smooth voice stopped me sharply. Hidden at the bottom of the steps, I could hear them upstairs in Peter's room. He was talking to Jack, and he didn't sound angry like he did in the living room. In fact, he sounded more sad than anything else.

"I'm not trying to be mean to her," Peter was saying, sounding small and apologetic.

"But you are! You should've seen how terrified she was to come over here, because of you!" Jack, on the other hand, definitely was angry.

I winced at the sound of him confessing my embarrassing secrets, but I stayed longer to listen to their argument.

"Maybe she shouldn't come back then." Peter was saying it reasonably, as if he was only thinking of what was best for me, not because he didn't want me around.

"You're such an ass," Jack said. "I like her, Ezra likes her, Mae's practically in love with her. She's going to be around. I don't know why you're fighting everything so much."

"None of you understand, okay?" Peter's voice had gotten sharper. "Ezra has Mae, and you're too young. And this is like a holiday for Mae! She's always wanted a daughter."

"Look, it doesn't matter!" Jack had grown exasperated. "She's going to be around, and you're just gonna have to find a way to deal with it. Without hurting her."

"You know I don't want to hurt her." Peter had gotten so quiet, I could barely hear him, but his voice was unmistakably sincere. He truly didn't want to hurt me, or even hate me. So why did he?

"Yeah, I do!" Jack snapped. "So knock it off!"

"Okay!" Peter relented.

The conversation appeared to be winding to a close and I could hear footsteps getting closer to the stairs. I couldn't have them catching me eavesdropping, so I ran to the bathroom. At least I felt less like crying now, even though I felt even more confused about what was going on.

When I came out of the bathroom, both Peter and Jack had returned to the living room. Peter remained cordial but distant. Jack played with the dog and tried to get everyone involved in some other video game. Ezra continued to ask me questions about myself, ranging from what my mother did to what television shows I liked the best, and Mae seemed contented to play with my hair for the rest of her life.

It was after eleven o'clock when Jack declared that we should get going. Even with the anxiety, the night had passed amazingly fast.

They all walked us to the garage door, even Matilda, making me once again feel self-conscious. They were constantly putting me in the center of the attention, when they were all far more beautiful and fascinating than I could ever dream of being.

Mae hugged me tightly to her, and she looked almost like she was going to cry because I was leaving.

"You will come back, won't you?" Her hands were still on my arms, squeezing them a little too tightly, and Ezra put his arm around her waist, gently pulling her back from me.

"We really enjoy having you over," Ezra said, managing a much less frantic invite than his wife.

"Oh, she'll be back," Jack answered for me, grinning broadly.

Peter, who had been standing off to the side, took a step closer to me, and his piercing green eyes met mine. For one irrational, euphoric second, I thought he might kiss me, but he stayed frozen several feet from me.

Then, very softly, but so strong that it was definitely a command, he said, "Come back."

"Okay," I nodded. He must've established his human interaction quota with that, because then he turned and walked out of the room. I regained some sense of composure and forced a smile at Mae and Ezra. "I'll be back. I promise."

"We'll see you soon then," Ezra smiled at me. Mae looked as if she was going to explode with glee, and Ezra kept his arm firmly placed around her to stop that from happening.

"I told you Ezra would like you," Jack said when we were in the garage. We were heading down to his Jeep, and I had a long tirade of questions to ask him, so I kept my mouth shut until we were safely inside. I didn't want my thoughts interrupted at all. "Do you disagree?"

"I do not," I replied, then hopped into the Jeep and waited for him. He had barely gotten in when I turned full on to face him. "Okay. What the hell does your family want with me?"

"What do you mean?" Jack asked carefully. He didn't want to accidentally give away too much.

"You're all fawning all over me, like I'm a shiny gem or something." That wasn't the right way to say it exactly, because I felt like they genuinely liked me.

"I don't know how to answer that." He started the Jeep and backed out of the garage.

"Jack! I have a right to know what exactly you're doing with me!" My voice sounded shriller than I had meant it to, but some small part of me was actually afraid. They were powerful and beautiful and they wanted me. It was flattering but terrifying.

"No, I know. I'll answer you. Just give me a minute to think about it." The radio still played Smashing Pumpkins, and he turned it down as we started the drive home.

"You guys aren't really brothers are you? I mean, not in the blood relative sense." It was more of a statement, but Jack laughed and shook his head. "You're trying to tell me that you all have the same parents?"

"No, we don't," Jack said, still chuckling over my question.

"You're more like a fraternity or something?" I asked.

"Kinda, but more than that." He was vague, as usual, and I sighed.

"Jack, what's going on?" I asked him earnestly. "What is all of this? Why are you guys so different? And why do you think I'm special?"

"Do you trust me?" He looked gravely at me.

"Yeah, you know I do." My heart raced. He was finally going to tell me something.

"Okay. Then… I will tell you, very soon. But you just have to wait a little bit longer."

"Why? What's going to happen in a little bit longer?" I demanded to know. "I've met your family, I hang out with you all the time, and I know that you're not exactly human. What's left?"

"It's complicated," Jack sighed. "And I… I don't want to scare you off."

"What could possibly scare me off after all I've seen with you?" I insisted incredulously.

"There are still parts of me you don't know." He kept his voice even, but it sounded more like an ominous warning. He gave me a sidelong glance to see how I'd responded, so I tried to look brave, but he could tell that he'd rattled me. "It's about more than just trusting me, or even trusting my family. It's about who you are."

"What's that supposed to mean?" By now, I was getting frightened and confused, and I just wished he could be straight with me, for once.

"'When you dance with the devil, the devil doesn't change. The devil changes you.'" The way Jack said it, it didn't sound like it came directly from him. He was quoting someone, so I took a stab in the dark.

"What? Is that like Dylan Thomas you're using to confuse me?"

"No, it's Joaquin Phoenix, and I'm not trying to confuse you. I'm just trying to prepare you." For some reason, that sent chills down my spine, and I really wondered what he had in store for me.

"You didn't answer my question," I told him when I finally found the will to speak. We'd already pulled up in front of my building, and I knew he wouldn't answer anyway.

"We don't want anything with you." He bit his lip and looked over at me. "We just want you to be one of us."

- 10 -

"What does that mean?" I know I looked terrified despite my best efforts, but he just smiled at me.

"I answered your question." He nodded at my building. "Get some sleep. I'll talk to you tomorrow."

"Yeah, right, like I can sleep after that," I muttered opening the door. "When did you get so damn ominous? Were you watching Vincent Price last night or something?"

Jack just laughed, and I got out of the Jeep. When he drove off, I stayed outside for a minute, letting the cold air seep into my skin. My whole life was changing. I could feel it. Everything about me was going to be different, and I had no idea what I was going to become.

For the first time ever, I woke up before Milo but not by choice. I had been dreaming something about Peter's emerald eyes and gnashing teeth, but by the time I woke up in a cold sweat, I couldn't really put it together.

My heart pounded horribly and my head was swimming. It had taken forever for me to fall asleep last night, and I couldn't shake the feeling of impending doom.

They wanted me to be one of them? What kind of horror movie crap was that? Did they expect me to marry into the family (and if so, was I supposed to marry Jack… or Peter?)

Or was it something more horrific, like they were in a cult or something? Was I expected to be some kind of virgin sacrifice?

While taking a shower, I tried to wash away my trepidation. Despite all the unusual and sometimes frightening occurrences, I couldn't imagine that Jack would ever hurt me. Mae and Ezra seemed sincere in their unexplained affection for me, and even Peter had shown a reluctance to hurt me.

All of it reminded me of a story I had read once. A young rather unattractive girl climbed a mountain and accidentally stumbled into a village of the most beautiful people she'd ever seen.

Everyone in the entire town was absolutely perfect and amazing, but since everyone looked that way, they had grown bored with it. Being perfect was ordinary, but all the things about her that made her ugly in her old life made her stand out as beautiful and revered. Everyone fell in love with her and had sex with her, and eventually she died of exhaustion and depression.

The story had some kind of moral about how everyone used her for the way she looked, and being liked for the way you looked is worse than not being liked at all.

That wasn't what stood out to me about it now. Jack and his family were flawless, and I was just ordinary and boring. Maybe they spent too much time keeping to themselves, and my general homeliness was new and refreshing for them. It was the only explanation I had for why they'd want me around.

But then, how exactly would I go about becoming one of them? And why would they even want me to? Just what the hell did he even mean by "one of them?" One of them what?

By the time I got out of the shower, I had used up all the hot water. I muttered an apology to Milo, but he shrugged and said he didn't mind cold showers.

Going to school had never seemed so much like a chore, but at least it was Friday. I could stay out as late as I wanted tonight, and I would spend every second of the night interrogating Jack if that's what it took. I wouldn't stop until he told me everything.

The day went by surprisingly fast, but that was in a large part because I slept my first three hours. Over my lunch break, I text messaged Jack and asked him when we were going to hang out.

Even though he usually responded to me within seconds, he didn't this time, but that's what I had mostly expected since he stayed up all hours of the night. Still, I couldn't help but check my phone every ten minutes and feel a twinge of disappointment that he hadn't answered.

When I got home, I turned the TV onto old *Speed Racer* cartoon reruns, but I didn't even really pay attention to it. My phone was on my lap with the volume turned up full blast, and I kept bouncing my foot anxiously up and down. I crossed my arms tightly over my chest to keep from biting my nails, but it was a very hard battle.

"Are you going over to Jack's tonight?" Milo sat on the couch, absently watching the cartoon. He glanced over at me, and even in my distracted frame of mind, I noticed the pained expression on his face.

"Probably." Then I looked down at my phone and sighed. "Maybe not."

"I could make us supper if you stayed in," Milo offered hopefully.

Even though his voice had already changed, his face still carried all that baby fat that made him look like a little boy, and I couldn't wait for him to grow out of that. Then it wouldn't hurt so much when I broke his heart.

I really had been neglecting him a lot lately, and it had to be horrible sitting in this tiny apartment all by himself night after night. But I had to get to the bottom of things with Jack.

"That's a nice idea, but not tonight." I let him down as gently as I could, but his face crumbled anyway, and he looked away. "Maybe we can another day this weekend."

"You're gonna be out all night with Jack." Milo tried to keep it matter-of-fact, but there was a bitter edge. "It's the weekend, and you're seventeen. I really shouldn't expect any different. And pretty soon, you'll be out on your own and have your own life and all that. I should just get used to it now."

"Come on, Milo. You know you'll always be a part of my life." Before I had met Jack, I would've said that with a 100% certainty. Milo was my brother and a huge part of my life, and nothing could change that.

At least that's what I thought until Jack had half-warned/half-promised me that my life was going to change, that I was going to change. There might be somewhere that I went that Milo couldn't follow. As much as it would kill me to leave him behind, the thought of life without Jack and Peter sounded worse.

"Whatever you say," Milo replied, and he was completely unconvinced. Maybe it was starting to show on my face, that I already had one foot out the door.

I considered arguing with him more about it, but what was the point? Things were changing, and we both felt it. I didn't want to lie to Milo, so we sat in silence, watching the TV. I expected him to get up and go in another room, or at least somewhere else to mourn my impending absence, but he stayed out there with me.

When my phone finally jingled Jack's ring tone, my heart skipped a beat and I jumped at it, but Milo just rolled his eyes.

When do you wanna hang out? Jack texted me.

As soon as possible.

You know what I think would be fun? Why don't you bring Milo with? Jack messaged back, and I felt a wave of conflicting emotions run over me.

Bringing him along would definitely satiate my guilt, but it would also mean even less alone time with Jack where I could drill him for answers. Plus, I still hadn't figured out what they wanted with me, let alone what they could possibly want with Milo. But he would like them, especially Mae.

Finally, I decided that there was only one way to make a decision.

"Milo, do you wanna come with me to Jack's tonight?" I tried hard not to sound reluctant about asking him, and I even smiled when I turned to look at him, trying to make the offer sound somewhat enticing.

"What do you mean?" His eyes lit up and his voice raised an octave, but he wanted to make sure he understood what was transpiring before he agreed to it.

"Just go over to Jack's house and hang out. He has *Guitar Hero* and stuff ." That would be an added bonus for Jack. He'd have someone to play video games with him that didn't get irritated by it or totally suck at it.

"Do you really want me to?" Milo hesitated, and I smiled reassuringly at him.

"Yeah, of course I do." I wanted to be around him, but I wasn't sure that this was the best idea.

But it was the best one I could come up with, and nothing bad had happened to me when I'd been with Jack. In fact, he'd saved my life twice. There shouldn't be anything to worry about. So why was I worried?

"Then okay. Yeah. That'd be great." Milo jumped up and ran into his room to change his clothes. He still had that crush on Jack to contend with, and I'm sure he'd forget all about it once he met Peter and Ezra.

He's in. When are you picking us up? I replied to Jack.

Five minutes. I'm already on my way. That was Jack for you, not being psychic.

"You better hurry!" I shouted at Milo and went into the bathroom to fix my makeup. The clothes I was wearing would have to do, but at least I wouldn't go there with smudged eyeliner. "He's gonna be here in five minutes!"

"Ready!" Milo responded a second later. I peeked out the bathroom door to see him wearing almost the exact same outfit he was before – a long sleeved white shirt with a green polo over it and a pair of jeans.

"You're sure you want to come with?" I asked him, once I had finished getting ready.

146

We walked out of the apartment, and Milo doubled check to make sure the door was locked and that he had his house keys in his pocket, something that I never did.

"Yeah, why wouldn't I?" Then Milo shot a nervous look at me. "Do you not want me to?"

"No, that's not what I meant!" I said quickly and smiled at him. "Of course I want you to come with." I pushed the call button for the elevator and turned back to him. "There are just a few things you have to know before we go."

"Okay?" Milo raised an eyebrow at me, but I thought it'd be best if he were prepared. The elevator doors sprung open and we stepped inside. Thankfully, we were alone, because I would feel silly saying this stuff in front of complete strangers.

"First, his brothers are really hot. I mean, like movie star hot, except even hotter. I know that you think Jack is amazing, but his brothers blow him out of the water." I looked over to gauge his response, but for the most part, he just looked skeptical.

"Second, his family is super rich. One of their cars easily costs twice as much as Mom makes in a year, and they have five of them and this super fancy house. It's really intimidating."

"Like how rich?" Milo started to look nervous, so my point was getting through. "Like Bill Gates rich?"

"I don't know. I didn't ask," I said. Their wealth was inconsequential to me.

"Well what do they do for money then?" Naturally, Milo wanted to know all the practical reasons for everything. I had always meant to ask Jack what they did, but something else always sidetracked me.

147

"I didn't ask that either," I sighed, and the elevators opened to the lobby.

"Is there anything else I should know about them?" Milo asked as we walked out.

"Um, Jack drives super fast, but he's perfectly safe." I pushed open the glass doors that led outside.

"Really?" Milo wrinkled his nose. "Like how fast?"

"You'll probably see," I told him offhandedly, and then hurried over to Jack's Jeep and jumped inside before Milo could ask anything more.

As soon as I realized what happened, it dawned on me why Jack had invited Milo along; he knew I wouldn't say anything in front of Milo. Jack was trying to get off the hook about last night.

Someday, I'd probably have to tell Milo everything, but that day definitely wasn't today. Maybe when I had the answers myself, and I could actually explain everything. Until then, I didn't feel like letting that much out in the open.

"Hey," Jack smiled at me, then turned back to Milo. "Hey, Milo. It's good seeing you again."

"Yeah, you too," Milo replied. He stared at Jack for a moment, but he was much better at controlling his crush on Jack than most people. I wondered if it had to do with the fact that he was gay. Or maybe he just had really amazing self control.

"So what did you have planned for tonight?" I asked as Jack sped off down the highway towards his house.

"I don't know," Jack shrugged. "I just thought it was time that your family met my family."

"Why?" I asked.

"Why not?" Jack countered.

"I don't know. We haven't known each other that long, and it's not like we're getting married or something." That would be the logical time for families to mingle, not when two people have known each other for a couple weeks and are just friends.

"No, it's definitely not like that." Jack breathed deeply, and then turned up the stereo, blasting out the Violent Femmes.

We were silent on the short car ride, but when we pulled up in front of his house, I heard Milo gasp in the back seat and whisper, "It's like a castle."

I'd already been there a couple times, and it still felt breathtaking. The turret really set it off, but it completely suited them. After meeting Ezra and knowing that he built it, it all seemed even more perfect.

"Is Mae gone?" I asked.

We had pulled into the garage, and I noticed her black Jetta gone. Every other time I'd come here, the garage had been full, and her empty spot stood out.

"Yeah, but I thought she would be back by now." Jack's face flashed confused and concerned, but he instantly smoothed it out with a broad smile for Milo and me. "She'll be back soon. And Ezra and Peter are still here." He got out, and we followed suit.

"Hey, wait." I lowered my voice then grabbed onto Jack's arm to stop him. Milo was a little bit behind us, admiring the Lamborghini. He'd never been much of a car person before, but the Lamborghini had that power over anyone. "Is Peter going to be nice to Milo?"

"Oh, yeah, he'll be fine," Jack nodded.

"So it's just me that he has a problem with?" My heart tightened.

I had been hoping that Peter's icy demeanor had something to do with the fact that I was an outsider, but if he had no problems with Milo, then it had to be me personally.

"You are far more complicated," Jack whispered.

"Is 'complicated' like your go-to word or something?" I muttered, making him laugh.

"Why are we just standing in the middle of the garage?" Milo piped in. He wasn't that into cars, so it hadn't held his attention for long, and he stood behind us looking confused.

"We're not." With that, Jack quickened his pace towards the house, and Milo and I followed more slowly.

Jack threw open the door, and he was instantly greeted by Matilda jumping into him. Without Mae there to stop her or dampen her enthusiasm, she was free to jump and slobber all over Jack as much as she wanted.

"Oh, and they have a dog too," I told Milo and gestured to the giant white ball of fur in Jack's arms. Jack remembered that Milo was there, and he put her on the ground much sooner than he normally did.

"Yeah, I figured that out," Milo said dryly.

"This is Mattie!" Jack scratched her head roughly. "She's a good girl. She's just a big baby."

"I can tell." Milo stood off to the side, watching Jack wrestle with his dog.

Ezra magically appeared in the doorway, and after taking a moment for myself to admire him, I looked back to see Milo's reaction. His eyes had widened and his jaw had even gone a little lax. I wondered if I looked that awestruck when I met Ezra.

"Oh, it's just you," Ezra said.

"Thanks," Jack replied sarcastically and stood up, temporarily ending his roughhousing with Matilda.

"No, sorry, I didn't mean it like that," Ezra's face broke into a smile that made it hard for me to breathe. "I thought that you might be Mae." At the mention of her, his lips got tighter, and he and Jack exchanged a pained look. "But she's not back yet."

"I don't know what could be taking her so long," Jack added, growing irritated. Ezra dismissed him and turned to Milo.

"You must be Alice's brother." Ezra's smile returned and he walked over to Milo to shake his hand. I watched to see if Milo noticed how weird (but good) their skin felt. If he did, it didn't register on his face. He just smiled dumbly at Ezra. "It's a pleasure to meet you. I'm Ezra."

"I'm Milo." It was difficult for him to form the words, and he sounded out of breath. For once, I wasn't the only one gawking at everyone.

"So, Jack," I said, interrupting Milo's awkward staring, "Milo really loves video games."

"Really?" Jack's face lit up, and I half expected him to throw Milo under his arm and dash off into the next room. "Come on. I've got like everything, and I mean everything. From *Grand Theft Auto* to *Pong*, I've got you covered." He started to hurry into the living room, and Milo gave Ezra one last longing look before following him.

"Really? You have *Pong*? Why?"

"Cause its awesome!" Jack sounded mildly offended at being questioned.

"Finally, someone for him to play with." Ezra smiled gratefully at me, and I looked away so I wouldn't blush. "You wouldn't believe how much time he spends on those damn things. Mae's always trying to get him to go out and do something, anything, but it's near impossible. She was so relieved when he met you and actually left the house."

"Well, I'm glad that I could help," I replied timidly. "Where is Mae?"

"Um, she's out." Ezra's normally open face closed up a bit, and it was a familiar expression that I'd seen written on Jack's face every time he didn't want to tell me something. "She really ought to be home soon."

"I just wanted to make sure Milo meets her." I rubbed my arm, afraid that I had encroached on territory they'd rather I didn't. "I know he'd really like her."

"Everyone really likes Mae," Ezra grinned, and then I felt stupid. Obviously everyone really liked her, so it was a silly thing to point it out.

"Oh, yeah, of course," I fumbled. He laughed, and it was a tremendous laugh, but it wasn't as spectacular as Jack's. I doubted that anyone could ever match his, though, not even someone as perfect as Ezra.

"I am a lucky man." He looked wistful for a moment, thinking of Mae, and I longed to have something like that. It was pure, unadulterated love. Then, his expression changed as he thought of something. "Peter's upstairs, if you wanted to talk to him."

"Oh." I hadn't really planned to talk to Peter, since he had this horrible way of simultaneously making me want to run to him and run away crying. But Ezra had said it in a way where I felt obligated to do it, and part of me really enjoyed the way Peter made me feel, even if it came wrapped in pain and confusion. "I'll go see him then."

"I'm just going to wait down here for Mae." Ezra stood by the door, watching me as I went, looking a bit like a lost puppy.

I passed through the living room, but Jack and Milo were too entranced by some war video game to notice me. As I made my way up the stairs, I remembered the first time I met Peter, and the way he glared at me from over his book. I hoped that this wouldn't be a repeat of that, but since Ezra had sent me up here, I had to believe that it wasn't.

Peter's bedroom door was open, and I leaned in the doorway, peering around for him. When I found him, my breath stopped and a burning flush went over me.

Wearing only a pair of jeans, he was drying his hair with a white towel. He wasn't overly muscular, but his chest was defined and hard. A thin trail of dark hair started just below his belly button and traveled downwards, and my eyes had never been so tantalized by the prospect of what fell below the waist of his jeans.

When he noticed me staring at him, he tossed his towel on his bed and just looked back at me, his green eyes shooting through me. I ached for him in ways I had never imagined.

"I just took a shower," Peter said.

His lyrical voice somehow managed to dampen the trance I had been under, but nothing could fully break it. He looked away and grabbed a white shirt off the chair, and much to my dismay, he pulled it on.

"I didn't mean to disturb you," I mumbled, finding it hard to speak clearly.

"No, you're okay." He sat back down on his bed and tousled his damp hair.

I waited in the doorway for him to say more, but that was a struggle. It felt like there was something inside pulling me towards him. Like a rope was attached to my heart and someone physically yanked on it. He looked at me with an expression I couldn't read, but his eyes definitely looked pained.

"You can come in, if you want," he said finally.

It didn't feel so much like I walked to his bed as I just gave in and let myself be pulled over to him. Then I was on the bed, sitting dangerously close to him.

I breathed in, and he smelled sweetly of apples. That was probably his soap, but there was something tangy and wonderful underneath that was all him.

Like a complete idiot, I told him, "You smell good."

He smiled the first genuine smile I'd seen him have, and it struck me with its utter perfection. Then softly, he laughed, sending astounding tingles radiating throughout my whole body. I almost shivered with pleasure.

"What do I smell like?" Peter leaned in closer to me, as if he was sharing a secret.

He was so close that when he exhaled, a damp tendril of his hair blew back and brushed against my cheek. My skin trembled expectantly, demanding more.

"Apples?" I wondered how I managed to find the strength to speak.

I knew the conversation was utterly pointless and dull, but most of my brain had become occupied by him. And I don't mean by thoughts of him, I mean him. It was as if he'd seeped in and somehow become a part of me, but it wasn't enough. I was desperate for all of him.

"Yeah." He smiled crookedly, and then leaned back a little, away from me.

Without any thought on my part, my body moved to correct the distance between us. I would've preferred that I stayed where I was, but my body insisted that I tilt closer to him.

"Why do you hate me?" The words came out of my mouth, but I couldn't believe that I'd asked them.

Inside my mind, I screamed Shut up! Shut up! You can't say that to him! But he'd managed to cut off the blood flow to the part of my brain that controlled my inhibitions. If I weren't careful, I'd very quickly be confessing my innermost secrets to him.

"I don't hate you." He looked embarrassed and lowered his eyes.

I had an awful pain at not being able to see into his eyes, but it came with some relief, as I'd be able to think a bit more clearly.

"Then why do you act like you do?" I pressed.

What the hell was I doing? I was normally an absolute coward, and now at the worst possible moment, I suddenly decided to be brave and corner this amazingly stunning man into hating me. He had said he didn't, but after I shamed and irritated him like this, I'm sure he would.

"I don't know." He looked up, staring straight ahead, but he wasn't really looking at anything. His beautiful features stiffened to a painful mask.

"You want to hate me, though." My voice was almost inaudible, but he'd heard me. I'd thought I hadn't had the strength to speak, but the words kept relentlessly tumbling out.

"That's not exactly true." His face softened again, and he turned to look at me.

His eyes were smoldering through me, and I felt my heart pound loudly in my chest. Very gently, he placed his hand on top of mine, and I felt that same electrical surge that I had the day before, but more intense this time. Pleasure rippled through me and I closed my eyes.

Then suddenly, he pulled his hand back, and my eyes flew open. His face was a few inches from mine, and something in him looked completely ravenous. He never wavered or moved, but when he spoke, his voice had gone into a very low snarl.

"Go before I do something very bad to you."

- 11 -

"You can do whatever you want to me," I whispered, and he flinched at that.

"Go!" Peter growled.

His voice stung, but it managed to get me moving. Using all my strength, I looked away and stood up. He still hadn't moved, but I could see the tendons in his neck and his arms standing out sharply.

It wasn't until I had started down the stairs, and I had begun to breathe, that I understood why he'd gotten so tense. He was using all his might not to move.

When I got downstairs, I felt dazed and I was panting. There was a very real chance that I had just barely averted danger. And the worst part was part of me still wanted to rush back upstairs and let him do whatever he wanted with me as long as I could still be with him.

"Alice?" Milo asked. He and Jack were standing in the middle of the living room, holding plastic guitars, but I could barely even see them. The whole world felt hazy and I couldn't tell if I was dreaming or not. "Are you okay?"

"You were with Peter?" Jack had stopped playing the game and turned to look at me. He eyed me over, and he saw something that made his face harden. "Come here." I felt frozen in place, so he commanded more harshly, "Come here."

This time I listened and walked over to him, moving like a zombie.

"Did something happen to her?" Milo's voice got higher the more scared he got.

Jack didn't answer him. Instead, he looked me over with this odd expression on his face, a cross between disturbed and jealous. He put two fingers underneath my chin and lifted it up, revealing my neck. He turned my head this way and that, inspecting me carefully.

When he was done, his expression had softened, and he looked satisfied.

"Come here," he repeated, but this time, he looped an arm around my shoulders and pulled me closer to him. "You're okay."

I threw my arms around him, hugging him tightly and relishing the safety of his arms. I sobbed into his chest, unable to hold it back anymore, and he kissed the top of my head.

"What happened?" I heard Ezra's melodic voice boom behind me, but I hadn't seen him when I came in. He seemed to have materialized at the sound of my crying.

"I don't know! She just came downstairs crying!" Milo explained plaintively. He was upset, and I wished somebody would just tell him that everything would be okay. Why wasn't Mae here when I needed her?

"Did something happen?" Ezra demanded, and there was an edge to his voice.

"No," Jack said softly, stroking my hair.

"Are you sure?" Ezra persisted.

"Yes, I'm sure," Jack replied, growing irritated.

"I'm going to talk to Peter." I didn't hear Ezra leaving, but I knew he had anyway.

"What's wrong with her?" Milo sounded panicked.

"Nothing." I pulled away from Jack a little but made sure to keep his arm around me. I wouldn't feel as safe or sturdy without it. Wiping at my tear stained cheeks, I forced a smile at Milo. "I'm fine."

"You're not fine!" Milo insisted with wide, worried eyes.

"It's just... girl stuff." I tried to shrug it off, and I couldn't tell if he saw through it or not.

It was a perfectly reasonable explanation that while I was upstairs, alone with a very attractive guy, he had said or done something to offend me, and that's what had upset me.

In fact, that would be much more plausible than what had actually happened, which was that I had become so entranced with somebody that I almost let him... I'm not sure what.

And I was pretty sure that he sent me away not because he hated me, but because he was attracted to me.

"Like what?" Milo narrowed his eyes.

"I don't wanna talk about it." I just shook my head and looked away.

"What's going on?" Mae shouted suddenly, and my heart soared at the sight of her standing in the doorway. She rushed over to me, placing her hands firmly on my shoulders to look in my eyes.

"She was upstairs with Peter," Jack explained. Mae's expression changed from one of worry to shock, and she turned to look at Jack sharply. "Nothing happened."

She softened, looking sympathetically at me. Before she pulled me into a hug, it finally dawned on me.

Whatever had happened or almost happened with Peter, they knew it. Ezra had sent me upstairs, knowing exactly what would happen. Meaning, he had sent me to my probable harm.

What the hell was going on here? And why didn't I feel as terrified as I should? In fact, as Mae stroked my hair and murmured words of comfort in her soft British accent, I felt nothing but safe. What was wrong with me?

"I'm okay, really," I insisted, and she finally released me.

"I hope you mean that." She smiled sadly and pushed strands of hair back from my face, and then straightened up.

"I do." I nodded firmly, and Jack playfully ruffled my hair, as if to reaffirm that everything was okay.

"And who is this?" Mae turned her attention to Milo. Just looking at her made his anxiety disappear, and he returned her open smile.

"I'm Milo, Alice's brother." He looked a little embarrassed by the look she was giving him, and I knew the feeling. She reached out and touched his face gently (his chubby cheeks were hard to resist) and grinned warmly.

"I'm Mae, Ezra's wife. You're so much cuter than I'd thought you'd be."

"Thanks?" Milo replied unsurely.

"Have you had a tour of the house yet?" Mae had already started looping her arm through his, and she'd missed her calling as a real estate agent. Milo shook his head no, and she laughed a little. With that, she led him away on a tour.

As soon as they were out of earshot, I turned to Jack and hissed, "What the hell happened?"

"You tell me," Jack countered evenly, and I might have overestimated how much he knew.

"You have an idea of what happened, don't you?" I asked. He didn't answer me, so I continued, "You have suspicions. There was something that you were afraid happened."

"I wasn't afraid," he answered quietly, but the fog of Peter was wearing off and I could feel how unnerved he really was.

"Jack, I trust you," I whispered fiercely. "Don't betray that trust." An amused but pained expression flitted across his face, and he shook his head.

"He's not gonna hurt you, Alice." Then he turned to look at me. "None of us are."

"Then..." I trailed off, trying to understand what was happening. "But Peter told me to go before he did something very bad to me." Jack let out a long breath through his teeth and stared off at some point above my head.

"Well... I guess we all just have different definitions of what hurting you means."

"Was that meant to be comforting? Cause it wasn't," I snapped, crossing my arms on my chest.

"Let me put it this way: You are a top priority for my family." Jack said, finishing the conversation.

He still had the plastic guitar hanging over his shoulder, and he unpaused the game and clicked out of the two-player level he'd been playing with Milo. He started playing a song, and when I asked him what that meant, he ignored me.

I flopped back on the couch next to Matilda and stroked her long, white fur. Everything with Peter had exhausted me. My skin flushed with embarrassment at the thought of running into him. I had made a fool of myself, and he was in trouble with Ezra.

But even with that, I still really wanted to see him. My very being wanted to be near him again, and it would be worth anything.

As predicted, Mae completely enchanted Milo. They seemed made for each other. She was all motherly love, and he was all motherless child.

When they made their way into the living room, Milo went back to playing video games with Jack. I curled up on the couch with Mae, resting my head on her lap, and let her play with my hair.

"I know you're hurting now, but things will make sense, love," Mae murmured, pushing my hair from my eyes. "Everything happens for a reason."

The nights of barely sleeping had caught up with me, and the soothing comfort of Mae was too much. I drifted off to a sleep filled with dreams of Peter. They were probably the best dreams I'd ever had.

When I woke up, I felt good, but incredibly disoriented. The living room was dark, and I was alone, except for Matilda, who snored loudly on the floor next to me.

I moved a little on the couch, preparing to start calling for Jack or Milo, but then I heard voices talking softly nearby. And then I heard my name, so I stopped moving and strained to hear.

"Well, we obviously can't leave Alice alone with him anymore." That was Jack, trying to protect me from Peter.

"No, I agree." Ezra's deep voice sounded like a lullaby when he kept it low. I imagined that it would be tranquil to have him sing me to sleep. "But they'll have to eventually."

"But she's not ready for it," Jack said. "He's not ready for it."

"You're not ready for it," Ezra countered.

"Maybe not," Jack relented. "But he feels too conflicted for anything to work. He's just making everything harder on her than it needs to be. I mean, you saw her today."

"It's incredibly painful, rejecting it," Ezra calmly said. "Peter's showing a tremendous will just going against it, but eventually, he'll give in. It's impossible. Whatever pain he thinks he's avoiding, this is far worse."

"How do you know?" Jack asked him suspiciously. "You never rejected it."

"I did at first," Ezra said, then backtracked. "I tried to ignore it, and that was brutal. But I saw Peter after what happened with Alice."

"And?" Jack pressed Ezra when he didn't say anything.

"He's not taking it well," Ezra said simply.

"How much longer will this go on?" Jack asked, and I couldn't help but notice a hint of sadness in his voice.

"Not much longer." Ezra breathed deeply. "We'll just have to keep an eye on both of them."

"Ezra!" Mae called from another room, down the hall from where Ezra and Jack spoke. "Come here! Milo's beat me at chess twice already! You've got to try against him! He's amazing!"

"I'll be right there!" Ezra shouted back to her, then spoke quieter to Jack. "You understand?"

"Yeah," Jack said reluctantly.

I didn't hear Ezra's footfalls when he walked away, but that didn't surprise me. Jack's silhouette appeared in the doorway, and I quickly closed my eyes, pretending I was sleeping.

Matilda whimpered as he walked past her, and he patted her head before sitting on the couch next to me. As soon as I felt the couch move, I stirred as if I was just waking up.

"Did you sleep okay?"

"Yeah," I nodded and moved so I was sitting on my knees facing him. My voice sounded thick from tears, but I hoped he would think it was from sleep.

"Hey are you okay?" Jack sounded sad and worried. My eyes adjusted to the dark, and I could map out the concerned expression on his face.

"Yeah, just tired."

"I gathered that when you passed out." He tried to keep his tone light, but he struggled.

What Ezra had said had gotten to him too, and when he felt anxious, I felt it even worse. It wouldn't be much longer before I started to cry.

"You sound upset," I said.

"Nah, I'm fine," Jack insisted, shaking his head in the darkness.

"Jack, promise me that I'll be okay. You know I'll believe anything you say, so just promise me that everything will be okay." My voice sounded more nervous than I would've liked.

"I know you can't understand right now, but you've got nothing to worry about." Then he put his arm around me and pulled me close to him, resting his chin on the top of my head. "I'm upset because I care about you too much. The problem is me, not you. You're gonna be better than fine. I promise."

"You're right. I don't understand," I said. He stroked my hair, and I moved my head on his chest. Then I realized something odd. "I can't hear your heart beat."

"Just listen harder."

Pressing my ear closer to his chest, I listened hard, and, there it was, very faint and incredibly slow. I wasn't timing it, but it couldn't have been beating more than ten or twenty times a minute.

"It's so slow!" I jerked my head back so I could look at him. "Are you okay? You're not having a heart attack, are you?"

"No," Jack laughed, this time sounding more like himself. "That's just the way my heart beats."

"But that's not the way it's supposed to be." I furrowed my brow, trying to understand. "That's not how my heart beats."

"I know." He was mildly amused, but my confusion always seemed to entertain him. "I can hear your heartbeat."

"How? You're way over there." He was actually sitting right next to me, but he was still too far away to hear. "You're hearing isn't that good."

"It is for this one thing." He reached out and put his hand gingerly on my throat.

At first, I didn't understand what he was doing, but then I felt his thumb stroking my jugular vein. He was feeling my pulse, and a look of sheer pleasure passed across his face. A warm hunger radiated from him that I didn't grasp.

"Jack!" Ezra's voice broke into the room, and Jack instantly dropped his hand, as if he'd been caught with his hand up my shirt instead of on my throat. "It's late. Milo's tired. Maybe you should take them home. Unless you don't feel up to it. In which case, I'd be more than happy-"

"No, I've got it," Jack replied gruffly and stood up.

Ezra gave Jack a disapproving look as we walked out of the living room, but Jack refused to look at him. For me, Ezra gave a reassuring smile and said he hoped that I would come back soon. Mae hugged me tightly at the door, but she hugged Milo even tighter.

During the car ride home, Milo rattled on endlessly about what an amazing house Jack had and how great Mae was and all the fun things he'd done while I had been asleep. I rested my head against the cold glass of the window, and found that for once, I had very little to say.

I still didn't know what Jack and his family were, but they definitely couldn't be trusted. Peter had been rude and kept me at a distance because he didn't want to hurt me. He was trying to protect me.

Despite this, I loved Jack and Mae and even Ezra, and I definitely felt something strong for Peter. And I knew that if being with them meant that I would die, I would still see them again. It would be worse to live without them.

When Milo and I went up to our apartment, I felt dazed. Part of it was coming to terms with my impending death, but most of it was just an after effect of being with Peter. He was like a drug, and I was still coming down from the high.

I flopped down on the couch while Milo buzzed about the kitchen. Being over there had the opposite effect on him, and he was totally energized.

"Aren't you hungry?" Milo asked from the kitchen. I heard pots banging, but I just buried myself deeper into the couch. "I'm starving. You know what's weird? We were over them from five o'clock at night until after two in the morning, and I never once saw them eat or drink anything.

"In fact, when I wanted something to drink, Mae had to rummage around the kitchen for a glass and some water," Milo continued, without pausing for a breath. "You know, I don't even think they have any food in that house. They must order a lot of take out. Which is weird cause Mae really seems like the Suzie Homemaker type."

Milo continued to ramble on but I was starting to drift to sleep. But then it all clicked. I understood fully what Jack and Peter were.

But before I could actually manifest the word and put it all together, I fell asleep, and lost it entirely.

Dreamlessly, I'd managed to sleep for thirteen hours on the couch. Whatever happened to me with Peter, it had been tantamount to overdosing on sleeping pills.

I stretched slowly, trying to work out the kinks and cricks in my back and neck. Milo sat at the computer, and he just smirked at my struggle to wake up.

"Morning, sunshine," Milo chirped. He still seemed hyper from the night before.

"Shut up," I grumbled.

Already, Peter filled the tired fog of my brain. Like some kind of hang over, my skin hurt and my head throbbed dully. When I breathed in deeply, I could still remember the way he smelled, like apples and something familiar that I couldn't quite place.

"What are you doing?" Milo jolted me out of my daydream. He looked at me like I had totally lost it, so I stood up and decided that I had to get myself in gear.

"Nothing," I told him absently.

Walking to the bathroom, I pulled my phone out of my pocket. It was almost four in the afternoon, so maybe Jack would be awake by now. I shut the bathroom door, but before I could even actually go to the bathroom, I had to text Jack first.

I need to see you today. I text messaged him, and then started the agonizing wait for him to respond.

After I showered, and he still hadn't responded, I started getting a nervous pit in my stomach. Maybe I had done something wrong, and I wasn't going to be allowed over there anymore.

Or maybe Jack had just grown bored with me. It was probably irritating him that I fawned over his brother, and I would hate me if I were Jack.

When he'd been talking to Ezra, they had said that I couldn't be alone with Peter. Maybe that meant that I couldn't be around him at all anymore. Somehow, I had ruined everything.

I couldn't take it anymore, so I decided to call Jack, and find out what was going on. When I got his voicemail instead of him, I was near tears.

"Jack, it's just me. Alice. Um… I just wanted to apologize for last night. I know that I… overreacted to everything, and I'm really sorry. I just… I really want see you today. We need to talk. Okay. So… just call me back, I guess. Bye."

Going through all the routine of getting ready, I managed to dress myself and apply makeup, but none of it felt real. It felt like some shell of myself going through the motions. My mind was completely locked onto the way Peter smelled and the way he looked through me and how my body felt pulled towards him.

When I had finished getting ready, I just sat on the couch, staring off into nothing, and tried to figure out what I would do if I never talked to Peter or Jack again.

"What's going on with you?" Milo still sat at the computer, but he couldn't ignore my zombie stare anymore. I shook my head and swallowed hard, so he got up from what he was doing and came over to sit next to me. "What happened last night over there?"

"Nothing," I mumbled.

"Alice, come on." He gave me a hard look, the one that said I-know-you-better-than-anyone-so-there's-no-point-in-lying. "Did Jack's brother do something to you?"

"No." I bit my lip and wondered if he had done something to me. Why couldn't I get him out of my head? It was as if he had crawled underneath my skin but not in a bad way. "I just really like him. Like more than I've ever liked anyone. It's completely... visceral."

"Did he blow you off or something?"

I wasn't sure if Peter sending me out of his room was rejecting me or done to protect me... or maybe both. My phone felt very heavy in my hand, and I looked down at it, willing Jack to call me and fix everything.

"I don't know," I answered honestly. "Jack hasn't texted me back. I think maybe he's mad at me or something. I think I did something wrong."

"You did not do anything." Milo was so incredulous that I looked over at him. "They love you over there, like crazy love. Mae talked non-stop about you, and Jack looks at you like you walk on water. It's a little sickening actually."

"Really?" That made me feel a little better, but Jack still hadn't called, so I wasn't over-the-top better.

"Yeah." He nodded, then looked down at my hands and wrinkled his nose. "Your nails are chipped really bad. Why don't I repaint them while you wait for Jack to wake up?"

"You think he's still sleeping?" I asked hopefully, and let my brother take my hands.

I had left my make up bag splayed out on the coffee table, and Milo leaned over and grabbed the nail polish remover, cotton balls, and dark blue nail polish.

"We left at like two-thirty in the morning, and everybody in that house was wide awake. Plus, he's some rich, young playboy that doesn't have a job. What does he really have to get up for?" He did have a point, and I finally started to relax.

"Considering this isn't the first time you've painted my nails, I probably should've figured out sooner that you were gay," I teased him. Milo had been painting my nails for as long as he could paint anything. When I really looked back at life with him, there were a lot of obvious hints that I should've picked up on.

"Probably," he agreed.

After he finished painting my nails, he sat with me on the couch. He talked a little bit about how much he liked Mae and everybody, and that he hoped that I wouldn't mind if he went back over there again. Honestly, I didn't mind at all. It was nice being able to be around him and Jack at the same time.

Milo pointed out that he'd never met Peter, and we both thought that was strange. He hadn't come down from his room all night, and Mae hadn't given Milo a tour of the upstairs. Like they were purposely trying to keep them apart.

My heart pounded painfully when I realized that Peter might actually be dangerous, and maybe it wasn't the safest place for Milo to be hanging out. I considered saying something to that effect when my phone rang.

"Hey, sorry, I didn't call you sooner," Jack said when I answered. Just hearing him made me elated, but his voice had a tightness to it. Something was bothering him. "I ended up having a really late night, so I just woke up."

"Sorry. I hope none of it's my fault." But I knew it was my fault. I had done something wrong last night.

"No, it's not," Jack reassured me warmly. "It was just … a little family crisis, I guess."

"What happened?" Anxiety gripped me, and Milo shot me a confused, concerned look, but I just shook my head at him.

"Um… I'll tell you when I pick you up, okay? Will you be ready soon?" He was definitely keeping something from me.

"I'm ready now." I was glad that I had gotten up and gotten ready before he called. If I had heard this when I first woke up, I would've rushed to his house in last night's clothes with greasy hair.

"Good. I'll be there soon." He hung up, probably to prevent me from asking more questions, so I flipped my phone shut.

"What happened?" Milo's worried expression mirrored my own, but I was too frazzled to answer him. Hurriedly, I slipped on shoes and grabbed my dark blue cardigan to throw on. "Alice?"

"I don't know. He wouldn't tell me."

Why did I have to feel like crying? I swear, I didn't really cry this much. Most of the time, I was a really sane, normal person. But something about Jack and Peter made me want to burst into tears all the time.

My emotions seemed to be on overdrive. It was like I had lived my whole life using just the bare minimum, and now this family had switched them into max.

"Is everyone okay?" Milo leaned over the back of the couch, watching me rush about. I probably had everything I needed, but I kept feeling like I was forgetting something, then running back to make sure I had it.

"I don't know, Milo!" I snapped. "He didn't tell me anything!"

"Sorry." He sounded hurt, and I wanted to apologize, but I didn't have time. Jack would be here "soon," which could mean anywhere from five seconds to fifteen minutes. "Do you want me to come with?"

"Not today." I finally managed an apologetic smile, and he slumped down in the couch. "Another time, I promise. Just... not today, okay?"

"Yeah, yeah, just go."

"Sorry. I'll talk to you later." And with that, I was out the door.

I should've said more, but I couldn't even wait for the elevator today. I pushed the call button, and when the doors didn't immediately open, I ran down the stairs.

Even in the rush I had been in, Jack had still managed to beat me outside. He'd driven the Jeep, and I practically dove into it. I looked at him expectantly, and he just smiled grimly at me.

"What happened?" I demanded as we pulled away from my apartment building.

"And a 'how do you do' to you too," Jack replied dryly.

"Jack!"

"Sorry." He stared out straight ahead but kept taking sidelong glances at me. "So... last night, after you left... Peter left."

"What do you mean left?" My heart had already started pounding and my stomach twisted in knots, and Jack just groaned. "Jack? Where'd he go? Why'd he leave? Because of me?"

"You have to calm down," Jack sighed. "This is why I didn't do it over the phone, but maybe I should've." Then he looked at me somberly, his eyes pleading with me. "Please calm down."

"I will if you just tell me what's going on!" I said, but I tried to slow my breathing and the frantic beating of my heart.

"We don't really know where he went." He had waited for me to calm down a bit, but he kept his eyes fixed on the road, like he was trying really hard not to be distracted by me. His knuckles had gone white from the way he gripped the steering wheel.

"Ezra has some ideas because..." He trailed off and rubbed his temple. "He left because of... You can't take this the wrong way. I know that you will, though. You always take everything the wrong way. If I said, 'hey you look nice today,' you'd say, 'and what, I don't look nice everyday?'"

"Jack, please focus." I wanted to yell at him and make him just hurry up and tell me what was going on.

"Yeah." He quickly glanced at me, but I didn't understand what he meant so I just stared at him. "Yes. Peter left because of you. Because of what happened, well, almost happened yesterday. But it's not because you did anything wrong, or there's anything wrong with you. Peter's just going through his own thing and I don't know. I think he's just being an ass, but Ezra says…" He trailed off, probably realizing that he hadn't really said anything but he'd almost said too much.

My eyes had welled with tears. No matter what Jack said, Peter left because of me, because of something that I had or hadn't done, and it was devastating. Everything about me craved him, and I drove him away.

"What did almost happen yesterday?" I asked quietly.

"Well…" Jack laughed hollowly, and his hand gripped the wheel even tighter. "What do you think happened yesterday?"

"I don't know. Honestly, it's hard to remember. When I try to think about it, I just remember being in his room and feeling this incredible pull towards him and this… yearning."

I tried hard to focus on what had sent me in a tailspin, but it felt so foggy. I could remember Peter's eyes and the way he smelled and wanting him so much it hurt. My heart raced, throbbing painfully, and I had gotten short of breath.

"Stop, Alice," Jack whimpered, and he was in total agony. His blue eyes had gone almost translucent, and they had that hungry look that was very reminiscent of the one that Peter had given me last night.

"Stop what?" I asked breathlessly. He groaned and looked away from me, and I was about press him further, but then the Jeep started skidding horribly across the road.

"Ah, hell." Jack gripped the wheel and tried to correct it, but I felt it start to tilt to the side, and he gave me a frantic look.

Before I could really understand what was happening, he lunged at me, wrapping his arms tightly around me and pressing me against him. I closed my eyes and buried my face in his chest, and I felt his body curl protectively around me.

There was the sensation of moving and I felt cold wind whip through my hair. The sound of crunching metal and shattering glass and this sickening thud filled my ears, but I could barely hear anything over the pounding of my heart.

I finally felt Jack's arm relax around me, and I lifted my head, looking at him in the face. He was worried and scared, but there was still that underlying hunger.

"Are you okay?" Jack asked, pushing the hair from my eyes to inspect for wounds.

"I think so," I nodded. I felt dazed and scared, but nothing really hurt.

"Good. Then I need you to get away from me for a minute," Jack said, not unkindly.

I hurried to do as he asked, pushing myself off him and standing up. He jumped up and took several steps back from me.

For the first time, I looked around. We were on the shoulder of the highway, and there were bits of broken glass and metal all over the road. Another car had been crushed against the cement divider in the middle, and there was an SUV farther down that looked like it had some minor damage. Headlights of stopped cars blinded me.

At first, I couldn't figure out where the Jeep was, and then I saw it. About thirty feet back from us, the crushed remnants of the Jeep were engulfed in flames.

I gasped, realizing that if Jack hadn't grabbed me, I either would've stayed in that car to get smashed and burned up, or I would've been thrown from the Jeep going well over a hundred miles an hour and landed on the pavement.

"Are you okay?" I looked back at him.

Jack had taken the brunt force of everything, and if he hadn't, I would've been killed. My body was much more fragile than his, but he had to have sustained some wounds.

"Yeah, I'm great." He tried to compose himself and looked at the carnage around us.

There appeared to be some cuts on his arm, and when he turned away, I saw the back of his shirt was shredded and covered in blood. When he'd hit the road, he must've landed on his back and skidded for awhile.

"You're covered in blood!" I shouted and took a step closer to him, trying to inspect his wounds, but he just waved me off.

I remembered the dog bite, and how the major wounds had looked so minor. I wasn't really worried about him, but he had just been thrown from the car.

"I'm fine." He held his arm out for me to see. A thick line of blood ran from where a gash should be, but there wasn't one. There wasn't even a mark.

"What about your back?" I asked, but he shook his head.

"It tingles. It'll be fine in a minute." All the skin and the muscles should've been ripped from his back, but it would be fine in a minute.

"You saved my life. Again." I wrapped my arms tightly around myself.

The adrenaline, confusion, and Peter's sedative all mixed through me, on top of Jack's apprehension and fading hunger. I was on the verge of hysterics.

"Well, this time, I almost killed you too. So... it kinda evens out." Jack meant he'd almost killed me by crashing the Jeep, but I could still feel his hunger. I remembered that ominous conversation he'd had with Ezra about how this all wouldn't last much longer.

"Why do you keep saving my life?" My voice trembled, and hot tears slid down my cheeks. Jack looked at me like he didn't understand what I meant, but I went on talking, and the more I talked, the harder I cried. "I just don't get it! Why do you keep saving me if you're just going to kill me? Why don't you just hurry up and get it over with already? Is this some kind of sick game for you? Do you always have to play with your food before you eat it?"

His jaw dropped and his eyes widened with shock and hurt.

"Do you know..." Jack trailed off, trying to get a handle on what I meant. "We're not going to kill you."

"Then what's going on?" I was almost shrieking by then. "What the hell are you and what do you want with me?"

"Alice, we're vampires."

Jack gave me an even look, and I almost burst out laughing, but then I realized that he was completely serious. I lapsed into a stunned silence, which was just as well, because suddenly there were wailing sirens and flashing lights of the police and ambulance.

- 13 -

The paramedics thought that I was in shock, and if I had been able to speak, I probably would've agreed. They couldn't explain how either of us were alive, or where the blood all over Jack's body had come from. They wanted to put us in an ambulance and send us downtown, but since Jack wouldn't pass any kind of medical test, he fought them until they finally relented.

He allowed them to check me over, but when they said I was fine, except for the shock, he demanded a ride home in a police car.

He sat next to me in the backseat, and while he whispered my name several times, I never responded. I just stared out the window and tried to make sense of his confession.

Some things fit. Like his superhuman strength, his miraculous ability to heal, the way he never ate or drank anything, and I'd only ever seen him at night.

But they were all tan (except for Mae, but she was British), and I'd actually heard Jack's heartbeat last night. He didn't have fangs, and he hadn't bitten me.

That did kinda explain what had happened with Peter, except why did they want him to bite me? What was so damn important about that? Couldn't anybody just bite anybody?

Mae must've seen the police car, because she was at the front door waiting for us when they dropped us off. Matilda jumped all over Jack, but he wasn't in the mood, so he pushed her off.

"Jack, what happened?" Mae was talking to him, but she was looking me over.

I didn't even have a scratch on me, but when I'd caught my reflection in the rearview mirror of the squad car, I was completely white and my eyes were frantic and red-rimmed from sobbing.

"I totaled the Jeep," Jack answered vaguely. We stood in the entryway, but he pulled off his shirt and started wiping off the blood with his ruined shirt.

"Again?" Mae sounded exasperated and looked over at him. "Jack, you've really-"

"She knows," Jack cut her off.

He looked at me, then quickly looked away. Even though there were still patches of blood on his back, he'd given up on that and balled up his tee shirt, then walked into the kitchen.

"What?" Mae turned back to me, her face unsure.

"He told me that you're vampires." It was the first time I'd spoken since he told me, and my voice sounded hoarse and foreign to me.

Mae let out a long shaky breath and looked down.

"Oh." That was all she said. She didn't tell me that Jack was insane, as I had hoped and half-expected.

"So it's true?" I asked. The words came out even, but I knew there were hysterics hiding behind them.

"Your throat sounds dry." Mae forced a smile and put her arm around me, but she did it like she thought I'd push her away. I didn't, but I knew that I probably should've. "Why don't we go in the kitchen and get you some water and we can sit down?"

"I'm already on it," Jack informed us as she led me into the kitchen.

He had filled a giant glass with cold water and ice cubes from the Pür filter in the fridge. He handed it to me, but I stopped and opened the fridge first. Just as Milo had predicted, it was completely empty. I stared into it for a minute, and Jack prompted me to drink the water.

I shut the fridge and greedily downed the water. My thirst had kicked in, and I turned to look at them. Jack was shirtless, leaning against the island, and Mae wrung her hands, but both of them watched me.

"Jack, I really wish you would've waited for when Ezra was home, or Peter even." Mae told him quietly.

"It couldn't wait anymore," Jack said dully.

"I know, but Ezra and Peter know so much more." Mae exchanged a nervous look with Jack, and then smiled at me again and pulled out a stool. "Here, love, why don't you sit down?"

"Where's Ezra?" I sat on the stool and decided to start with the simplest questions first, the ones that seemed sane and rational. Not like, so, do you guys wanna suck my blood? That was the kind of thing I definitely didn't want to think about.

"He's out looking for Peter," Jack answered, and Mae looked over at him.

She fidgeted with a wavy strand of her hair, and I knew that she desperately wanted to touch mine. My water glass was almost empty, so I set it on the island and sighed.

"So… you're vampires?" I asked, feeling incredibly foolish. It sounded so stupid coming out of my mouth. This was a family of normal, healthy people, and there were no such things as vampires.

"Yes, love." Mae smiled at me, and it had to be the saddest, most terrified smile I'd ever seen.

They were waiting on edge, and I didn't understand why. They were the big powerful vampires, and I was just one small human girl. If anyone should be scared, it should be me.

"All of you?" I looked from Mae to Jack, who just nodded solemnly. "Then why did you say that it would be better if Ezra or Peter were here? Don't you know just as much?"

"They're older, much older," Mae explained, and her strained expression started to relax a bit.

"How old are you?" I remembered the first time I had asked Jack that, when we were waiting in the booth at the diner, and the way he had laughed at the question.

"Well, um, I was twenty-four when I turned, and that was in 1994. So I guess that puts me in my forties."

"You don't seem like you're in your forties," I said and he laughed at that, which went a long way to alleviate the tension in the room.

"Vampires age differently, obviously." Jack gestured to his bare chest, which did not look a day over twenty-four.

"Physically, we don't age much at all," Mae elaborated. "We mature in a much different way. When we first turn, we almost regress emotionally. Jack is closer to that of someone in their teens than of one in their twenties.

"Part of that has to do with his personality," Mae smiled at him. "But part of it is his age. And since our minds always stay sharp, we don't ever really get old. We learn from our experiences and we mature, but not the same way people do. Jack will never really act like a man in his forties, no matter how old he gets."

In retrospect, a lot of what he did made sense when I thought of him as being more around my age. Which is why it never seemed creepy that he was hanging out with me, even though he was older. He never acted older. He was, after all, at my maturity level.

"How old are you?" I turned to Mae.

"I was twenty-eight when I turned, and that was... wow, that was fifty-two years ago." She looked a little surprised herself, as if she hadn't thought it about in awhile, and then smiled at me. "So, I'm eighty. Wow. Well, that's not as bad as Peter or Ezra."

"How old are they?' I couldn't help but lean in close, scrutinizing Mae's perfect porcelain skin. It was hard to believe that she'd even been twenty-eight.

"Oh, gosh." Mae looked over at Jack for help, but he just shook his head.

"I only know the age they were when they turned." Jack had been leaning forward onto the island, but now he stood up and leaned back on the kitchen counter behind him, crossing his arms over his chest. "Peter's nineteen and Ezra's twenty-six. You're the oldest."

"Thanks," Mae gave him a wry look, then turned back to me. "Well, Peter's not quite two-hundred. Maybe one-ninety or something like that. And Ezra is… Gosh, it's so horrible that I don't know how old my own husband is. Oh! Jack, you remember! We had that big party a few years back when he turned three-hundred? When was that?"

"I don't know," Jack shrugged. "Like… five years ago? Time's really hard to keep track of anymore."

"You're telling me that Ezra is over 300 years old?" I asked.

Ezra, who had to be one of the most perfectly attractive people I've ever seen and drove a Lamborghini. He'd been around for over three centuries. I had never felt so small or insignificant in my entire life.

"Yep. I'm the baby. By a lot." Jack grinned broadly, and part of that made sense. Ezra and Peter's eyes looked so much older, and everyone seemed to indulge Jack the same way you would indulge the baby of the family.

"But you call them your brothers, and they can't be." I remembered when I asked Jack about it being a fraternity, and slowly, it dawned on me what I had said that had made him laugh. They're blood relatives.

"Not in the human sense, no," Mae explained. "But as vampires… 'brother' still isn't exactly the right word." She looked back over at Jack. "You understand this better than I do."

"It's hard to explain until it happens to you, or if you don't know the person that turned you," Jack took a step towards the island and nodded at Mae. "Ezra turned Peter, and Peter turned me."

186

He laid his hands flat on the countertop and watched me, gauging my response to everything they were telling me.

"You mean Peter turned you into a vampire?"

Whenever I said the word vampire, I felt like a complete tool. Like I was in a bad horror movie or I was being Punk'd. It just wasn't a possibility.

I was having this conversation because it was like when I had a dream and everyone was made of cotton candy or something. I just kinda went along with it. Once I suspended my belief, I just had to go with the flow and pretend like everything made sense.

"Yeah." He nodded.

"So what does that mean? He bit you?" Just the thought of Peter biting anyone made my heart rate speed up. That's what he'd been trying to do when I was in his room, and even now, knowing exactly what he meant to do, it somehow made me want him more.

"No, biting doesn't do anything," Jack shook his head, but he raised an eyebrow and gave me an odd look. Then it dawned on me.

"You can hear my heartbeat," I said. When we had been in the car, right before the accident, my heart had been racing like mad because I was thinking about Peter, and it had been distracting Jack.

"And when you..." Jack's expression changed, and he looked away from me, but I could already feel his desire.

"You're thinking of Peter," Mae caught Jack's response. "When you're around Peter or you think of him, you release a kind of pheromone. I don't know how to explain it."

"It entices us to bite you," Jack said bluntly.

187

My heart had slowed, but he still looked strained. Meanwhile, Mae didn't look effected by it at all.

"So… is it just when I think about Peter? Or when I think about… anything like that?"

"Ezra will have to explain all that," Mae said suddenly. Jack had looked as if he was about to say something, but she cut him off.

"So how do you turn into a vampire then?" I returned to the topic we'd been on before I'd distracted them with my beating heart.

"I drank Peter's blood. So it's Peter's blood, and Ezra's blood, mixed with my blood coursing through my veins." Jack gestured to his arms, as if I could see through his skin to his veins. "It's not like a father-son thing, because it's not part of who they are. It *is* who they are. My blood is their blood."

"Does that actually have any bearing on who you are?" I leaned on the island, looking intently at him. I was starting to give myself to their fantasy completely, and I was interested in them as if I actually believed.

"They don't define my personality." Jack looked over at Mae, who nodded at him. "But we… Remember when you first came over to meet them and I said that I knew Peter and Ezra would like you? It was because I liked you."

"So they'll like whoever you like?" I was skeptical, because Peter still didn't like me.

"No, no, that's not it either." Jack sighed, and he debated how much he was going to tell me. I didn't understand what he could still possibly be hiding from me since he'd confessed vampirism. "Because I don't just like you. My blood likes you."

"Okay, what the hell does that mean?" I actually leaned away from him a little bit, and I'm sure I looked afraid.

"Jack, maybe Ezra would be better suited to talk about that," Mae gave him an even glare, and he lowered his eyes. Then she turned back to me, smiling warmly. "Ezra really is a bit of an expert on everything. Jack and I still have so much left to learn."

"You guys aren't really vampires, are you?" I asked apprehensively, and Mae laughed.

"Oh, love, I'm sorry, but we are." She tucked a strand of hair back behind my ear, and since I didn't push her away or flinch, she smiled.

"But you guys don't sleep in coffins or have fangs and you're not pale." I said, then quickly corrected myself. "Well, except for Mae, but even she's not that pale."

"We kind of have fangs." Jack opened his mouth wide and ran his tongue along his teeth, emphasizing the pointed incisors. They weren't longer or bigger than any other teeth I had seen, but they did look awfully sharp.

"And coffins are just a ridiculous legend. Beds are much more comfortable." Mae scoffed at the notion.

"But you're tan. You can't go in the sun! Wait, can you go in the sun?"

"We can, in fact, but we don't usually," Jack continued. "The sun kind of makes us tired, but we won't burst into flames or die or anything like that."

"That doesn't explain the tan," I pointed out.

"We don't change from when we were turned, and I skateboarded a lot so I was out in the sun. When I turned, my skin was full of melanin, and now it always will be." Jack thought about it for a moment, then corrected himself. "We do change a bit. We improve. I wasn't quite this handsome, and I had more of a farmer's tan. But somehow, it evens things and smoothes everything, like gleaning off any fat I had. It's impossible for a vampire to be overweight. We no longer require the storage of anything, so it all dissolves pretty quickly after the turn."

"We drink blood, so it's more fat-free," Mae added.

"You drink blood." Until then, I had been trying hard not to really think of it.

When I thought of Peter biting me, it had been more about the feeling of everything, and not about the actual act of him drinking my blood. It was almost impossible to imagine Mae or Jack doing it.

"It is a necessity," Mae whispered sadly.

"But like animal blood, right?" I asked hopefully, but Mae kept her eyes down, so I looked up over at Jack, who just shook his head.

"We can't live on animal blood." Jack kept his pale blue eyes on me, so I had to focus not to look even mildly revolted. "It's the same reason a person can't live on a blood transfusion from a dog or rat. Essentially, we require a weekly blood transfusion to survive. We just have to ingest it."

"You... you kill people?" I know my voice was trembling, but then Mae's eyes shot up and both her and Jack looked appalled.

"No! No, of course not!" Mae vehemently denied it. "People can lose huge amounts of blood before they die."

"We just drink blood from people," Jack elaborated. "It's a painless process. Our saliva works as like an anesthetic and makes the wound heal crazy fast."

"And Ezra's so good at it that most people don't even know they've been bitten," Mae explained, somewhat proudly. "Jack and I live mostly on blood from the blood bank anyway. It's not quite as good, but it's much less complicated."

"You get blood from the Red Cross?" I pictured Mae and Jack going down to a Red Cross and asking for a pint of blood for the ride home.

"No, not exactly." Mae gently touched my knee and smiled at me. "There's a vampire blood bank. People think they're donating to some place like the Red Cross, but it's for us. So we have a fridge in the basement full of blood."

"Not that Peter or Ezra ever really get into it," Jack muttered, and Mae shot a look at him.

"They lived too long in the times before blood banks," Mae said, looking rather apologetic. "They're purists."

"So... they... what? How does that work? They just find some random person and bite them?" The thought of Peter biting anyone else made me feel vaguely nauseous.

"No, they have clubs where people willingly donate, and a lot of times, they can pick up girls, who think they're going on a date and getting a long kiss on the neck, but really they're just getting a snack," Mae clarified.

"You're okay with that?" I asked Mae. "Ezra's out and about dating and drinking other women?"

"It's not pleasant," Mae admitted, with a pained expression. "But it's the nature of who we are. And I'd rather have him seducing a woman than just attacking someone and killing them. It's the price of eternity, love. I can be with him forever, but he has to kiss other women." She smiled sadly at me, and I wondered if I'd ever be able to come to terms with it like she had.

"I drink almost entirely bag blood," Jack interjected brightly, and I turned my attention back to him.

"The night you picked me up, were you going to bite me?" Then, remembering how suddenly drowsy I was and that I couldn't remember how I'd gotten home, my eyes widened. "Did you bite me?"

"No!" Jack put his hands up defensively under the scrutinizing glares from Mae and me. "No! I didn't! Honest!" Then he looked sheepish. "I'd actually just come from the club, and I'd … fed, right before I saw you."

"You mean the clubs I was trying to get into?" I wondered if Jane had ever been picked up by a vampire without knowing it. She probably had, and that served her right.

"No, it's a vampire one. Well, I guess I don't know where you guys were trying to go, so you might've. Most people don't know it's a vampire club. That's how I turned."

"Peter picked you up at a club?" I raised my eyebrow skeptically.

"Nope," Jack grinned. "I followed these two hot chicks in, and they turned out to be psychotic vampires. Peter was there, looking for something to eat. But the girls went crazy and left me for dead. Peter found me in the alley behind the club, and for some reason, he decided to save me."

"Do you have to be dead to turn?" I asked.

"No, you can't be dead," Jack clarified. "Once you're dead, you're dead. That's it. Vampires aren't undead. We're just a different form of people. Ezra explained it to me that vampirism is a virus, sorta like AIDS, except whereas AIDS makes you sick, this makes you better."

"It's a virus?" I looked skeptical.

"I guess." Jack shrugged. "That's what Ezra told me. It's like an evolutionary mutation. His theory is that people have no predators. The only thing that really takes people down is weather and disease. The plagues actually helped keep the population in check. When cities were overflowing, a plague would come and knock the numbers down. A vampire is just another kind of plague."

"Yeah, that's great and everything, but a virus?" I shook my head in disbelief. "How can a virus do this to you?"

"Again, Ezra is more of an expert than I am," Jack said. "But it just makes you more efficient. We get exactly what we need all the time. We don't have to process anything. We live on pure, fresh nutrients. And it stops decay. When we die, we're like Styrofoam. We're here forever. When we get injured, we heal at an alarming rate, because we're all blood."

"You guys are really vampires?" They had been explaining stuff to me for a long time, but I still couldn't wrap my head around it. Jack laughed and leaned on the counter.

"That was my reaction at first, too," he grinned.

"I think that was everyone's," Mae agreed.

"But ... this is a normal house. I mean, it's really nice, but it's normal. And you guys are just like a family. And you-" I pointed at

Jack. "-you sit around playing video games all day. In a house in the suburbs of Minneapolis, Minnesota? Come on. Vampires are cooler than that."

"Thanks a lot," Jack laughed loudly.

"Well, you know what I mean. You guys have eternity, and you spend it like this?"

"Exactly. We have forever. How would you spend it?" Jack cocked his head at me.

"I don't know," I admitted. I had never really thought of it before. Trying to figure out what I wanted to do with my measly little human life had always seemed like enough. "But something more glamorous than this."

"Peter and Ezra have seen everything, at least a hundred times, and Mae doesn't really wanna go anywhere," Jack shrugged. "I mean, I've traveled a little bit, but I'm not in any rush. I'll be able to see it all one day. I went to the pyramids with Peter a couple years ago." He rolled his eyes. "He's been there like thirty times. He's like 'oh big triangles in the sand, whoopee.' So that was kind of the end of my traveling, for now, at least."

"So you just sit here and play video games?" I asked incredulously.

"What do you expect us to do?" Jack laughed. "We just have more time than you. What do you do with your life?"

"I don't know." I lowered my eyes and thought about it. "This all just seems weird to me."

"Of course it does, love." Mae gently stroked my hair. "It's a lot to take in."

"You guys aren't gonna eat me, are you?" I didn't sound afraid, because I wasn't. I was merely curious, and Mae laughed.

"No, of course not," she smiled reassuringly at me.

"But Peter wanted to last night," I pointed out. "And Jack really wanted to tonight, before the car crash."

"Jack!" Mae gasped, glaring over at him. Funny, she didn't look even remotely appalled when I told her Peter wanted to.

"I did not!" Jack insisted, but he was a bad liar.

"Jack, you know you can't do that," Mae growled, and I wondered what the big deal was. They said that when they bit people it didn't hurt and it didn't kill them. So what did it really matter if Jack bit me?

"It wasn't my fault!" Jack said defensively. "She was getting all crazy thinking about Peter. And you know what? I didn't bite her. So, you can just wipe that look off your face."

"Why does thinking about Peter make me more delectable?" I asked, and they both lowered their eyes. "Come on! I know you're vampires! What's left?"

"Delectable," Jack mused. "That's a very good way to describe it."

"Why are you even telling me this?" I narrowed my eyes at them. "Why did you tell me you were vampires? Isn't it like some big secret or something?"

"Hardly," Jack snorted. "I hate it that in movies when they're all like, you can't tell anyone that we're vampires or the high council of snooty vampires will kill us all! There's no high council. There's not a big vampire society. There isn't one council governing every human on earth.

"And you know what?" Jack continued. "People don't believe in vampires. Do you think that we have to hide anything about us? Did I ever really try to hide anything with you?"

"No, but you wouldn't tell me things," I told him pointedly.

"Yeah, cause I liked you. The first day we met, if I had told you that I was a vampire, you would've thought I was insane and wrote me off."

"Why did it take so long for you to tell me?"

"I wanted to make sure you trusted me, so you wouldn't just think I was insane and never want to talk to me again." Then he got a pained expression on his face and sighed. "I was gonna tell you that night in the park. Then that stuff happened with that damn dog. And you got so upset when I killed it, and I thought if you react like that to me hurting a dog, how are you gonna feel when you find out that I bite people?"

"Oh." I thought back to that night, and I remembered the way he had threatened to end our friendship because I was crying. It had seemed rather harsh at the time, but in retrospect, that must've killed him. "Well, I know now. And I don't think you're a monster."

"Good." Jack was genuinely relieved. He rubbed his bare skin. "I'm gonna go put on a shirt. I'll be right back." Jack darted out of the kitchen and I heard his feet pounding up the stairs.

"You doing okay with all of this?" Mae looked at me earnestly, and I nodded. She touched my cheek gently, cupping my face, and then kissed my forehead. "Good. Did you need more water?"

"Yeah, sure," I nodded, and she picked up my glass and took it over to the fridge to refill it. "There's just one thing that's bothering me." That was a lie. There were about fifty things bothering me, but there was only one that I wouldn't let go for tonight.

"And what's that, love?" She brought the glass of water back of to me, looking curious.

"Why did Peter leave?" I asked, and her expression faltered and she lowered her eyes. "Jack told me it was because of me."

"Jack doesn't know what he's talking about," Mae replied tersely.

"Mae." I stared at her until she'd look at me and then she sighed.

"This really is a conversation for another day." She forced a smile at me. "I've had a very long day, and I'd really just like to take a hot bath. I'm sure that you and Jack can think of something to amuse yourselves with."

"Always!" Jack beamed, suddenly bursting into the kitchen wearing a fresh tee shirt and shorts.

"And behave," Mae warned him as she walked past him. "I mean it."

"Yeah, yeah," he muttered. When she had her back to him, he stuck out his tongue at her. Then he waltzed over to me, grinning like a fool. "I am so glad you know. Do you have any idea how hard it is keeping anything from you?"

"Not really, no." I still didn't know everything, but it didn't bother me anymore. Jack was in an incredibly good mood now, and it was taking me over as well. "Do you have any idea how hard it is to have things kept from you?"

"Yes!" Jack insisted, still smiling. "Ezra and Peter keep stuff from me all the time. They think I'm too young for anything. If they had it their way, I probably still wouldn't know that I was a vampire."

"You're forty?" I wrinkled my nose.

"Does that freak you out?" He held his chin up high, checking for my response.

"No. It doesn't. I know that this all should completely freak me out, but it doesn't. I feel stupidly safe with you."

His lips curled mischievously, and I knew that I had accidentally dared him to scare me. He twirled the stool around so my back was to the island, and then he stood in front of me, placing his arms on either side of me, trapping me between him and the island. His face was right in front of me, and his eyes were dancing.

"What about now? Are you scared?"

"Nope. Am I supposed to be?" I smiled back at him.

"You probably should be." His voice had gone low and husky, and his eyes were almost translucent as he studied mine.

Then I saw his eyes lower, looking at my neck, and my heart, beating of its own accord, sped up. I breathed in deeply, and he smelled so clean, like Ivory soap and mint toothpaste. His expression changed, growing more somber, and his face inched closer to mine.

- 14 -

"You can hear my blood," I said softly. He didn't answer but slowly pulled his eyes away from my throat so they met mine again. His hunger rolled off him, filling me with a strange desire. "What does it sound like?"

"It sounds like..." He let out a breath that sounded suspiciously like a moan. "...music."

"What does it feel like?" I whispered. "When you're bitten? What would I feel?"

His eyes got that wistful look, almost like the one Ezra had when he thought about Mae, and my heart fluttered. A look of pleasure passed over Jack's face, and for a moment, I felt flush with the warmth of his hunger and adoration.

"You..." He exhaled deeply, then smiled sourly. "... really need to get going." Abruptly, he pushed back from me and turned around, walking away from me. The sudden shift, along with the lingering desire, startled me.

"What? Why?" I jumped off the stool and scampered after him. "It's not that late."

"No, it's not," Jack agreed, continuing out into the garage. I caught the door before it swung shut and ran after him. "But I only have so much will power left."

"You can bite me if you want," I offered helpfully. I knew he really wanted to, and it didn't really seem like that big of a deal if he did. "I want you to."

He stopped in front of the Jetta, and I stood a few feet away from him, watching him. He laughed darkly and turned to face me, scratching the back of his head and smiling incredulously.

"You're killing me here!" Jack shook his head, then pointed his keys at me as he walked towards the car door. "You are far more dangerous than I am!"

"What?" I demanded. He had stopped at the driver's side door, and I looked over the top of the car at him. "Why won't you do it?" His desperate want made me want him too, and I didn't understand why he wouldn't just bite me.

"I just can't, Alice." His expression was grave, and he dropped his eyes from mine, looking rather ashamed. "And if you're not going to stop, then I'll have Mae give you a ride home." He shook his head. "I won't be able to say no."

"Fine, I'll drop it."

Grudgingly, I opened the car door and got inside. A few seconds later, Jack got in and started the car. I could feel how much he wanted me, the deep hunger brewing painfully inside of him, and the shame at feeling that way. I sat in silence, feeling embarrassed tears sting my eyes.

"Are you crying?" His breath caught in his throat. "Why are you crying?"

"Is there something wrong with me?" I wiped at my eyes.

"What are you talking about?"

"There has to be something wrong with me. Peter can't even be around me, and you can't do it either. Is my blood like poison or something?"

"Oh my god, Alice." He rubbed his temple, laughing emptily. "You have no idea what you're doing to me." He looked over at me again and shook his head. "I can't even take you home. I can't even-" Then he just turned and jumped out of the car.

"What?" I scrambled out after him, wondering what I had done to drive him away. He stood just outside the car, trying to shake it off. "What did I do?"

"You're not poison! You're the opposite of poison!" Jack exhaled, but it was more like he was gasping for air. "I can't be in that car with you. You did this thing to me and I need to get back down, but you're so..." He shook his head, unwilling to say it aloud.

"I don't understand. If you want me so much, then why can't you just have me?" I felt what he felt, so I wanted what he wanted. It was raw and pure and so intense it was suffocating.

"Alice..." He had his hands on his hips and he let out a shaky breath. "Peter would kill me. He would literally tear me to shreds. He wouldn't want to, but he would."

"What? What does Peter have to do with this?"

I thought of Peter, feeling strangely excited by the fact that he would express jealousy over me, and my heart sped up. Jack's face contorted miserably, and he shook his head.

"You're thinking of him. You're fucking thinking of him." He clenched his fists.

"I'm sorry!" I cried, trying to slow my heart down. Jack looked as if I was actually killing him, and his agony ripped through me. "Can't you just bite me and make this stop?"

"Alice!" Jack lamented. "He is my brother! And you are his! You belong to Peter, not me!"

"What are you talking about?" While there was something very thrilling about his words, I felt like I had been slapped in the face. "You picked me out for Peter?"

"No, I had no choice in the matter. None of us did." He looked away from me, but I could see his face breaking. "It's the blood. Your blood, his blood. They react to each other. It's why you get all crazy when you think about him. And it drives me crazy because it's in my blood too."

Everything that happened with Peter had felt so physical because it was. There was a chemical reaction between us that I couldn't explain. But then I had started thinking about it, and it was more than Jack could take, so he rushed past me and into the house.

"Mae!" Jack shouted when he got inside. Stupidly, I kept following him. Part of him wanted me to, because so much of him still wanted me. "Mae!"

"What?" Mae rushed into entryway, wrapping a bathrobe tightly around herself. Then she saw his pained expression, and her face went pale. "Jack, you didn't."

"Just get her away from me!" Jack snarled, and I saw there were tears in his eyes.

"Just go upstairs," Mae nodded. "I'll take care of her."

"I'm sorry," I mumbled through my own tears, but Jack was already gone.

"Did he bite you?" Mae rushed over to me, inspecting my neck much the same way Jack had the day before.

"No," I shook my head fiercely. There was a loud banging upstairs, and Mae looked apprehensively at the ceiling.

"Come on. We need to get you out of here." She put her arm around me and started ushering me out to the garage.

"You're wearing a bathrobe."

"He can't take much more, love," Mae whispered. The Jetta was still running, so we got inside of it and pulled out of the garage.

"I'm sorry," I repeated.

"Oh, love, it's really not your fault," Mae smiled reassuringly at me. "Jack should know better, but he's still so young." She reached over and stroked my hair. "It's really not so bad. Honest."

"I feel what he feels," I said quietly. "I know how hard that was for him. I felt how much he wanted me, so ... I wanted him to, and I was making it harder."

"You what?" Mae looked at me with a startled expression on her face. "You feel what he feels?"

"Yeah," I nodded. "Is that okay?"

"It doesn't matter if it is or not if that's the way it is," Mae replied matter-of-factly and looked straight ahead.

"He told me that I'm meant for Peter."

"I thought he might," Mae sighed. Then she smiled at me again. "You would've found out eventually. We just didn't want to surprise you with too much new information, especially with Peter being the way he is."

"If I'm supposed to be for Peter, then how come Jack is the one that wants me around?" I asked. "And why didn't Peter just bite me? Why did he run away?"

"Peter is a very complicated man, but he's a good man." She swallowed hard, and I could tell there was something she was still keeping from me. "And Jack is very young. And they may not seem like it lately, but they were very close to each other."

"Would Peter really kill him if he found out Jack bit me?"

"Yes." She licked her lips and refused to look at me. "And he would know. It's not something you can hide. He could smell Jack on you." Then she turned to look at me. "So if something happened, I need to know, so I can try to protect you both."

"What do you mean? Peter would kill us both?" For the first time since meeting Jack, I felt really scared for my safety. "I don't understand. If I am meant for Peter.... None of this makes sense, Mae!"

"As soon as I drop you off, I'm going to call Ezra and make him come home to sort this all out." Her eyes filled with tears and she gripped the steering wheel. "I should've never left you alone with Jack. He's just been alone with you so much, but I knew things were changing."

"He didn't bite me. Honest," I tried to reassure her.

"Everything is still getting out of control. I told Ezra not to go and that everything is different this time."

"This time?" I asked.

"Not right now, Alice." The car suddenly jerked to a stop, and I realized we were in front of my building. I had been so wrapped up in my thoughts that I hadn't even noticed it. "You need to go home, and Ezra or Jack or somebody will be in contact with you tomorrow."

"How did you know where I lived?" I looked over at Mae, but she just stared straight ahead.

"I have to get home and take care of Jack before he hurts himself."

"He might hurt himself?" I gasped.

"I have to go!" Mae pleaded. "We'll talk to you tomorrow, okay?"

"Okay, go!" I jumped out of the car and watched her speed off, praying Jack wouldn't do something stupid.

Everything about me felt so confused and jumbled, and I collapsed onto the cold sidewalk and sobbed.

One hot bath, two PM Tylenol, and a hot tea and brandy (courtesy of Milo and my mother's alcohol cabinet) later, I managed to fall asleep. Milo saw the wreck I was when I came home, and I promised him that I would tell him another day, but I couldn't muster the strength to do it then.

When I woke up, my pillow was soaked and I knew I had been crying in my sleep. Milo informed me that I'd been moaning all night long, but thankfully, he couldn't understand anything.

I stumbled around the house most of the day, and I'm surprised that I didn't bump into any objects. Milo forced me to eat, but swallowing felt like a massive chore.

I put on comfy sweats and a tee shirt and didn't even bother with showering. It would be too much work, and I didn't even know if I'd see Jack or Peter today. There was a very good chance that I'd never see either of them again. Peter had run away, and Jack...

"Alice, I don't think you should go over there anymore." Milo stood next to the couch, frowning at me. I had curled up in a ball and stared blankly at the TV with my phone gripped in my hand. "You keep coming home looking completely drained. I don't know what they're doing to you, but it can't be good."

"You should see what I do to them," I mumbled.

"What?" His brown eyes were filled with concern, so I just looked away from him.

"Nothing."

"Alice, I'm serious." Milo had that parental vibe going on, and normally, I'd cave under it, but I was too numb to react to anything. I just pulled the blanket up over my head so I wouldn't have to look at him.

Eventually, he walked away, and I stayed buried underneath the covers. The horrible truth was that I didn't really want to be alive anymore. Last night had devastated me too much.

Everything was confusing and it hurt, and I couldn't shake the feeling that this was all some kind of bad dream.

Then, my phone played "Time Warp" and my eyes snapped open.

Ezra's back. He'll be there to pick you up in fifteen minutes.

Why not you? Are you okay? Is everything alright? I demanded, feeling my heart race painfully.

I'm fine. Ezra will explain more. I'll see you soon. Jack messaged me back, but I still felt relieved.

"You're not going over there!" Milo watched me as I pulled on my Famous Stars and Straps zippered hoodie, the one I had worn the night Jack had been attacked by that dog.

"Yeah, I am," I replied flatly, searching around for my shoes.

"Dressed like that?" Milo asked in disbelief.

"Yeah." Finally, I found my shoes and slipped them on. "Things have changed. I don't need to impress them anymore."

"Are you like breaking up with them or something?"

"I don't know." I hadn't really thought about me not choosing to see them, but as soon as I did, I dismissed it. It would be impossible for me to ever end things with them. I was inescapably tied to Peter, and I'd probably fallen in love with Jack.

"We have school tomorrow!" Milo called as I opened the door.

"I don't care," I said and then left.

- 15 -

Ezra didn't drive quite as fast as Jack, or maybe he felt it was more polite to actually give me time to get ready. Either way, I beat him outside.

I sat on the curb, shivering in the cold and trying not to envision the worst, when he finally pulled up in the Lexus. I had never been in the car, but I recognized it instantly from the garage.

"I hope I didn't keep you waiting long," Ezra smiled warmly at me when I got inside. He saw me shiver, so he turned up the heat. "Let me know when it gets warm enough for you. We don't really feel the cold the way you do."

"Okay." The seat felt warm and comfortable, especially after freezing on the curb, and I sunk deeper into it.

"How are you doing?" Ezra asked sincerely, and I tried to answer him as honestly as I could.

"I'm… absorbing a lot of things. Is Jack okay?"

"Yeah, he's fine," he nodded. "He just needed some time to get himself together."

"Is he going to be okay being around me again?"

"Yes. Last night, there were a lot of emotions going for you both. It's very new territory, for all of us, and there's going to be some missteps." He spoke evenly, and his deep voice managed to soothe me in a way that had been lacking since I came home last night. "But you both will have to be more careful around each other. It should be easier now that you're both aware of the limitations."

"I hope so." I pulled my sweatshirt tighter to me, even though I wasn't cold anymore. "Is Peter back?"

"Not yet. But he will be soon."

"Jack said that I'm meant for Peter. What does that mean?" I looked over at Ezra, and half-expected him to give me the same run around as everyone else.

"Mythology has set us up to be extreme loners, but at our core, emotionally, we're very human. We desire companionship, but ours has to be more selective." As he spoke, he kept one hand on the wheel, while the other one bobbed a silver ring over his fingers. "Our blood is almost magnetized to our – for a lack of a better word – soul mates. We feel it intrinsically when we find each other."

"Is Mae your soul mate?" I asked quietly.

"She is." His eyes had that faraway look again, and the corners of his mouth curled up ever so slightly. "I lived 255 years before her, but now, I couldn't imagine existing a single day without her. I even 'dated' before I met her, but it was impossible to make lasting relationships. That was part of the reason that I turned Peter. I was desperately lonely, and he traveled around with me for awhile. But then he met his mate."

"Wait," I interrupted. "I thought I was Peter's 'mate.'"

"I told you this was new for all of us," Ezra looked over at me. "Peter met a vampire named Elise, and they were together for only a brief time. Maybe ten or twenty years. He knows it to the exact day, but he never speaks of it."

"What happened?" I glanced out the window, and I realized we weren't taking the normal route to his house. In fact, if my guess was right, he wasn't taking me anywhere near their place. "Where are we going?"

"I thought it would be better if the two of us had some time to talk before we went back." Ezra must have read the confusion on my face because he continued. "Some of this would be better if Jack didn't hear."

"Oh," I said. Jack had mentioned that they didn't like to tell him anything, and he wasn't kidding. "So what happened with Peter?"

"Elise was killed." Ezra heard my sharp intake of breath and smiled humorlessly. "Fighting broke out amongst vampires, arguing over who had control over a certain area. Vampires are notoriously territorial and possessive, but then again, so are humans. In most ways, we are just heightened versions of yourselves."

"So you're saying that another vampire killed Elise?" My eyes were wide, and he nodded.

"It nearly destroyed Peter. He went into a very dark period for awhile." A troubled expression darkened his face, and I didn't want to know what Peter had been through or what he had done.

"He's fought in every major war since WWI, up until this last excursion in the Middle East," Ezra continued. "He had blood lust or a death wish, or some combination of that, for a very long time, but he's mostly come out of it now. He's not the same man he once was, though."

"It must've been terrible for him," I said. I had spent hardly any time with him, but it would be agony for me if anything happened to him.

"It was," Ezra agreed solemnly. "But he had moved on, as best he could. After Elise died, he assumed that that part of his life was over. We all had. But then you came along."

"How did you know I was meant for Peter?" I asked. "Jack stumbled upon me long before I met Peter."

"We didn't, not at first, although Mae suspected immediately." With that, Ezra gave a small shrug. "None of it really made sense."

"What do you mean?" I crinkled my forehead, trying to understand.

"For starters, you're human." Ezra gave me an even look, and I shook my head. "We're never intended for humans. Both Peter and Elise were vampires when they met, and so was Mae when I met her. We're not callous, exactly, but we just don't feel attachments to humans the way we do to other vampires.

"When Jack came home and said he'd met you, we couldn't figure it out," Ezra went on. "He connected with you instantly, but he didn't feel that… physical need, the way we do."

I nodded, knowing exactly what he'd meant. I felt it the instant I saw Peter, and it only got more intense with time.

"But the connection was something we all understood," Ezra explained. "Because Peter is of my blood, I felt connected with Elise, and both Peter and Jack feel connected with Mae."

"Do you feel connected with me?" I thought that I felt connected with him, but it was hard to tell what was a real connection and not just falling under the spell of his perfection.

"Yes." Ezra smiled warmly at me, and I flushed. "I feel more connected to you than I have with any human since I've been a vampire."

"Jack said my safety was top priority for you," I mumbled dazedly. It was insanely flattering and intimidating knowing that I had fallen into Ezra's favor.

"He wasn't exaggerating," Ezra grinned wider. "You are in a very unique position."

"Is that what the issue is about biting me?" I asked.

"Yes and no." Ezra tilted his head. "Remember when I said that we were possessive and territorial? As soon as Peter met you, you were his. He felt it inside him, the way you do.

"Peter lost Elise, and it devastated him completely," Ezra continued. "He vowed never to feel that way again. To be perfectly honest, I doubted that he could survive it." Ezra exhaled, looking rather sad. "He doesn't want to want you. It doesn't change the way he feels, because nothing can.

"On top of everything, you're so fragile." He eyed me up seriously. "When you're with someone, the way we are, we frequently drink each other's blood. But for you, it is dangerous, especially with Peter feeling the way he feels. It would be very easy for him to get caught up in the moment and take things too far.

"He ran the other night because he didn't want to hurt you," Ezra continued. "It's not supposed to be this hard, Alice. It's usually a very simple, clean process. But this is much, much more complicated."

"Because of Elise?"

"Yes, and because you're human." He had a drawn expression and he sighed. "And because of Jack."

"Because Jack wanted to bite me last night?"

"It's more than that." Ezra looked at me knowingly. "Alice, Jack's fallen in love with you."

"What?" Startled, I blushed randomly. I had considered the possibility that I was falling for him, but as Ezra had just explained, vampires didn't fall in love with humans. "I-I didn't think that was possible."

"Neither did I," Ezra admitted soberly. "He shouldn't feel anything for you. You're human, you're meant for Peter, and you're not his. Maybe it was because he spent so much time with you before you met Peter and fully melded with him."

"So... what does this mean? Does it transfer? Can I just be with Jack instead of Peter?" I asked, and Ezra looked very shocked by my questions.

"You would want that?" He looked at me evenly. "You want to be with Jack instead of Peter?"

"I don't know," I confessed uneasily. "I mean, if Peter doesn't even want me, it just seems stupid to force something."

"Peter still wants you," Ezra was quick to clarify.

"Then why isn't he with me?" I demanded. "Why was Jack the one I wanted last night?"

"I don't know," Ezra said at length. "Peter will be home soon, and hopefully, we can get some of this straightened out then."

The car had started gliding into familiar territory, and I knew we weren't far from their home.

"What about Jack?" I asked softly.

"Peter can't know how he feels or how close he came to biting you last night," Ezra warned me. "And he can never bite you. Peter will be able to smell him on you, and that won't be good for either of you."

"Am I still allowed to be around Jack?" My heart broke at the thought of a life without him, even if I had Peter.

"Yes, of course. You both must be very in control of yourselves."

"Are you sure that I am meant for Peter?" I asked him carefully as we pulled into the driveway.

"Yes." He answered definitively. The garage door closed behind us, but we stayed in the car. "Something's off this time, but there's no other explanation."

"Oh." It was strange how one sentence could exhilarate and devastate me.

"Are you in love with Jack?" His voice was barely above a whisper, as if he was afraid of someone hearing.

"I don't know," I admitted honestly. Tears welled in my eyes, and I bit my lip.

"Alice, listen to me very carefully. If you care anything for Jack, you mustn't act on it." His deep brown eyes settled on me, conveying the severity of his words. "I'm not trying to frighten you, but... it's just the way things are, and I am very sorry."

"It's alright." I wiped my palms across my eyes, trying to smear away the tears.

"Are you okay to go in?" Ezra asked.

"Yeah, I'm fine," I said. He waited for me to open the car door and start getting out before he got out. "So, does Mae like me so much cause of the whole blood thing and her being yours and all that?"

"No. Mae loves you because she's Mae, and that's what she does." Ezra smiled brightly me, relieved to talk about a subject he was quite fond of. Putting his hand on the small of my back, we walked into the house. "Honestly, are we what you envisioned when you thought of vampires?"

"Hardly," I scoffed, and he laughed warmly.

"You're home!" Mae shouted, running into the entrance and throwing her arms around me. For the first time, Matilda didn't run and greet us, but I realized that's because Jack wasn't with me. "I was a little afraid we'd scared you off last night."

"You can never scare me off," I said into her shoulder. She finally released me and cupped my face in her hands, staring at me as if to make sure I was real.

"Oh you look so tired! Did you sleep at all?" Her eyes were anxious, so I nodded and forced a smile. "You know what you need, love? A nice warm bath. We have a fabulous Jacuzzi tub in our room, and I'll get some bubbles going and you'll be as right as rain."

"How right is rain really?" Jack wondered dryly, and I pulled my head away from hers to look over at him.

He leaned against the doorway, smiling crookedly at me. My heart swelled just at the sight of him. Last night, I had been so afraid that he would be gone forever, and I couldn't contain myself. I rushed over to him and threw my arms tightly around his waist.

"Hey, I'm okay, I'm okay." He gently pushed me off, holding his hands on my shoulder until I was a foot away from him. "Okay? I'm okay."

"I was just worried." I blinked rapidly, fighting back tears, and swallowed hard.

"Yeah, you look like it," Jack said quietly, and his concern washed over me.

"She just needs a nice warm bubble bath!" Mae wrapped an arm tightly around my waist so she could pull me away from Jack, and it did require some effort on her part. "We have some wonderful lilac bath salts that just melt the tension away."

Mae continued telling me all the amazing features of her tub as she led me away, but I glanced back over my shoulder at Jack.

"You've really got to be more careful," Ezra warned him.

"I didn't even do anything!" Jack protested, and I wondered dully how this all could possibly work out in the end.

The hot Jacuzzi wasn't quite as magic as Mae had professed it would be, but it really did help relax me at least. All of this seemed so bizarre. In a time not so long ago, I hadn't even known these people, and now it would be impossible to imagine the rest of my life without them, however long that life might end up being.

When I finally pulled myself out of the relaxing waters of the tub, I wrapped myself in one of their gigantic plush towels. Mae had filled her bedroom with lilac scented candles, and it was all aglow with candle light.

Laid out on the white bedspread, she had left satin pajama pants and a matching blue camisole for me. Since their house generally ran cold, I put my hoodie on over it, but it almost felt like sacrilege to put something so ordinary over her extravagance. They lived on a whole other plane from me, in every way possible.

"I merely stated that you rolled the Jeep." Ezra's words wafted down the hall towards me when I opened their bedroom door. "It's not asking that much that you pay for it."

"You just want me out of the house more," Jack grumbled.

"That wouldn't hurt you either," Ezra said.

I made my way down the hall to the kitchen, and they all stopped talking when I came in. Mae stood amongst a mass of dishes and food splayed out all over the counter tops. She had white powder on her cheeks and some kind of red sauce dripped all over an elegant white apron.

Jack sat on a stool pulled up to the counter, and I'm sure he fancied himself helping, but I'd imagine that he spent more time playing with the ingredients. As it was, he was juggling a tomato and a lemon when I walked in.

"Oh, you look so much better!" Mae beamed at me. Jack dropped the tomato on the counter and deliberately looked away from me. "Wasn't that bath fabulous?"

"Yeah, it was pretty great." I ran my fingers through my tangles of wet hair, and I could almost see Mae longing to play with it. Walking over to the mess she was making, I was careful to keep a distance from Jack. "What are you doing?"

"Trying to make you some kind of comfort food," Mae smiled grimly at me. "I used to be an amazing cook, I swear! Everyone in my neighborhood loved my cooking!" Jack scoffed, and she reached across the counter to slap him on the arm. "I was! You would've been thrilled to eat anything I made!"

"Whatever you say." Jack leaned back in the stool, moving farther out of arm's length, in case Mae decided to swat him again.

"It's just been so long since I've cooked anything." Mae looked sourly at the mess around her, which consisted of everything from cucumbers to pears to pie crusts. "I've just forgotten what everything tastes like." A spoon was in a bowl of something red, and she gave it one superficial swirl, then looked apologetically at me. "I don't think that I've made anything that you can actually eat."

"What about this?" Jack held up the tomato towards me, but I just shook my head.

"I'm okay. I'm not even hungry."

"Oh!" Mae shouted, her eyes glittering. "Your brother is a cook, isn't he?"

"Not professionally, but yeah, he's really good," I told her hesitatingly. I liked Milo and all, but there was too much going on over here, and I didn't really want him to come over. At least not tonight.

"Oh fantastic! And I'm sure he knows all of your favorite recipes!" She overflowed with her own genius. "Here. Why don't you just give me his phone number and I'll give him a call. Oh, what time is it? It's not too late is it?" She glanced around for a clock, and it was only a quarter to nine. "He's still awake, isn't he?"

I nodded, and Mae whipped her phone out of her pocket, and I gave her his number.

"Oh, Milo!" Mae smiled so wide, it looked almost painful. "I'm so glad you answered! Oh, I didn't wake you, did I? I'm sorry, love. I don't want to disturb you." He must've answered with something positive, because she laughed lightly, and continued about making me the perfect meal to make me feel better.

"I'm really not very hungry." I lowered my voice considerably, just in case Mae might hear, but she was talking to Milo and swooping around the kitchen, gathering pots and pans and whatever she thought she'd needed. "Why do you guys have pots and pans anyway?"

"It makes us look more normal." Jack rolled his shoulders. "I mean, we don't really need kitchens, and in a household of four people, we have seven bathrooms."

"Bathrooms add resale value!" Ezra said. From his tone, I gathered that this wasn't the first time they'd had this argument. "We're not going to live here for that long, so its best if we get our money's worth."

"What do you mean you're not gonna live here long?" I had been leaning on the counter, but I snapped my head sharply and looked over at him.

"I can only be twenty-six for so long before the neighbors start to notice," Ezra elaborated, but it still took a minute for it to sink in. They were never going to age, but everyone around them would. "We move every five years or so, but we've been staying around Minneapolis for quite awhile."

"I've never lived anywhere else," Jack added.

"You were born here?" I gave him an odd look. For no real reason, I had just always kinda imagined that he was a transplant from California or Vegas or something like that.

"Stillwater, actually, but it still makes it tricky living that close to my family." He had said it casually, like it was no big thing, but something had just dawned on me, and he noticed the shift in my expression. "We can't see our families. We change, at first to look better, and then we don't change at all."

"And it's too hard watching them grow old." Ezra had somehow managed to take something that was really terrible sound at least vaguely soothing, but my heart still clenched.

I looked over at Mae, standing at the stove and chatting amicably with my brother, and felt the full ramification of what he was saying.

"It's not as bad as it sounds," Jack said gently.

There were things that I hadn't thought about when I got involved with them, and I'm sure there would be even more things that would come up later. Nothing about this was going to be easy.

As if to solidify my point, Peter suddenly walked into the kitchen. His jeans and shirt were slim fit, revealing the slender lines of his gorgeous body. His blazing emerald eyes landed on mine, for just a second, then flitted away, as if he couldn't stand to look at me.

Just being this close to him made my skin tremble and my blood pound heavily in my ears. Out of the corner of my eye, I noticed Jack flinch, but for once, I didn't feel it. When Peter was around, he eclipsed everything else, including the feelings that I sometimes borrowed from Jack.

"What's all this?" Peter gestured to Mae's attempts at cooking. She'd been too distracted with her food preparation to notice him walk in, but when he spoke, she shot him a nervous, startled look.

"I'll call you back," Mae muttered into the phone, then quickly hung up and dropped it in her pocket. "Peter, you're home!"

"I am." Peter chewed the inside of his cheek, and he deliberately had to keep from looking at me. I wondered how he could even fight the urge. For me, it was so overpowering that I could barely breathe. "Am I to assume this is a feast for my return?"

"Peter, she knows," Ezra told him quietly.

His eyes turned on me sharply, sending a rush through me so rapidly that I felt dizzy. Behind me, I heard a stool clatter to the floor, but I didn't look back to see Jack storming out of the room. Peter didn't really seem to notice either but walked slowly over to me, his eyes never leaving mine.

"So, you're feeding her now?" Peter was looking at me, but he was asking someone else, not that anyone bothered to answer. He reached out and touched a wet strand of my hair and breathed in deeply. "And she's showering here too. Is she living here now?"

"No." Ezra let the word hang in the air.

Peter just kept staring at me. In the back of my mind, I was aware that there were other people in the room, and it should be embarrassing that Peter was looking at me so intently in front of an audience, but somehow, it wasn't.

"So you know we're vampires?" Even though Peter smiled at me, there was an underlying edge to his voice. "You know that we kill?

You could've just as easily been food for us, but with a bit of luck and chance, you're standing here instead."

He narrowed his eyes at me. I could feel heat radiate from his body in a way that the others seemed incapable of. My skin tingled and that tugging feeling encircled my heart. Every single part of my body screamed out for him, and painfully, I was starting to believe that he didn't feel the same way.

"Why are you here?" Peter asked huskily.

"I-I-I want to be," I stumbled.

He occupied my brain, and it was all but impossible for me to form a competent answer. His scent, tangy and tantalizing, washed over me, blinding almost all my other senses.

"You want to be," Peter repeated flatly. "You want this?"

I opened my mouth to answer, but then I felt his hand around my throat. There was a rush of air and then I felt something hard slam into my back.

He'd picked me up by my neck and pressed me against a wall. His eyes burned with conflicting passions, but all I could really feel were his fingers on my throat, and the way my pulse felt pumping underneath them.

"This is really what you want?" he snarled.

This time I couldn't answer because his hand was so tight on my throat. I couldn't even breathe, but I barely noticed. He pressed up against me and I could feel the hard contours of his body against mine, and his intoxicating smell suffocated me. If I stayed like that for too long, I would probably die, but it seemed completely worth it.

- 16 -

Without warning, Jack slammed into Peter, sending him flying across the room. My lungs burned as they filled with air, and I leaned back against the wall, gasping.

Peter stumbled back into the fridge, but he quickly regained his footing and flew at Jack. Jack was ready for it and lunged back towards Peter, pushing him back away from me once again.

"Jack!" Mae wailed, sounding utterly panicked.

Ezra stepped forward to intervene, so Peter backed down slightly. Jack stood between Peter and me, his body unbearably shielding me from Peter.

For his part, Peter had a look of barely controlled rage contorting his beautiful features. His fists clenched at his sides, and he glared past Jack at me.

"He's not going to hurt her!" Ezra told Jack, and both of them stepped back, but neither was willing to relinquish his stand entirely.

"He had his hand around her throat! She couldn't breathe!" Jack yelled.

"I would never let her die!" Peter shouted. "I could feel her heartbeat and it never waned!" Something occurred to him, and he took a step closer to Jack. "What do you even care? How did you even know she wasn't breathing? What did you do?"

"Stop!" Mae ran in between the two of them, putting one of her hands on each of their chests, while Ezra stood off to the side. "Nothing happened, okay? Nothing!"

"What the hell is going on?" Peter looked to Ezra for an explanation. "Why does he care about her?"

"We don't really know what's going on," Ezra admitted quietly, casting a look back at me. "This is unlike anything I've encountered."

Peter studied me curiously, and my heart started to speed up. I saw his eyes register it, and then I heard Jack moan. Instantly, Peter's eye flicked over to him.

"You're reacting to her!" Peter didn't sound angry as much as bewildered. He leaned in closer to Jack, eyeing him up. "You didn't bite her?"

"No!" Jack groaned, exasperated.

"How is this even possible?" Peter was totally amazed.

When he looked back at me, his eyes softened and grew even more confused. That didn't help slow my already quickened pulse.

"Alice!" Jack snapped.

"I can't help it!" I lamented.

"Jack, go over there," Mae commanded, pointing to the far side of the dining room. He grumbled something in protest but did as he was told. She walked over to me and hugged me to her.

"She might have… somehow become attached to Jack," Ezra explained slowly. Pain and confusion spread over Peter's face when he looked back and forth from me to Ezra. "She reacts the strongest with you still, but it seems that some of it may have transferred."

"How is that even possible?" Peter repeated, and Jack scoffed.

"Why do you even care?" Jack growled. "You don't even want her!"

His words sliced through me like a knife, and I flinched, so Mae tightened her arms around me. What hurt the most is that I knew Jack was right. Peter only felt things for me because his body made him.

Peter snarled, and Ezra took a step closer to him, just to make sure he wouldn't lunge at Jack.

"Enough!" I shouted. "I'm not going to let you kill each other over something as stupid as me. If one of you could please just take me home, I'll be happy to leave you all in peace."

"Alice, none of us wants that." Mae stroked my hair and held as me close to her as I would allow. "We don't want you to go."

"We're trying to sort this all out," Ezra agreed.

"I'm going for a drive," Jack announced suddenly and strode across the kitchen. "I'm taking the Lamborghini."

"Be careful!" Ezra called after him. The garage door slammed in response, and he stared after it indecisively. "Maybe I should go with him." He looked over at Mae, who nodded in approval, and he started hurrying after Jack.

Mae still had her arm around me, and I knew that she would be one of those moms that would never let go.

One of the benefits to being a vampire was that she'd never really have an empty nest, although she'd never exactly have a full one either. She played mother and nursemaid to the boys, but in reality, they were grown men and needed very little of her.

The great appeal of me was that I was very fragile and dependant, and on top of that, a girl. For her, I was some kind of enchanted doll,

227

and that explained the great deal of time she spent playing with my hair.

"I still need to make you supper!" Mae burst into life and rushed over to the stove. Fortunately, she had yet to turn it on, or whatever she would've been cooking would've been completely burnt.

"I'm really not that hungry," I repeated for the tenth time.

"Nonsense!" Mae had her back to me and was already flitting about with ingredients. "Why don't you go in the other room and relax, and I'll call you when the food is done."

"It's easier to just go along with what she wants," Peter told me. He took a step towards the living room and paused, waiting for me. "Come on. We need to talk."

I walked with him into the living room, breathing in how wonderful he smelled. My body felt relieved just to be so close to him. It was exhausting staying away from him. Every part of me felt pulled to him, and I had to use all my strength to keep me any distance.

"How is your throat?" Peter asked sadly, admiring my neck.

"It's okay," I lied. It felt like I had terrible whiplash, but I didn't want him to feel bad about hurting me. I sat down on the couch, so very purposefully, he sat in the chair on the far side from me.

"I'm sorry." He looked at me sadly, then dropped his eyes. "I shouldn't have done that. But you should know that's what I'm like." When he spoke again, his voice was barely audible. "I'm not very nice."

"I don't believe you."

"You should." He met my eyes evenly. "You'd be so much better off with Jack. I'm..." He shook his head, unable or unwilling to say exactly what he was.

He knew how I felt about him, that I had no control over it, and yet he still tried to convince me that he was bad. The choice had already been made, and whether he was good for me or not didn't matter.

"But I want to be with you," I insisted, and something about my voice startled him into softening a bit. But he quickly recovered, and his face hardened again.

"You don't know who I am. I'm not like them. I'm not good."

"How are you different?" I asked.

I hated that he was so far away from me, and it had finally gotten to be too much. I got up and walked over, kneeling directly in front of him.

He smiled at me, a rather sweet, sincere one, then reached out and touched my cheek gently, brushing back my hair. It sent shivers of pleasure through me, but I fought to keep my eyes open, to keep them locked on his.

"You should be so afraid of me, but you're not," he murmured, bemused. He studied my face, his hand resting wonderfully on cheek. "If you weren't..." He licked his lip and sighed. "If I didn't feel this way about you, I wouldn't hesitate to kill you. Do you fully understand?"

I'm not sure if I would've told him that I did or not, but I had started trembling too much to speak. He leaned in closer to me, and his hand moved back, so he was burying his finger in the thickness of my hair.

"I am a real vampire. I've killed people."

"You… you have?" I whispered. My heart, which still pounded desperately for him, twisted with fear and revulsion.

"Mmm." He sighed again, this time more resignedly. "They didn't tell you. I'm surprised Jack didn't, but Ezra always tries to protect me. After…" Raw pain flashed over his eyes. "Elise died, I went on a rampage of sorts. Eventually, I got myself under control, but there's still that thirst."

"But that was a very long time ago," I said softly.

"I don't want to hurt you."

"You won't," I promised him.

All of his resistance shattered, and his vulnerability made him look impossibly young. He stared at me for a minute, and unexpectedly, he kissed me.

His mouth pressed forcefully to mine, and his hand knotted in my hair. My body exploded with pleasure. I loved the insistent way he held me to him.

Just as abruptly as he started kissing me, he stopped. Peter moaned and jumped away from me. Before I could say anything, he left the room.

Every part of me wanted to follow him, but I just lay back on the hard wood floor and stared up at the ceiling. Even as my head reeled from the ecstasy of his kiss, I didn't want to feel this way about him. Peter would just keep hurting me and pushing me away until there was nothing left.

Something in me had been chosen for him, but I started to wonder if it had been a mistake.

Mae came in a few minutes later to tell me supper was ready, looking distressed but not surprised that I was alone. She had made some kind of pasta that I recognized as Milo's recipe, but hers didn't do it justice.

After I ate, Mae cleaned up the kitchen, and I helped her as much as she would allow. Every now and again, I'd hear Peter upstairs, and I'd feel a sharp pain in my side. The fact that he was so close but refused to be with me was devastating.

In the living room, Mae put on the Beatles, claiming that they could heal any mood, and sat on the couch. I sat on the floor in front of her and let her play with my hair. Theoretically, it was meant to comfort me, but like the meal she had just made, it was done more as a way to get her mothering out.

When Ezra appeared in the living room sometime later, I was relieved. He kissed Mae warmly, and I found my chance to escape.

I slipped out from her and went to find Jack. He had crouched down on the dining room floor to rub Matilda's belly, and I stood in front of him, wrapping my arms around myself.

"Did you have a nice drive?" I asked Jack.

He looked up at me, then glanced over at Mae and Ezra, who were busy in their world, murmuring things to one another. At that moment, I hated them for being so easily in love.

"Yeah. Did you have a nice time with Peter?" Jack raised an eyebrow at me, trying to seem playful, but I saw the hurt behind it. More than that, I felt it, like a burning regret in the back of my throat.

"I've had better," I said.

His smile came more naturally after that, and I felt some of the tension ease up between us. Giving Matilda one last pat, he stood up and looked down at me.

"Do you want to give me a ride home?" I asked.

"I do…" Jack trailed off, and nodded up at the ceiling, towards Peter's room, and then he shook his head. "I don't think I should. At least not right now."

"Are you like banned from ever picking me up again?" I had never thought that I would really miss his speedy trips around the city, especially after he almost killed me last time, but it saddened me to think that it might never happen again.

"No," Jack scoffed, as if anybody could ever ban him from anything. "I just think it'd be better if I didn't for awhile. He needs to figure out what he's doing, and so do you."

"I didn't think I really had a choice in the matter," I admitted honestly.

My understanding of things was that I was completely at the whim of Peter and Jack. I would be whatever they would let me be as long as it was in their lives.

"Everyone has free will." He leaned in a little closer to me, looking at me earnestly. "Even you."

"You really think so?"

"I have to." His hopeful smile faltered, and he turned to Ezra. "Alice is ready to go home."

"Sure." Ezra jumped up from the couch, smiling at me. "Sometimes I forget that you don't live here."

Putting his hand on the small of my back, Ezra ushered me away from him. Looking back over my shoulder at Jack, I wished that things could just go back to the way they were. I wished I didn't know about vampires or Peter or that my blood had ever been meant for anybody.

- 17 -

On the bus on the way to school, I decided to broach the subject. The ride had a finite amount of time, followed by a full day of school to keep his thoughts from settling too long.

Milo had his textbook open on his lap, doing some last minute cramming for a test. I wanted to make everything seem normal, so I had in my ear buds and the iPod played the Yeah Yeah Yeahs, but it was quiet enough where I could talk.

"Hey, Milo?" I tried to keep my voice as casual as possible.

"Huh?" Milo grunted, his attention unwavering from the textbook.

"What do you think of… vampires?" I hesitated before the word, as if by saying it aloud to someone other than them, it would make it real.

"I don't," Milo answered flatly.

He didn't express the vaguest interest in this conversation, but I pressed on anyway. I hated not telling him things, and it was nearly impossible for me to carry around a secret this life changing.

"You don't think maybe they're real?" I pulled at the straps of my backpack and bit my lip, waiting for his response.

"No." He looked at me like I was a total idiot, which is what I kinda expected. "Do you think werewolves are real?"

"There's no such thing as werewolves," I replied.

"Yeah, and there's no such thing as vampires." Milo shook his head and went back to studying.

"But you don't think that, like, there's even the possibility that they might exist?" I asked. He lifted his head, looking confused about why I would be talking about nonsense.

"Creatures that live on only blood and never age?" He shook his head again. "That's not even biologically possible. And then they sleep in coffins? That just seems unnecessary."

"Well, maybe they don't sleep in coffins," I suggested, picking at a chipped piece of nail polish on my finger.

"That doesn't make it any more plausible." He looked over at me with narrowed eyes. "Okay. What's this about? Did you stay up late watching *The Lost Boys* again?"

"No." I ran a hand through my hair, trying to think of how I could explain this away. "I just had a bad dream last night. That's all."

"You know, maybe if you didn't stay out all hours of the night running around with Jack, you would be able to sleep like a normal person without any ridiculous dreams."

"Right." I decided that maybe hinting would be my best bet. "All hours of the night."

"Yeah, that's what I said," Milo went back to looking at his book, growing irritated.

"Yep. I had vampire dreams cause I was out all night with a really attractive guy!" I tried emphasizing everything so he would get the point, and when he lifted his head again, I thought I'd finally gotten through to him.

"Wait. I thought you said you didn't think Jack was attractive?" Milo asked, and I sighed.

"Just forget it." I shook my head.

He started to ask me about Mae's cooking last night, but I turned up my iPod. I guess I didn't really feel like talking about vampires.

Over lunch, Jane made a point of telling me that I looked like hell and I hadn't been acting like myself. She brought up Jack for the first time in days, but I didn't feel like talking about him, so I said that I wasn't feeling well and went to the bathroom.

When I looked at my reflection in the mirror, it didn't really seem to look like me. My skin was pale with dark circles under my eyes, and I had visibly lost weight.

Since I spent most nights over to Jack's and they never ate, it never really occurred to me to eat. Maybe it would if I didn't spend so much of the time with my stomach twisted in knots.

I didn't know how much longer I could go on this way. My normal human life felt like a total sham, and the vampire parts that had once felt fun and exciting were growing painful.

Everyone had been so nice to me and they all claimed that they cared about me, but why were they hurting me so much?

Again, I was reminded of the story of the ugly girl in the beautiful people village. Only this time, I related much more to how dried up and used she must've felt by the time they were done loving her.

After school, Milo proceeded to launch into a speech about how I'm never home anymore and how Mom's even starting to notice. At least he seemed to have forgotten entirely about the vampire conversation on the bus, which made me feel a little better.

I didn't think that anybody would really care if I told Milo. I just figured that he'd probably have me locked away in a psych ward, and I'd never be able to see them again.

Good news. Peter and Ezra are on a business trip. Jack text messaged me, and Milo rolled his eyes.

"You know I really like Jack, but have you considered what this is doing to your school work?" Milo asked.

He sat at the kitchen table, working on some piece of homework, but I lay sprawled out on the couch half-asleep. My lack of nightly sleep was starting to result in afternoon naps.

"Nope!" I said.

Schoolwork didn't really seem to matter anymore. It was starting to look like I'd probably marry into money, or maybe I'd just die. Either way, education didn't seem that important.

Why is that good news? I messaged him back. Knowing that I wouldn't see Peter hurt, but it was also a relief. I could only tolerate so many rebuffs.

We can hang out and I can take the Lamborghini. Are you game?

Definitely! I'll meet you outside! Hurry! I responded and jumped up from the couch.

Milo started in with a lecture about school and sleep, but I didn't even pretend to listen. After the stress of the past weekend, I could really just go for a night of silly Jack fun.

I burst outside just as the red car pulled up in front. Throwing open the car door, I leapt inside and smiled broadly at him. Jack laughed at my exuberance, and my heart swelled at the sound of it.

"You're in a good mood today," Jack grinned. We didn't drive right away, and he just sat there for a minute looking at me. "What do you wanna do?"

"I don't care! Just as long as we get there fast!" I said, and his eyes glimmered.

"You don't have to tell me twice." He threw the car into gear and we sped off so quickly, I pressed back against the seat.

Even though we'd just been in a car wreck, I still felt safe with him. After all, he had saved me from the crash, even if he had also been the cause of it.

"This weekend felt so long," I said drearily.

"Tell me about it." Jack was just as tired and frustrated as I was, and that was easy to forget.

Generally, I considered him to be a culprit in all of this, but he was just as much a pawn as I was. We were trapped in an unyielding battle with biology.

"I just want everything to go back to normal." I had expected him to agree with me, but he just laughed.

"I'm assuming you mean normal in that you were running around with your new vampire best friend," he smiled. "Yeah. Cause that's the baseline for normal."

"Well, it feels more normal than all this business about my blood being meant for Peter," I muttered. "How is any part of me meant for anything? Who decided that?"

"I wish I knew." His expression slacked for a second, but then he shook his head. "Look, let's just not think about any of that. You look exhausted. Why don't we just do something nice and relaxing this evening?"

"Like what?" I turned to face him and leaned my head against the seat

"How about we just go back to my house and watch a movie? I have like a million. I'm sure there's a couple in there you'd be up to watching."

"That sounds fantastic," I admitted. The thought of spending the evening just curled up somewhere with Jack sounded positively wonderful. "How long are Ezra and Peter gone for?"

"I don't know," Jack shrugged. "Probably a week, I guess. Why?"

"What do they do? For business, I mean. How did they make all your money?" I had spent so much time talking about the supernatural that I never really had a chance to ask about the practical things, like how they supported themselves.

"Ezra's been working for, you know, hundreds of years doing various things, so he managed to build up quite the nest egg before I was even born. Right now, they're doing a lot of stocks and trading, and I just never bothered to follow.

"They own a couple companies overseas," Jack explained. "Everything they do gets shifted and moved around all the time. They can't stay with the same people for too long, or people'll catch on that they haven't aged."

"Why don't you have a job?" I asked.

"Cause I don't really need to work. Whenever I find something that interests me, I do it, but we have plenty of money. Ezra and Peter don't even have to work. But Ezra thinks that since we're going to live forever, we might as well be prepared for it," he shrugged, then looked over at me. "Why? Does it bother you that I don't work?"

"No, I'm just curious about your life," I said.

We reached his house, and he drove up into the driveway. Turning off the car, he grinned wickedly.

"Well, you know pretty much everything about my life." He got out of the car, preparing to escape with that total fabrication of an answer.

"I know hardly anything about your life!" I scoffed, hurrying out after him.

"I'm a vampire and I drive too fast and I'm awesome on the Xbox." He spread his arms expansively, as if that explained it all. "That's all you really need to know about me."

"I hardly think that's true." I raised an eyebrow at him, causing him to laugh, but he just shook his head and went into the house.

Matilda was already waiting at the door for him. He just gave her a quick scratch and kept on walking, so she followed at his heels.

"Mae, I'm back!" Jack announced, going into the kitchen.

"I'm just doing some laundry!" Mae shouted from down the hall by her bedroom.

"I hate it when you guys are mundane." I wrinkled my nose. "Vampires are supposed to be big and powerful and sexy and dangerous."

"And buy a new outfit every day?" Jack crouched down so he could give Matilda the attention she was dying for, and I leaned back against the counter. "That doesn't really seem practical."

"Exactly! Vampires aren't supposed to be practical! You're supernatural beings with magical powers! You don't do laundry or play video games! You jump off cliffs and have sex with really attractive women!"

"I get it," Jack laughed. "I had this notion about what a vampire should be, but it was all based on glamorized Hollywood ideals. Nothing could be sexy and cool all the time, especially not something that's immortal. Do you know how exhausting and expensive it would be to wear designer gowns and crowned jewels every day for six hundred years?

"And what would be the point? Who would I be trying to impress? I'm a damn vampire! I'm not gonna put on black eyeliner and grow my hair long just so some stupid humans think I'm sexy. They think I am anyway." He winked exaggeratedly at me, so I laughed and started walking away.

"Where are these alleged millions of movies anyway?" I headed towards the living room, even though I hadn't seen a single movie in there.

"Most of them are in my room." He stopped me at the stairs and nodded up to his room. "This might surprise you, but I'm the movie buff in the family. Well, Mae is a little bit, but she only likes things with Ginger Rogers and Cary Grant." He rolled his eyes. "Sometimes, she really does act like she's eighty-years-old."

"I heard that!" Mae was walking towards us with a laundry basket overflowing with clothes, and she thrust them at Jack. "These are yours, by the way. You had a pair of tan Dickies that were covered in blood and I couldn't get it out."

"That must be from when I went to the club." He sifted through the basket of clothes absently, but my eyes widened.

It was one thing to know that he drank blood. It was a different thing entirely to know that he'd ruined clothes by drinking blood from a human being.

"Sometimes Jack goes down to the vampire club on Hennepin Ave." Mae had noticed the shocked look on my face, so she tried to explain. "A lot of the girls down there are donors, and the ones that aren't don't mind. But sometimes when you hit an artery, things can get a little messy."

"But if you hit an artery, don't they die?" I must've continued looking freaked out, because Jack started getting frustrated. He shifted the basket to his other arm and shook his head.

"Our saliva has chemicals in it. Like mosquitoes and vampire bats have anesthetic in theirs. We have that, plus more to make the wound heal fast. The marks are usually completely gone within an hour or two of the bite." He grew bored with the conversation, so he turned and jogged up the stairs. "Come on, Alice, if you want a say in what we watch."

"I'd go with him, or he's liable to make you watch *The Lost Boys*," Mae warned me.

"Hey, it's a good movie!" Jack shouted, and I was inclined to agree.

Just the same, I'd rather watch something a little less blood sucking. The whole point of the night was to not think about all the weird stuff going on.

I hurried up the stairs after him and fought the urge to go into Peter's room. Even standing in the hall, I could smell that tangy, sweet aroma that Peter left behind, but I quickly pushed it out of mind before my heart would beat all funny.

"I'm just gonna put these away real quick," Jack informed me when I came into his room. "I wouldn't want my vampire image to be spoiled by wrinkled clothes."

The door was open to his massive walk-in closet, and he had started hanging up some of his shirts. I walked over to peer inside, and I wasn't surprised to find that his wardrobe consisted almost entirely of tee shirts, Dickies, and various shades of Converse.

"You have a billion dollars, and you have the wardrobe of a twelve-year-old."

"Yeah, well, I have the emotional maturity of a twelve-year-old too, so-" He stuck his tongue out at me and then went back to hanging up his clothes.

"You showed me." I rolled my eyes and went over to flop down on his over-stuffed bed.

It was completely unmade, but it had to be the most comfortable thing I had ever laid on. The sheets were probably Egyptian with a ten million thread count. Not that I knew what any of that meant, but I know it made things more comfortable for some reason. My sheets came from Target, though, and I slept just fine on them.

"I'm glad you like my bed." He had finished hanging his things up and walked out into his room. "I would've made it if I'd known you'd be rolling around in it."

"I'm not rolling around," I muttered, but I sat up so I wouldn't be tempted to.

I looked around his room. There were a few posters on his dark blue walls (one of which was a tour poster from the Cure playing at First Ave on July 12, 1984, and I wondered if he had actually been there). Underneath his massive flat screen TV, there was lots of gaming equipment strewn about a slick black entertainment center, but I didn't see any movies.

"So did you just make up the stuff about the movies?"

"Oh, no, check this out." Jack picked up a remote control off the entertainment center and hit a button. The entire wall to the left of the TV slid back, like a pocket door, and revealed a gigantic shelving unit overflowing with DVD's. "That's cool, right? This was Mac's idea, because she said having all the movies out in the open was 'tacky.'"

"But Peter has tons of books out in his room," I said.

"Right?" Jack shook his head and walked over to inspect his movie collection. "Books are 'sophisticated.' It's what I get for living with people who were born before television. They just don't understand this modern age."

"Yeah, you have a rough life," I mocked.

"Hey, my favorite pair of shorts just got thrown away!" He looked back at me, pretending to be heartbroken. "It's been a pretty sad day all around."

"About that..." I wanted to segue into asking him more questions about the club, even though I wasn't sure if I should.

"I didn't kill her, if that's what you're thinking," Jack explained quickly. "Most vampires don't kill people. It would make eating

245

impossible. If we killed every time we ate, the vampire population in Minneapolis alone would kill at least a thousand people a week. We'd eat ourselves into starvation in less than a decade."

"I didn't think you'd killed her, but that's good to know." A shiver ran down my spine anyway.

In order for a thousand vampires to eat, a thousand people had to be bitten each week. Even if some of them lived on blood banks, the way Jack and Mae mostly did, that was still impossible to fathom.

"How could all those people be bitten? Why aren't they talking about it?" I asked.

"Very few know they're bitten." He wouldn't look at me, and he shifted his weight uncomfortably. "We don't go around blood raping them or anything. They just think they're on dates. Lots of vampires – not me – but lots have 'girlfriends' or 'boyfriends,' but really, it's like… having a cow, so you don't have to buy milk."

I gasped and instantly thought of Jane. She went home with all sorts of guys, and most of them were attractive and kinda creepy. She could easily have been a vampire's cow, more than once.

"But how do they not know?"

"Well, they just think…" He rubbed his forehead and sighed. "They just think that they're with really good lovers. It feels really good. So if you incorporate it with sex, especially with drunk or high people, they have no clue. And it doesn't really hurt them. You're a little weak and woozy, but otherwise okay."

"So that girl that you bit…" I felt strangely jealous. Knowing that Jack was with a girl, that he'd fed on someone made my stomach twist. "Did you have sex with her?"

"No," Jack said, but he turned away from me and looked ashamed. My heart sped up, and he tilted his head, so I knew he heard it. "But we did… stuff. The stuff doesn't matter, though. I know guys say that, but for us it's really true. It was just a way to get what I wanted."

"Because for you, it's not the sex. It's the blood that's intimate and… erotic." When I said that, he realized he'd actually made things worse and grimaced. "So what's it like?"

"It's like drinking blood," he sighed.

He rubbed his eyes, and I could feel how nervous this made him. The topic upset me, and he knew it. Just thinking about drinking her blood made him thirsty. On top of that, he could hear the quickening of my pulse.

"It's hard to explain. You'll understand when you're a vampire," he said finally.

"What is it like for her then? What's it like for a human to be bitten?" I moved so I was sitting on my knees, leaning more towards him. His hunger filled the room like a fog, permeating through me.

"I don't know." Swallowing hard, he glanced over at me and almost instantly looked away.

"Did she enjoy it?"

The thought of her, some faceless girl, being with Jack in a way that I never had made me ill. Maybe that's why I did what I was doing. I wanted to know, in some twisted way, but I also didn't think it was fair that she got to feel something with him that I couldn't.

"Yeah. I mean, I guess she did. I don't know." He ran a hand through his sandy hair and gave me a pained look. "Why do you wanna know? What are you trying to find out?"

"What would I feel?" My voice had gone low and soft, sounding strangely seductive, especially for me. I don't know if I'd done it on purpose really, or if it was just that I could feel everything that Jack felt, and it was playing with my mind. "If you bit me right now. Would it hurt?"

"For a second." Licking his lips, he kept his eyes locked on me, and his breathing got heavier. "But then there's the most wonderful sensation you've ever felt. It radiates from the bite like a warm heat and your heart speeds up so fast, it should hurt, but it doesn't. Your senses go into a frenzy, but it all feels amazing…" He trailed off and swallowed hard.

"What would you feel?" I asked, and the corner of his mouth turned up just slightly.

"It's like that, only better. Nothing else can even compare."

His eyes touched on the hunger that I had seen in Peter's eyes when he wanted to bite me, and I knew thinking about Peter was a bad idea, but I did it anyway.

Jack had a sharp intake of breath, and he noticed the changes, the way my pulse got louder and faster, and some special scent that was supposed to drive him wild.

I'd been biting my lip, trying to control my own feelings of desire, and then I felt a sharp pain in my bottom lip. I can't say whether or not I did it on purpose, but Jack noticed instantly. His pupils dilated and he exhaled shakily.

I had bitten my lip hard enough to draw blood. It wasn't very much, but any amount would be enough to send Jack over the edge at this point.

- 18 -

He rushed towards me so quickly I didn't see him move. His face just suddenly appeared directly in front of mine, his blue eyes staring straight into me. They were completely ravenous, but there was something more behind them than lust.

"You're going to be the death of me," he murmured in a voice so slow I could barely hear it over the pounding of blood in my ears.

Defiantly and provocatively, I raised my chin in the air, revealing the smooth skin of my throat. I tempted him brutally, even though I knew that it could only lead to our demise.

Closing his eyes, he leaned forward and very tenderly, he licked the fresh blood off my skin. He wrapped his mouth around my lip, drinking as much of my blood as he could, and he moaned softly.

As soon as his lips touched mine, a wonderful weakness spread through me, and I arched my back. An intense quivering started in my heart but radiated out all over me, so my whole body shuddered.

When he kissed me fully on the mouth, I thought I would explode. I could taste my blood on his tongue and the intense excitement that went along with it.

His mouth felt hungry and needy, but there was nothing forceful or rough. His muscles trembled with restraint. I knew the things he wanted to do me, the things that I would gladly let him do, and I could feel how hard he had to fight that off.

Carefully, he pushed me back onto the bed, his lips never leaving mine, and he pressed me into the soft mattress. His body laid on me, and I felt his heart pound against mine.

Burying my fingers in his hair, I tried to pull him to me. No matter how close he got, I knew he'd never be close enough. I wanted him underneath my skin, and when I breathed in deeply, I smelled that tangy perfect scent I associated with Peter.

I slid my hands under his shirt, desperate to feel him. His normal temperate skin burned hot. It felt amazing, so I dug my fingers into his flesh, and he moaned against my mouth. His hands found their way under my shirt, smoldering against the trembling skin of my belly.

He managed to pull his lips from my mouth, and they traveled down to the exposed skin of my throat. He pressed his lips against my veins, feeling the pulse against his skin.

There was a hunger so strong it was painful. I thrust my body against his, begging him to drink, and suddenly, he growled and sprang from my arms.

"What?" I cried, sitting back up on my knees. He stood on the other side of the room, panting heavily and shaking horribly.

"He's going to kill you." Jack let out an unsteady breath, and his eyes were wild with passion. "I want to so bad, but he would kill you."

"So?" It was hard to breathe, let alone speak, and I barely managed. "It would be worth it. I want you to, and I don't care what the cost."

"Yeah?" He looked unsure, then nodded. "Yeah. Me neither."

I was at the edge of the bed, and h

wrapping his arms so tightly around me

Oxygen didn't feel much like a necessity any

All that mattered was the way his lip

He kissed me so hard that my lip sprung

desperately.

My fingers dug into his hair and I waited for him to bite me.

"You're going to get yourselves killed!" Mae hissed, and I whipped my head over to see her standing in the doorway, glaring at us. Jack had stopped kissing me, but I was reluctant to untangle myself from his arms.

"We didn't do anything." Jack kept his eyes on me and his voice was husky, so I knew he was still locked in a trance from the bloodlust.

"Yet," Mae glowered.

"Yet," Jack agreed, and he kissed my throat again, right where my pulse still pounded heavily.

My body slacked in his arms, but Mae rushed over, smacking Jack hard on the arm before he could do anything.

"Jack Allen Townsend!" Mae shouted.

"Okay, okay!" He took a step back from me, causing me to collapse backwards on the bed, and held up his hands defensively, but Mae swatted him again. "You can quit now! I stopped!"

"You better!" Mae obviously didn't trust him because she stood directly in front of me, blocking his path to me. "You're going to get her killed! Is that what you want?'

"You know that's not what I want," Jack groaned, but a guilty expression passed across his face. The heat of the moment was rapidly

nd the realization of what he had almost done to me, to
king over.

Then what the hell did you think you were doing?" Mae
manded. He scratched his temple and sighed.

"Being a vampire?" He kept his tone sarcastic, but I could feel
how afraid he really was.

"You are such an idiot!" Mae turned away from him to inspect
me for bite marks. When she saw the blood on my lips, she gasped and
turned back to him. "Did you do that to her? You drew blood?"

"No!" Jack insisted, his eyes wide. "She did that! She bit her lip!"

"Why would you do that?" Mae whirled on me, and I'd finally
regained enough strength to sit up. "Do you have any idea what that
does to him? Do you both have a death wish?"

"It was an accident," I mumbled.

"You need to shower and use a lot of mouth wash." Mae held her
hand to her face, looking distressed but sounding matter-of-fact. "If he
even hints at smelling Jack on your blood…" Her eyes welled with
frightened tears, and she pointed to the bedroom door and snapped,
"Go! Right now! Go downstairs and use my shower!"

"Sorry." I scrambled out of Jack's bed, which was easier said than
done since my ankle tangled in a mass of blankets. "Sorry." As I
stumbled down the stairs, I heard Mae yelling at him.

"How can you be so careless with her life? With your own?" Mae
admonished him. "She's only a girl, Jack! What were you thinking?"

"I wasn't!" Jack said.

"I know how hard this is for you-"

"You have no idea how hard this is for me!" Jack growled fiercely, and I winced.

By kissing him, I had only made it harder. It was impossible for him to ever be with me, unless we wanted our life expectancy reduced down to a matter of hours. Still, that kiss had hinted at how amazing those hours would be, and maybe it would be worth it...

I shook the thought from my head and hurried into Mae's bathroom. Immediately, I opened the medicine cabinet and pulled out the Listerine. The alcohol burned my lip, but I used it until it went numb.

After a shower so long and intense that my skin came out red and raw, Mae decided that it was time that she sat down and had a long talk with me.

She admitted that she didn't understand what Jack and I had gone through because she'd only been turned for six months when she met Ezra, and they had been together ever since.

There was obviously something very different going on with us, but as long as Peter felt a claim to me, I couldn't do anything with Jack, or I was risking both of our lives.

Jack and I would have to find a way to be friends without ever being caught up in any moments, and that would probably be easy if I didn't do anything stupid like, say, bite my lip so he's attracted to my blood.

I ended up staying most of the night over there anyway. I couldn't sleep after that, so we decided to pretend like nothing had happened.

Jack put in *The Crow* and *The Dark Knight*, and I curled up on the couch with Mae. He sat on the floor on the far other side of the room with Matilda because that seemed safest.

Even with everything that had happened, Mae let Jack drive me home. She had decided not to tell Ezra about the "incident" so we'd have to go on like normal, and that meant that we'd have to get used to being around each other without being stupid.

When the sky started to lighten, I finally agreed to go home.

"This is my favorite time of day," Jack mused, looking out the windows of the Lamborghini as we sped away from his house and towards mine. "The sky is so pretty right before it changes."

"It reminds me of a dream," I said and turned to him. "I'm really sorry about what happened earlier."

"Don't be. That was my fault. I have to learn how to control my impulses. You might not believe this, but that's something that I struggle with," Jack laughed dryly.

"I bit my lip. I shouldn't have done that. I'm sorry."

I had done it on purpose, whether I was ready to admit it to myself or not. He wanted me to, and I could feel that the same way I could feel my own heartbeat. I had made the choice to do it, knowing exactly what it would lead to.

"No, it's okay." He paused for a moment before adding, "You taste really good."

"We're not talking about that. We're not even thinking about it," I corrected him.

"I'm not. I wasn't. I was just making conversation." That's what he said, but I could feel the hunger ebbing when I stopped him.

"Well, we can't talk like that. We can talk about anything but blood or biting or sex."

"Sure, take out all the fun things," Jack grumbled.

"It's for your safety as well as mine." I shot him a warning look, and he stiffened a little

"Okay. You're right. Sorry."

"Do you think maybe we should stop hanging out?" I didn't want to, not even slightly, but it would be the safest way to avoid anything.

"No," Jack answered too quickly. He let out a deep breath, then looked nervously at me. "Why? Do you?"

"I don't know. I mean, I still want to hang out with you but..."

My answer hurt him, and at times like that, I hated that I could feel anything he felt. When we had been making out upstairs, it had been amazing, but these situations were murder. His emotions were always so raw and intense. He had very little self-control when it came to the way he felt.

"Honestly, I don't know if I could stop even if I wanted to," Jack said finally.

The sky glowed oddly blue-gray as the sun neared the horizon, and the color seemed to match perfectly with Jack's eyes when he looked over at me.

"Yeah, me neither," I agreed and forced a smile at him.

For good or bad, there would be no way I could ever go back to my life before. If it meant that I had to die trying to live this one, then so be it.

But who can really go back to studying for history exams and flirting with drunk guys at a party when there are vampires and the ecstasy that goes along with bloodlust?

Could anyone really shut the door on immortality?

When he dropped me in front of my house, he smiled grimly, and promised that he'd talk to me later. As I rode up the elevator to my apartment, I had to believe that everything would work out, one way or another.

Ezra was insanely smart, and he'd been around forever. He had to be able to figure out something that didn't involve anyone dying. Well, at least not Peter, Jack, or me.

They were vampires, after all. No matter how much they tried to convince me otherwise, I knew that there had to be a rather high mortality rate for the humans in their lives.

It wasn't until I opened the door to the apartment that it really occurred to me what time it was. Milo was dressed and ready for school, looking relieved to see me. His happiness was short-lived because my mother cleared her throat loudly, and he grimaced.

Sitting in the darkened corner of the living room, she reminded me of some kind of James Bond villain. The dim light from the window hit the cloud of smoke above her head, and a light from the kitchen touched only her slippered feet, leaving the rest of her to hide in the shadows. If she had been stroking a large white cat and spoke in a German accent, she'd be perfect.

"Well, well, nice of you to drop by," Mom greeted me.

"You're welcome," I said unsurely, despite the warning look Milo gave me.

"Where were you all night?" Her tone had gotten even harder, dropping any pretenses of her being even mildly happy to see me.

Milo had to be pretty upset that I wasn't around, especially since he'd had to deal with Mom first thing in the morning, but even he'd been relieved to see that I was still alive. (And there was becoming a very real threat that I wouldn't be for much longer.)

"Why didn't you answer any of my texts?" Milo blurted out. I'm sure he'd been texting me and warning me of Mom's impending tirade.

"Sorry. My phone was on silent."

"That doesn't tell me where you were!" Mom snapped.

The sun had finally peaked over the building next door, and light glinted in through the window, revealing the furious expression on her face. She took a long drag from the cigarette, waiting for an answer good enough to explain where I had been until after seven in the morning on a school night.

"I was at Jack's." I crossed my fingers, hoping that she still had an infatuation with him that could buy me at least one more Get Out of Jail Free card.

Unfortunately, her scowl only deepened, so I knew I was completely out of luck.

"So you're out all night having sex with a boy that's way, way too old for you, and I'm just supposed to turn a blind eye to that?" As she spoke, her words kept getting louder and louder until she was shouting by the end of the sentence.

"Yeah," I replied blankly.

There would be no way I could soothe her anger, so I didn't even bother trying. Milo looked at me questioningly, although I'm not sure if he was questioning my suicidal tendencies or if I'd actually had sex with Jack. Knowing him, it was probably both.

"Alice!" Mom got to her feet, pointing her finger at me. "Go get changed and get ready for school!"

"No!" I protested. "I'm tired! I'm going to bed!"

"Alice, I really think you should listen to her," Milo whispered plaintively.

"I'm tired, too, but I had to wait up for you! And if you think that you can go gallivanting around just because you finally found a boyfriend, then you are sorely mistaken! When you're under my roof, you abide by my rules!" Her eyes were so angry they were bulging from her skull, but after what I'd seen in the past few days, she no longer seemed all that scary.

"Fine. Then I just won't live under your roof," I shrugged.

It was only a matter of time until I moved in with Jack's family or died, so I didn't really need to keep this address anyway. I was hardly ever home anymore. I hadn't actually consulted Jack or Mae about this, so I wasn't really sure how the idea would go over, but I plowed ahead with it anyway.

"Alice!" Milo hissed.

"You are still under eighteen, missy!" Mom didn't even miss a beat. "You are not going anywhere, and if you even think about it, I'll have your little boyfriend turned in for statutory rape."

"It won't stick," I said. "Why do you even want me here? I'm gone all the time, and I just cost you money. I mean, you only saw me for like five minutes all of last week. What exactly do you want me around for?"

"You've got it all figured out then, do you?" Mom shrugged at me. "You got a boyfriend with a little bit of money? He's gonna take care of you now? Is that what you think? Yeah, well maybe you've forgotten, but I had a boyfriend like that once. You know what I got? Two ungrateful kids and not a damn cent from him! So don't try and tell me things you know nothing about!"

"I'm not trying to tell you anything! I'm just saying that I'm a burden to you! You don't want me here, I don't wanna be here, so why am I here?" I asked her emphatically.

She looked hurt at that, but nothing I had said wasn't true. We barely saw each other, and she didn't know anything about me. The only one that would be hurt was Milo, and I'd still see him.

"Go. Go ahead," Mom said evenly. I started walking towards my room, and she held up her hand. "Don't even think about! That room is full of my stuff. You never paid for a damn thing in your life. So when you leave, you take what you got on your back, and that's all."

"Fine, whatever." I tried to act like it didn't bother me that I'd be leaving all my personal belongings behind. Like CD's, diaries, underwear, and everything I had ever owned. But I had made up my mind, and that was it. "I'll see you… maybe never." Then I turned and waltzed out of the apartment.

"Alice!" Milo burst out of the apartment after me before the elevator even came. He dragged his half unzipped backpack and raced towards me. "Why did you do that?"

"It just seemed really pointless to stay there any longer." I tried not to look over at him, so I wouldn't have to see the pained expression his face. Leaving home meant that I was leaving him, too.

"You're really gonna go live with Jack?" He sounded simultaneously surprised and resigned by the idea.

"I don't see what choice I have." The elevator doors opened and there were several passengers on it, which I was kinda grateful for. Milo would be less likely to press me for answers, so it'd be easier for me to leave details out.

"You definitely have a choice!" Milo insisted, ignoring the crowd in the elevator. "I know Jack and his family are super amazing, but you haven't really known him that long. I mean, they're almost too good to be true. There's got to be a dark secret hidden there."

"You just might be right."

I bit my lip to keep from smiling, and I realized with surprise that it didn't hurt. Running my tongue along my bottom lip, I searched for any bump or scratch from when I had bit it earlier, but there was none. Jack's saliva must've healed it.

"Come on, Alice," Milo pleaded when the doors opened. "Be reasonable."

"When have you ever known me to be reasonable?" I shot him a look while stepping out of the elevator, and he just rolled his eyes.

We walked outside into the cold, and I wrapped my sweater more tightly around me. All I had on me were the clothes on my back and my cell phone in my pocket, and there was a very good chance that my only rides anywhere were a pair of vampires that had just gone to bed.

"So what?" Milo was walking to the bus stop, and since I had nothing better to do, I walked with him. "This is it? This is like the last time I'll see you?"

"No, of course not!"

"Be serious." He had pulled his bag onto into his back, and he readjusted the straps. "You're going to move in with him and have all these fabulous adventures and completely forget about me."

"You're my brother, Milo. I can never forget about you." And I wouldn't, but I had a sinking suspicion that he probably wasn't that far from the truth. "Look, I'm not saying things won't be different or that I won't see you less. But that doesn't mean things will be bad."

"Maybe you can just stay there for a night or something," Milo suggested hopefully. "Give Mom a chance to cool down, and then you can come home.

"But she's not completely off base, Alice. You have school and you stayed out until seven in the morning. I don't care what you were or weren't doing with Jack — well, okay, I do, and you'll totally have to tell me later. But it doesn't matter. You're still in high school. You should be coming home before the sun comes up and getting an education."

"I am way too tired for you to lecture me about school, okay?" I groaned.

"Just think about it, alright?" Milo asked as the bus came towards us. I didn't want the bus driver to try to make me get on, so I started backing away from him. "And turn your phone on! If you don't come home tonight, maybe you could at least get some of your things while Mom's at work."

"Okay!" I waved at him, then turned and walked down the block, away from my apartment, away from my brother, away from my life.

- 19 -

I just walked around the tree lined streets. Spring edged ever closer, with warm temperatures and longer days. The nights would get shorter, too, and I wondered how Jack contended with that.

I was definitely cold and tired, but I was way too wired up from everything that had happened. My lips still tingled from kissing him, and I wondered dully if I'd ever be able to kiss him again.

Moving out of my mother's had been rash, I'll admit it, and she was justified in her anger. I just didn't have the strength to deal with stuff that didn't matter anymore.

Maybe I would've reacted a little better if I hadn't had the reminder of Jack's nearly-forgotten words ringing in my mind. When I asked what it was like to bite a vampire, he'd responded with, "You'll understand when you're a vampire."

It would only be natural that I eventually segued into vampirism. Even if I didn't move in with them today, I would some day. They were welcoming me into their folds for a reason, and as Jack had so ominously pointed out, they wanted me to be one of them.

I sat down on a bench and pulled my knees up to my chest. The sun spilled over the buildings, warming my skin, and I wondered how much longer I'd be able to enjoy the sun like this.

Being with them would mean missing a lot of things, but it didn't really feel like it. There would be so much more I'd be getting in return.

Pulling out my phone, I hoped that Jack would still be awake.

"Hello?" Jack answered groggily.

"Sorry. Did I wake you?"

"Nah, I'm just about to go to bed, though. Why? What do you need?" He still sounded awfully tired, and he yawned into the phone.

"I was just... wondering if I could stay with you for awhile." I grimaced at my own question. Maybe I asked too much from them. Maybe I should go home and try to make amends with my mother before she changed the locks.

"Yeah, sure. What's wrong with your place?" Jack replied without even thinking about it.

"I got in a fight with my mom about coming home so late, and I'm not exactly welcome there anymore."

"Oh, man, I'm sorry," Jack apologized. "Yeah. Sure. You can stay here as long as you want. Do you need a ride right now?"

"It would be nice, but it's not necessary." I still didn't completely understand his deal with sun, and I wasn't sure if he could drive out in it to come get me.

"Yeah, yeah, okay. I'll be there in like five minutes." He yawned again and I heard a rustle of movement as he got up, meaning that he'd already been in bed.

"I'm not at home, though. I'm on a bench a couple blocks away." I looked around for a street sign so I could tell him what intersection I was at for sure, but he could always find me.

"Cool. Hang tight." He clicked off the phone, and I shoved my phone back in my pocket.

I felt better knowing that I wouldn't be stuck on this bench all day like a homeless person, but it was still hard to know if I was doing the right thing.

Nothing in my life had prepared me to deal with situations like this. Up until now, my life consisted of sitting at home with Milo, shopping, partying, hating myself with Jane, and that's about it.

I'd barely even kissed a boy, I'd never driven a car, or been out of the tri-state area. My father left before I was two, and my mother spent my whole life working continuously so we'd have just enough to survive.

I knew nothing about life, and here I was, preparing to give it up in exchange for something I didn't truly understand.

Jack pulled up in front of me within six minutes of me making the phone call, and I didn't understand how he could possibly get around that fast. But here he was, grinning at me tiredly behind gigantic sunglasses. I hopped in the car and decided that I was too tired to question anything.

When we got to his house, Jack showed me to my room. It was the guest room at the end of the hall upstairs, the bedroom in the turret. I felt like Juliet or Rapunzel.

The walls were rounded and there was a balcony in the back. It'd been painted a soft lilac that eerily matched the walls of my own room, and the four-post bed had been made in all white, luxurious comforters. Mae had even left satin pajamas on the bed.

"Wow, this is really perfect." I touched the blankets and admired the room. "It's exactly like me."

"It should be." Jack stood in the doorway, leaning on the frame to make sure that I had everything, and he yawned. "Mae did it for you."

"Like just now? I called and she painted the room?" I furrowed my brow in confusion and disbelief.

"No," he laughed, shaking his head. "Originally, she kind of thought you'd just be staying in Peter's room, but when that started seeming like less of an option, she did up this room for you. You were gonna end up here eventually, right?"

"Yeah." I nodded, but it felt weird knowing that someone had been preparing for me before I even knew I'd be here.

"Mae likes to nest." Jack noticed my unease and smiled to settle me down. "It's her thing. This was just her way of nesting. She doesn't get to decorate for girls very often, you know."

"Yeah, I guess not."

"Alright, well, I'm gonna get some sleep. But I'll be right next door if you need me." He took a step backwards and grinned mischievously. "But don't you get any ideas."

"Yeah, I'll try not to." I was being sarcastic, but I knew that I'd really have to try not to.

Jack laughed and walked into his room, which was just one thin wall away from mine. Peter was gone, and Mae was downstairs. It would be almost too easy to just go next door and finished what we started earlier...

But thankfully, my body decided to remember exactly how tired it was. I shut the bedroom door, put on my borrowed pajamas, and almost as soon as my head hit the pillow, I was asleep.

When I picked up clothes from home the next day, Milo hugged me like a hundred times, and his eyes welled with tears. Jack waited in the kitchen for me while I packed my things. I'd thought that his presence would somehow cheer Milo up, but it had the opposite effect. It reminded him that not only would he be seeing less of me, he'd be seeing less of Jack as well.

When I finally convinced Milo that I would see him again, he hugged me tightly once more for good measure, and then I escaped.

"We could've just bought you new clothes," Jack pointed out on the car ride back to his house. "That probably would've been easier and less painful."

"I know, but Milo needed to see me. I needed to prove that I wasn't just gonna forget about him." I looked over at Jack to see if he understood my sentiments, but he just stared ahead and didn't say anything. "I will see him again."

"I'm not arguing with you." He wasn't, exactly, but his tone wanted to contradict my claim.

"You don't think I will." Just saying it aloud hurt. "Why would you let me promise Milo anything if you knew it wasn't true?"

"I don't know anything," Jack said. "But I do think that Ezra will be home when we get back. And it might be good for you to talk to him."

"You always know more then you let on," I grumbled, crossing my arms over my chest and sinking low in the seat. "You pretend to be dumber than you actually are."

"Have you considered that I really might just be that dumb?" he asked playfully.

"I have. Many times."

He laughed at that but didn't say anymore until we got to his place. There would be very little he could say that would comfort me anyway. I was beginning to realize that I might have underestimated the cost of being with him.

When we went into the house, Jack called for Ezra and Mae, and they appeared in the living room almost instantly. Mae swooped in to hug me as if she hadn't seen me in ages when in reality it had been an hour.

Ezra smiled at me, and somehow, it still made me blush. He had returned today early from the trip, citing that he couldn't stand to be away from Mae for that long, but Peter wouldn't return for a few more days. He could apparently stand to be away from me until the end of time.

"So I heard that you're going to be staying with us for awhile," Ezra said, and I tried to decipher if there was any disapproval in it.

He sat on the couch and Mae curled up next to him. They had only been apart for a matter of days, but being around him made her giddy.

I wondered if Peter would react anything like that when he returned, but I'd probably be lucky if he even looked in my direction.

Something tugged painfully at my heart, and it amazed me that I still even wanted into this.

"Yeah." I sat on the chair across from them, and Jack sat by my feet, rubbing Matilda's belly. "Is that okay?"

"I don't see why it wouldn't be." Ezra played with a long, wavy strand of Mae's hair absently, and she buried her head in his chest. I realized that I hated people who were so comfortably in love, especially when my "love" life was bogged down by all sorts of unnecessary stipulations.

"What's going to happen?" I asked bluntly.

"You'll have to be more specific. A lot of things are up in the air for you." He didn't mean anything by it, but it stung just the same.

Nothing for me was set in stone, which should've been a relief, but I didn't like having everything feel so uncertain and precarious.

"Exactly." I took a deep breath. "Am I just gonna live here forever? What happens when Peter gets back? He doesn't want me around. Should I even stay here with him? What if he keeps rejecting me? Am I supposed to just go back to my life? Are you planning on me someday being a vampire?"

"You can stay here as long as you want, regardless of how Peter feels. He has other places he can go if need be. You have made yourself an indispensable part of this family." Ezra looked down at Mae, carefully choosing his words.

"Peter… No matter how any of us feels, there is a bond between you and Peter that is not easily broken. For his sake, as well as our own, it is essential that you remain a part of our lives." His russet eyes

271

rested warmly on mine. "As such, yes, it would be in everyone's best interest if you were to turn."

Looking down at the floor, I exhaled and tried futilely to slow the frantic beating of my heart. I knew they all could hear it, and Jack especially was susceptible to it.

The thought of being a vampire, which had crossed my mind much more frequently than I had ever imagined it would, both excited and terrified me,Nearly everything about them was simultaneously exciting and terrifying, and I could never seem to reconcile the two.

"Alice, it's really awesome," Jack chimed in helpfully. "You've seen me. I'm awesome."

"Jack," Mae scolded him.

"It's not a decision you can take lightly," Ezra went on, and Mae had gotten a particularly solemn expression. I didn't fully understand it, especially based on how much she loved having me around. "This is something that changes everything about your life, and it's irreversible. If you decide that this is what you want to do, you cannot go back. But if you decide not to turn, we won't hold it against you."

"It will make your life harder, though," Jack interjected.

"Jack!" Mae snapped. "You can't make this choice for her!"

"I'm not trying to!" Jack sighed dramatically and shook his head.

"If you do turn, the thirst is a bit overwhelming, as Jack can attest to," Ezra gestured to Jack, who nodded heavily in agreement. "All your senses become much more heightened, and all your movements feel exaggerated. Your emotions are stronger, too. They are all right at the surface, and you're volatile. You're libido increases, as does your general lust for anything."

"It's almost like being a child again," Jack elaborated. "Everything feels so new, and you're clumsy."

"Your body has to acclimate to a whole new way of being. It's not a simple process," Ezra continued. "The hardest thing to deal with at first is the bloodlust. The hunger you feel now can't even compare to what you'll feel then. It's a hard thing to learn to control, but it is very manageable once you do."

"So, you guys are always hungry?" I asked nervously.

"In a way," Ezra admitted. "But it's not that intense. If it was, you wouldn't have survived this long."

"Thanks." I wondered how I could feel so safe in the house with them.

"It's not meant to be a threat," Ezra laughed. "It's just the way things are. For the most part, being a vampire is a wonderful, amazing gift. But there are two things that are double-edged swords.

"The first is the blood," Ezra went on. "Its life giving, and there aren't words to describe how wonderful it makes you feel. But when you can't feed for any prolonged length of time, say several weeks, it is the most excruciatingly pain imaginable. Before you get your bloodlust under control, the frenzy of feeding can have horrendous ramifications. It is an immeasurable pleasure, but unless it's properly controlled, it is devastatingly dangerous."

"That's good to know," I swallowed hard.

"I've got it under control for the most part, and I have horrible impulse control," Jack offered.

"The second thing is immortality." Ezra breathed deeply and looked down at Mae. She had a faraway, sad look, and I hoped that someone would explain it to me. "We're not truly immortal. If you damage our brain or our heart, or we go long enough without feeding, we will die. But barring another vampire attacking us, there really is very little that stops us. We are slow to turn other vampires as a result of it. So, please, don't think this is a casual invitation we are giving you."

I felt humbled. It actually hadn't occurred to me that there would be a limit on vampire membership, but it was incredibly flattering knowing that I was even being considered.

"But there is a very heavy price with that," Ezra continued gravely. "Everything around you will die. Even this town, it will change, and things you loved and held dear will be destroyed. You will outlast everything. There is more of a burden in that than you can possibly imagine."

"Does that mean that I can't see my brother? Or just that it will be painful watching him grow old?" My voice felt small and shaky, and my hands trembled.

Ezra shared a look with Mae, who nodded, and then she stood up, saying, "I have to show you something."

"You're gonna take her?" Jack groaned and got up. "She doesn't need to see it."

"You're just saying that because you think she'll change her mind," Mae told Jack.

"Uh, yeah!"

"If it would change her mind, then it should!" Mae snapped. "If she doesn't have all the facts because you kept them from her, and she makes a decision that she later regrets, then she'll spend the rest of eternity resenting you. Is that really what you want?"

"No," Jack muttered and rubbed the back of his neck.

"What's going on?" I asked nervously, standing up.

"I'm going to take you to see something," Mae forced a smile at me. Then she turned back to Ezra and kissed him. "We won't be gone too long."

"Okay. Be safe." Ezra looked sad to see her go, but he smiled reassuringly at me. "It'll be alright."

"What's going on?" I asked Jack, feeling strangely frightened as I followed Mae out of the living room.

"I guess you gotta go," Jack sighed and sat back down. "I'll see you in a bit."

"Where are we going?" I asked.s

"I'll explain in the car."

- 20 -

By the time I got into her Jetta, nervous anticipation filled me. Whatever she wanted to show me could scare me off becoming a vampire. I half-expected some horrifying monster or a stash of human corpses or something equally disturbing. What else could there be that would completely change my mind about turning?

The soft music of Nina Simone playing out of the car stereo did little to make me feel good, and I stared apprehensively at Mae, who in turn, stared straight ahead, looking rather tragic.

"I was born in Reading, England in 1928," Mae explained in a voice so sad, it barely sounded like her. "When I was very young, the second World War broke out. Towards the end, American soldiers were stationed all over England. Philip was the most dashing young man I had ever met." She smiled lightly at that, but it didn't reach her eyes. "Despite my best attempts at being virtuous, I ended up pregnant at sixteen, and Philip was an upstanding man, so we were wed. My first child, a son I named Samuel, was born while he was still fighting in the war.

"Samuel was five months old when Philip finished his tour of duty, and we moved to the US, to a small flat in St. Paul, where Philip and his family were from," Mae continued. "The first few months we lived here were truly wonderful. Then, one night, three weeks before Samuel's first birthday, I went in to check on him, and he wasn't breathing." A solitary tear slid down her cheek, but she chose to ignore it.

"The pain never gets easier. Don't listen to what anyone tells you. Losing a child is... an impossible loss."

"I'm sorry," I said, unsure of what else to say.

"Everybody kept saying, 'At least you're young enough to try again.'" Mae smiled bitterly at the memory and glanced over to me. "But I didn't want to try again.

"After Samuel died, I spent months curled up in bed. My family, everything I had known and loved, was a million miles away, and my husband, as much as he did love me, was very young himself and he was busy trying to work and start a life for us..." She had a faraway expression for a moment, but then she remembered I was there and snapped herself out of it.

"I was just a little older than you, so you can imagine what it would be like," Mae looked at me warmly, but I sensed an uneasy warning underneath her gaze. "I understand the excitement of being offered a whole new life with an attractive stranger. But you isolate yourself from everything you know."

"I don't feel isolated," I offered lamely.

I tried to understand her reasoning for telling me the story. My guesses were leaning towards Samuel's headstone, and she wanted to explain the immeasurable loss a person goes through when they out live everything around them.

But she would've outlived her baby whether she was a vampire or not. It had nothing to do with the choices she made.

"Nevertheless." Mae stared straight ahead, her knuckles turning white from the way she gripped the steering wheel. "Philip, bless his heart, stayed by my side, when a lesser man might've shipped me back home for my parents to deal with.

"Eventually, I managed to pull myself out of the depression and go on with my life. I got a job at a deli to keep myself busy and made a few friends. And one day, I decided it was time to start trying for a family again.

"Being pregnant was the most miraculous thing that ever happened to me. To feel this little life growing inside me..." She looked rather blissful, but her gaze got harder when she turned to me. "That's something you'll be giving up, you know. Vampires can't get pregnant. They don't have children. You will never have a family if you choose this life."

"I don't think I want kids anyway." I had actually thought about it very little, but for the most part, the idea of having a child didn't sound that appealing.

"Well, you might change your mind when the option is taken away from you," Mae replied thoughtfully. "It's just something for you to think about."

"I will," I promised her, but I doubted that it would affect my decision at all.

Even if she was right, if someday I regretted never having children, I could only make the decision now, based on my current state of mind. And right now, having children didn't seem that important.

"The day my daughter was born was the happiest day of my life." Her expression stretched into a deep smile, and her eyes filled with happy tears. "She was so beautiful. Her eyes were huge and blue, just like Philip's. And she had these soft, downy curls, the same as I had had when I was born. I remember the first time I held her in my arms, and the soft warm weight of her body... I promised her I'd never let anything bad happen to her." She exhaled heavily, and the sadness started seeping into her eyes.

"I named her Sarah, after my mother." She wiped at her cheek, trying to catch a tear before it fell. "Everyday with her was absolute heaven. I'm sure every mother thinks her child was perfect, but she really was. She rarely cried, and she woke with this beautiful smile on her chubby cheeks. I quit my job at the deli just so I could spend as much time with her as I could. Every moment with her just seemed so absolutely precious.

"One night, I was preparing supper, and I realized that we were out of milk," Mae went on. "We had a man who would deliver milk to our house, but with having a toddler, we went through milk faster than normal. Sarah was nearly two, and I had stopped breastfeeding not long before that.

"Philip had just gotten home from work, so I didn't want to send him back out. Besides that, the corner market was only two blocks down and it was a beautiful night.

"I remember that I had been wearing this beautiful spring dress with blue flowers that I'd made from a pattern. It was one of my favorites, and I had been meaning to make a smaller version for Sarah just as soon as I got more fabric."

She hesitated before she spoke again, and I almost thought she might not go on anymore. Whatever she had meant to tell me had become too painful, but finally, she continued.

"He was so attractive that I would've gone with him anywhere," Mae said bitterly, but she was angrier with herself than him. "I had barely made it a block, and then he just appeared out of nowhere.

"In retrospect, he wasn't half as handsome as Ezra is, but to my human sense, he was an Adonis. I never even put up a fight. When he led me away into the trees, I was too intoxicated by him to think of Sarah. He sunk his teeth into my neck, and I thought for sure I was dying, but it felt so good, that I didn't even care. I should've been pleading for my life, for Sarah, but I just…"

"You couldn't do anything," I tried to comfort her. While I had never been in the exact same position, I knew how impossible it was to think when a vampire wanted your blood. "It wasn't your fault."

"But I loved her!" Mae insisted fiercely. "I just wanted to spend the rest of my life watching her grow up and being a part of her life! But instead I went into a patch of trees, and let a vampire bite me.

"He drained me, but then instead of leaving me to recover and go back to my family, he offered his blood to me. He said I tasted too good to waste on a human life. I didn't understand what he meant, and I was still completely under his spell, so I did as I was told." She smiled painfully and rolled her eyes at her own ignorance.

"I had a choice!" Her voice broke sharply. "I'm the only one that did. Ezra was forced into it, and Peter and Jack were done to save their lives. But me, somebody asked me. I didn't understand what it meant, and yet I agreed to it. Willingly."

"But you couldn't have known." I thought about reaching out to touch her, but she was too angry.

"For two days afterwards, I laid in the trees, afraid to move," Mae went on. "The virus attacked my body, and everything changed and died. I was weak and in pain, and I had no idea what was happening to me.

"Then finally, my strength returned, only much more brilliantly then it had before. And this unquenchable thirst. All the while I had been writhing in pain, all I had been able to think about was Sarah and how much I wanted to get back to her. But as soon as I felt that hunger, I knew that I could never go back to her. I couldn't trust myself.

"Within my first few hours as a vampire, I nearly killed our neighbor, I was so hungry. After my bloodlust calmed down, I felt safe enough to check on Sarah. I hid in the backyard and peered in through the window.

"Before I even got near the house, I heard Sarah crying. Philip was carrying her around trying to calm her down, saying 'We'll find your Mama. She'll come back to you.'" Fresh tears streamed down her cheeks, and the car started to slow.

We were on a suburban street I had never seen before, and Mae parked on the side of the road, underneath a tree.

"I slept in the woods during the day, and at night, I would sit outside the window and just watch Sarah. She cried for me every night for a month. Philip had the police searching for me, so I had to be very careful that no one would spot me." She sighed heavily. "I lived that way for over six months. I wore the same dress, and fed on our neighbor, since he was nearby. If Ezra hadn't found me, I don't know what would've become of me. Maybe I'd still be living out behind that house."

"What happened to your family?" I asked quietly.

"Philip eventually remarried a girl I had known from the deli. She was very kind, and I'd like to believe that she was good to him. They had two more children together, and Sarah eventually started calling her Mom. I don't know if she even remembers me anymore. It's probably better if she doesn't."

Mae nodded towards a house in front of us, and I saw the silhouette of an older woman it the window. She carried a small child, a little boy, on her hip, and she looked happy. There was something familiar about her, and I couldn't quite place it.

Then it dawned on me. Her graying wavy hair, pale skin, and even the way she smiled – they were all Mae's.

"That's your daughter!" I gasped, looking over at her.

"It is." She looked pleased that I had been able to see the resemblance. "She's a teacher. She used to be married, but her husband left her years ago. Ezra threatened to teach him a lesson, but I told him not to. Sarah has to live her own life. She's fifty-four now. She has a daughter, Elizabeth, and that little boy on her hip, that's her grandson, Riley. My great-grandson." She smiled painfully. "During the week, she watches her grandkids, while Elizabeth works and goes to school. Riley is three, and Daisy just turned five."

"So you just come out here and watch them?" I asked.

"It's the only way I could watch her grow up," Mae explained sadly. "When she was little, I would come into her room at night and

283

watch her sleep. I even did that a little while with Elizabeth, but Ezra says that I need to start letting them go. Sarah has a wonderful life, and I should just be happy with it.

"I know Ezra's right," Mae said. "It will get harder watching her as she grows old and frail. Watching her die." She swallowed painfully. "I don't want to outlive my daughter. I outlived one of my children, and I swore that I'd never do it again."

She turned to look at me and whispered harshly, "It is so much harder to watch everyone you love die then it is to simply die yourself. Immortality is much more of a curse than it is a blessing."

"But you have Ezra, and Peter and Jack," I attempted to comfort her. "I know it's not the same as a child you gave birth to, but you love them too, and you get to spend forever with them."

"I know, and I am grateful that I have them. Without Ezra, I never would've made it this long." Mae had gone back to staring at her daughter. Through an open curtain, we could see Sarah chasing after a small girl with soft, blond curls.

"Three years ago, Philip died. I cried more than I had thought I would after all these years. But he had always been good to me, and he'd been a wonderful father to our daughter.

"That's when Ezra built the house that we live in, and he said it would be the last place we lived in Minneapolis," Mae sighed. "He doesn't like to stay in one city for this long, especially one that has family. Jack's mother launched a missing persons search for him after he turned, but they eventually chucked it up to another drunk kid falling in a frozen lake."

"How does Jack feel about leaving his mother and family behind?" I asked. He had never mentioned his family at all, but then again, neither had Mae, and they were incredibly important to her.

"He severed all contact with her after he turned," Mae said. "He'd never been that close to her anyway. She left when he was young, taking only his sister with her, and his father raised him. From what I understand, his father wasn't a very nice man either. Then his father got cancer, and his mother was forced to take him back in. Truthfully, I think he was rather happy that he has an excuse not to see her."

"So why did you all stay here for so long?" I asked, even though I thought I knew the answer.

"I refused to go," Mae said simply. "But the boys are getting restless. Jack has never lived anywhere else. Peter will go stay other places, but he's always been more of a drifter. In a few years, I'll have no choice but to move, and I suppose it will be better for me to remember my daughter this way, while she's still vibrant."

"Where will you move?" I asked.

"I'm not sure yet. Jack has a list of places he'd love to go, but there has been some talk of England since that's where both Ezra and I were born, and I haven't been back since I was sixteen." She turned her serious gaze on me. "In two or three years, at the latest, we will be moving, and we won't come back to Minnesota. We may not even come back to America for many years."

"I don't understand why that's a bad thing," I said. Moving to another country sounded ridiculously exciting. I didn't know why she made it sound like a threat.

"You will not be able to see your brother again," Mae explained softly. "Even if we stayed around here, the best you could hope for is watching him grow old from afar. Even as much as I've watched my own family, I never interacted with them. After you turn, you'll be unable to talk to Milo ever again."

"But…" I trailed off, trying to think of an argument that would win her over. "But he's met you all! And why can't I just tell him what you are? What I'll be? He'd understand. And he wouldn't tell anyone."

"Telling humans just makes their lives worse," Mae told me gravely. "If you decided not to turn, or if we'd never even offered it to you, can you imagine how you would feel? In a year or two, we just up and leave you behind. Knowing what we are, knowing that we exist.

"Every time you're enamored with a boy, you'll wonder if it's just because he's a vampire. You'll age, and you'll wonder what it would've been like to stay young forever. And you'll wonder if you just made it all up, if you're insane."

"But you think it would be better for Milo to think that I had been murdered or kidnapped or something?" I asked her incredulously. "That's the better alternative?"

"You don't want to watch him die, Alice!" Mae insisted with tears in her eyes. "I know that you don't love him quite the same way that I love my daughter, but even knowing that Philip died was devastating. Leaving them behind is hard, it is so very hard, and you'll question it forever. But there is no other option. Immortality requires you to leave everything behind."

"So you expect me to turn my back on all of this, all that you have to offer, because Milo will die? He's going to die anyway! Me staying human doesn't make him live forever!" I countered. "But you and Jack and Peter won't die. I don't know how I could possibly go back to living my life knowing that you're out there and I'm not with you."

"You just needed to know," Mae looked at me earnestly. "You needed to know exactly what you'd be giving up. It's not fair to ask you something that you don't understand. I wanted to give you a chance, so you wouldn't make the same mistake that I did."

"Are you saying that you don't want me to turn?" I asked thickly.

"No, no, of course not, love." She reached out and gently stroked me cheek. "I would want nothing more than to spend forever watching you turn into the amazing woman I know you'll be. But I know the price of turning better than anyone, and if I can spare you from any pain, I will."

"But as a human, people will still die around me," I argued. She dropped her hand from my face but kept her sad eyes on mine. "I'll be touched by even more death as a human than I would be as a vampire. At least you guys won't die."

"That is true. But that doesn't make leaving your brother any easier." She forced a smile at me, then turned the car back on and drove away from her daughter's house. "It's just something that I thought you should think about it."

"Thank you." I sunk low into the seat.

I stared out into the darkness, watching the houses and trees roll past us. Mae sang softly along with the stereo in attempt to alleviate her own sadness by the time we got back home. She had left me with an impossible choice. Leave behind my brother, or leave behind them.

- 21 -

The covers were pulled completely over my head in attempt to keep the daylight out, but when I finally poked my head up, there was no light spilling in. Part of it was because of the thick curtains that blanketed every window of the house, but the main reason, according to the clock on my nightstand, was probably because it was after six, and the sun had already set.

Last night, I had again stayed up with Jack, watching his DVDs of *Mystery Science Theater 3000*, and very deliberately not talking about the elephant in the room: whether or not I planned to ever become a vampire.

I couldn't understand all the ramifications of my decision when I couldn't even fully believe it was true. Last night, I had spent the entire time watching an old TV show on DVD and trying not to entice a vampire to bite me.

How could I possibly reconcile those two ideas? The utterly mundane with the totally supernatural? One of those things just didn't belong.

Instead of dwelling on it any longer, I rolled over and grabbed my cell phone off the nightstand. I vaguely remembered the jingle of my phone interrupting my sleep, but I had been too tired to answer it. When you're still human, staying up all night can be incredibly exhausting.

So what? Are you like really sick or something? That was a text message from Jane. Along with, **Hello? Are you ignoring me?** At least she still cared, which I found to be kinda surprising.

There were three from Milo, and I was reluctant to read them. I didn't want to think about him being alone in that apartment all the time. He didn't really have any friends, and on top of that, he had his current issues with his sexuality. It was a very cruel time for me to leave him.

Are you done going to school now?

Mom asked about you. She's worried. Maybe you should apologize to her now.

I'm worried too. When are you coming home?

I groaned and pulled the covers back up over my head. How would I answer that? I was probably never coming home, and I'd probably never talk to him again.

But I couldn't exactly say that. I didn't want to. Just yesterday, I'd promised he'd be in my life forever, and apparently, that was a total lie.

"Are you up yet?" Jack asked sunnily, and I assumed he was standing in my doorway.

"Define 'up.'"

"I'll take that as a yes." The bed heaved as Jack jumped into it, and I lowered the covers enough so I could peek out at him. My room was completely dark except for a light from the hall, and I could barely make out the cocky grin on his face. "Morning, sunshine."

"If you're gonna be this cheery, you can just go away," I grumbled, and he laughed.

I hated how wonderful his laughter sounded and the way it filled me with pleasant tingles. I didn't want to be pleasant. I wanted to be grumpy and stay in bed all day, avoiding the world until somebody else made a decision for me.

Having a choice in something as major as the rest of my life was far too much of a responsibility for me.

"Didn't sleep well, I take it?" He propped himself up on his elbow so he could smirk down at me.

"I slept great, actually." My phone was still in my hand, so I reached my arm out and extended it towards him. "Milo texted me."

"I see." He took the phone from me and scrolled through the messages. "Jane still talks to you? I thought you were over her."

"I was never under her. We just eat lunch together at school and stuff," I brushed off his disapproving tone. "Never mind her. That's not what has me all depressed."

"You didn't reply to him."

"What could I possibly say to him?" I asked honestly

"Whatever you want." He shrugged and handed me back my phone. "He's your brother."

"Ugh, you're no help!"

"Are you going back home?" Jack asked quietly.

"No. I don't know." I looked away from him. "I have no idea what I'm doing!"

"Why don't you just get up and take a shower? You'll probably feel better then. Besides, you don't have to decide anything right now." He rolled out of my bed and looked at me expectantly. "Come on. Get up."

"Yeah, you're probably right," I admitted and slowly pulled myself out from underneath the covers.

"You know, I really wish you'd catch onto the fact that I'm always right." To encourage me to move faster, he flicked on the lights, and I squinted at the sudden brightness.

"Get out of here so I can shower."

My bedroom had an attached bathroom, so I shooed Jack out when I started getting my clothes together. Like the other rooms, I had a massive closet, and my paltry wardrobe looked pathetic in there. Mae had offered to take me shopping, but their generosity was overwhelming, so I declined.

After I finished getting ready, I lay down on the bed and tried to think of a way to respond to Milo. Even if someday I would have to faze him out of my life, I wasn't quite ready for that day to be today.

But that didn't mean I was ready to move back home and pretend like nothing was happening. Life as I knew it had changed, and I couldn't go back and act like things mattered when they didn't. Milo still mattered, but school and curfews didn't.

"Are you done?" Jack knocked on the door and pushed it open without waiting for an answer. He leaned on the open door and grinned at me. "You're already back in bed? You just woke up."

"I'm not sleeping. I'm just thinking." I had my phone in my hands, and I was just staring at it, as if it could magically come up with an answer to all my life's problems.

"Well, I hope you don't mind, but I'm here to interrupt your thoughts." He opened the door wider and stepped inside a little bit, so I could see past him. Looking rather sheepish, Milo stood in the doorway and gave me a half-wave. "I thought you could use the company."

"Milo!" I sat up and smiled at him. "What are you doing here?"

"Jack called and asked if I wanted to come hang out with you for awhile," Milo shrugged and came into my room. "I hope that's alright."

"No! It's great!" It wasn't until I saw him, his nervous brown eyes and his chubby cheeks, that I realized how much I'd missed him. I'd only been gone for two days, but since I'd barely even seen him when I was at home, it felt much longer.

"I think I'll give you guys some time." Jack started backing out of the room, and I smiled gratefully at him, but he just nodded and shut the door behind him.

"Nice digs." Milo admired my new bedroom, and I knew he was thinking the same thing that I had; it was surprisingly me. "Did they do this for you?"

"I think Mae did some redecorating or something," I shrugged.

"So, how are they treating you?" He sat tentatively at the edge of the bed, afraid that I might kick him out at any minute for invading my privacy or something.

"Really good. They seem happy to have me around." I twirled my phone in my hands, watching Milo carefully. "How's Mom?"

"Good. She misses you, I think. I mean, she won't say it. But she wants you back at home." When he looked at me, his worried eyes looked sad. "Are you gonna come home?" Then he cast a derisive look around my room. "Nah, I guess not. This is probably all too much to pass up for our little apartment. There it's just me. Here, you have Jack."

"It's not like that." Guilt rushed over me. I pictured Milo sitting sadly in that apartment, making exotic meals just for one, and I wanted to cry.

"Then what is it like?" Milo demanded. He wasn't angry; he just wanted to know what was going on with me. "To be honest, I was a little surprised that you and Jack had separate bedrooms. Or is that just for show?"

"There's nobody to show," I grumbled, avoiding his insistent stare.

"Alice, why are you here?" he asked wearily.

That was the question at the heart of it all, the one that I couldn't precisely answer. As much as they'd given me the run around of being "meant" for Peter and "bonded" with Jack, and to a lesser extent, Ezra, none of it was really a suitable answer for Milo. It was just like I was supposed to be here, with them, but an answer like that would only lead to more questions.

"It's just where I want to be for now," I finally said. It didn't sound good enough, and I could tell by his expression that it wasn't. "They're really nice to me."

"And I wasn't?" Milo retorted, sounding a combination of hurt and incredulous. "I mean, if you're not with Jack, and you're not just about the money, then... What do you do here all night long? Are you drinking? Is it drugs?"

"No, no, it's nothing like that." I shook my head and had to fight the smile that wanted to creep up at the word "drinking."

"I'm just trying to understand why you won't come home." By then, he was nearly pleading with me, and it broke my heart. "I can get Mom off your back, if you could just try to get home before she does. And you don't have to hang out with me all the time, but I'll help you with your homework and I can make you supper. Then you could just come out here and hang out with them. You don't have to live here."

"I'm not living here." Swallowing hard, I tried not to look at him. When he was sad, he looked so young. He had big innocent brown eyes, and they were so forlorn. "I just need some time here to figure things out, okay? But don't think for a second that I'm going to leave you behind. You mean too much for me to walk away from you, not even for a foxy guy and a lot of money."

"What do you need to figure out?" Milo furrowed his brow, but I could tell that he'd relaxed a little.

I decided to tell him the truth on this one. "What I'm going to do with the rest of my life."

"You're thinking about college?" He brightened at that, and I knew that I'd inadvertently opened the door for all sorts of college talk that I really didn't want to listen to.

"Among other things." College had vaguely crossed my mind, as in, hey since I'll be a rich vampire I won't have to go to college anymore.

"I know you were mostly being sarcastic, but I started doing some research on med school and psychiatry for you, and there are lots of fabulous opportunities because we're so close to the Mayo Clinic." The tangent had started, and he was moving his hands and talking excitedly.

"Milo, you've seen my grades," I tried to nip his enthusiasm in the bud. "There's no way I could get into med school."

"You've got time to turn it around," he brushed me off. "The U of M has a lot of great programs too, and if you really worked hard your first couple of years, it would be so fantastic for you."

"I'm sure it would," I mumbled.

I decided to let him just go on, nodding and agreeing when the conversation required. He was happy to be talking about something he was an expert on, and something that still included me in his future.

After awhile, he finally managed to run out of steam and informed me that he'd brought over some leftovers to eat. Mae had gone grocery shopping yesterday, so there was some food in the house for me, but it didn't compare to anything that Milo made, particularly since nobody here could cook.

When we went downstairs to eat, Jack joined us, claiming that he had already eaten, of course. He sat with us at the table, scratching Matilda's head and chattering along with Milo.

It had been days since Milo had been able to have a real conversation, so he had plenty to fill us in on. Like the impossibility of a level in *World of Warcraft* (something about orcs and letter abbreviations that seemed completely random to both Jack and me, but sounded very grave when Milo said them), and how bitchy Jane has been at school since I've been gone.

There was also some rather juicy gossip about this boy, Troy, at school, who Milo deemed "utterly foxy" and then blushed so red, it looked like he'd been burned.

Apparently, the young man in question had made some rather flirtatious advances towards Milo in gym class, and he didn't know how to reciprocate. Jack advised him not to make any moves at school, in case things are being misinterpreted, he wouldn't want an audience. Milo agreed that he should do some fact checking on Twitter and Facebook, and then maybe he'd escalate to text messaging from there.

It was getting late, and Milo started mentioning an Intro to Business test he had to study for, so Jack took him home. I rode with, just for the fun of it, and Milo was still an endless stream of conversation. He explained the finer points of running a small business, and Jack somehow managed to sound interested in all of it.

"That was fun," Jack grinned at me once Milo had gotten out of the car.

"I don't know if you're being sarcastic or not, but it really was." Then I smiled gratefully at him. "Thank you. I really missed him."

"It sounds like he missed you, too." Sadly, he sighed, and at first, I didn't understand why. We had all had fun, so I didn't see what could be so depressing about that. "This isn't going to be quite so clean cut for you, not like it was for me."

"You mean leaving your family?" I asked. Up until Mae mentioned his family the other day, I hadn't heard anything about them. The only thing Jack had ever told me was that he was from Stillwater.

"Yeah. My dad was a bastard, but he was dead anyway. My mom hated me because she hated all men, and my sister barely knew me. There was nothing to miss, nothing to leave behind." Pursing his lips, he turned to me. "Not like you. He'll be devastated when you go."

"I know." Tears were brimming at my eyes, and I blinked them back.

"Don't think that I'm saying this because I don't want you to turn. You know how badly I want you to." The way he said it made him sound desperate for me to turn, but I understood. "But I know this isn't going to be easy for you. And I don't want you to make your decisions based on me or anyone else."

"I won't."

My heart pulled me into separate directions, and the only solution seemed to be to tear it in two.

Peter still hadn't returned from the business trip, and I still hadn't made a decision. My entire life felt like it was at an impasse.

To keep me busy, Jack had taken me to a play and the zoo, but neither of those things really alleviated anything that was going on. Everything felt so up in the air, and I knew that I had to deal with things before the uncertainty killed me.

As soon as I woke up, I went downstairs in my jammies with my hair all messed up and my eyes full of sleep. Ezra sat on the chaise lounge, reading a book, and Mae sat near his feet, doing a large puzzle on the hardwood floor.

When I had gotten up, I heard the shower running in Jack's room, so I assumed that's where he was. He'd be otherwise occupied, making the conversation easier.

"Is something the matter?" Ezra looked me over.

"Are you alright, love?" Mae chimed in, looking equally worried.

"When is Peter coming home?" I asked.

"I don't know for sure." Ezra adjusted himself so he was sitting up fully. "Would you like me to call him and find out?"

"What's going to happen when he comes home?" I crossed my arms on my chest, trying to look tough, even though I knew it was as ridiculous as it sounded. "Well?"

"We don't know exactly," Ezra answered carefully.

"He hates me." Just saying it aloud it hurt, but it didn't change any of the facts. "Or if you prefer, he hates the way he feels about me. That's not gonna change when he comes home, is it?"

"We don't really understand what's happening with the two of you. I can't answer that," Ezra said evasively.

"What are you trying to find out?" Mae asked.

"If Peter doesn't want me, then what's the point of me turning?" I asked. They exchanged looks but didn't immediately answer me. "Are you expecting that he'll magically change his mind when he gets back?"

"Not really, no," Ezra admitted honestly.

"Then what is the point of all of this?" I gestured to everything around me, wondering what they were getting out of putting me up and hanging around me like this.

"All of what?" Jack bounded down the stairs and into the living room, running a hand through his damp hair, and I grimaced inwardly. I had decided to have this talk now because I knew he wouldn't be around.

"She wants to know what's going to happen once Peter comes back," Ezra explained when it appeared that I wouldn't.

I shifted uneasily and looked over at Jack, who had suddenly become very nervous. His blue eyes flitted over me, then he turned to Ezra and Mae for help.

Ezra had discarded his book on the chaise, and Mae smiled helplessly towards us. I knew they didn't have a good answer. Things had been set in motion, and while they didn't really have any plans to change them, there was no real reason for them to move forward anymore.

"He's not gonna want me, Jack," I said miserably. "What's the point of me turning?"

"What's the point of anyone turning?" Jack scoffed and looked away from me. "Come on, Alice. There isn't a point to any of this!"

"There has to be a point!" I shouted, surprised by the quavering in my voice. It was just starting to hit me what I was saying, what I was rejecting, and I could tell by the stunned, hurt expression on his face that it was sinking in too. "If I'm going to destroy my brother's life, it has to be for a reason!"

"You're not going to destroy his life!" Jack rubbed his forehead and closed his eyes. "So what if Peter doesn't ever change his mind? Good! I hope he doesn't! They want you here! I want you here!"

"Doesn't that give me even more of a reason not to turn?" I gave him a hard look. The kiss wanted to replay itself in my mind, but I couldn't let it, or Jack might react to my heartbeat.

"That doesn't even make sense."

He tried to pretend like he didn't understand, but the quick movement of his eyes led me to believe he did. That kiss had been incredible, and the risk of us doing it again was too great. He would've bit me if Mae hadn't walked in, and we couldn't count on her to walk in at just the right moment every time we were alone.

"Jack, it's not good for either of us for me to stay around," I told him with tears in my eyes.

"No!" Jack insisted fiercely. "That's just stupid! I don't know what went wrong. I don't know why your blood is for him, but it's a mistake! Okay? You're not supposed to be for him! And there's gotta be a way around it! It may take time, but we have all of eternity to figure it out! You really wanna throw that away just because I don't have the answer right now?"

"Why did you even introduce me to him?" I blurted out. "If I had never met him, this wouldn't have happened! This wouldn't have mattered! Why did you push me on him?"

"I never pushed you on him, never!" He took a step towards me, then changed his mind, and took a step back. Shaking his head, he breathed deeply. "I didn't know any of this. I wasn't reacting right to you, and they thought that you were for Peter. And I didn't realize what I..." He trailed off, looking at the floor.

"You two had connected in a way that none of had realized," Ezra elaborated. "It wasn't until he started feeling threatened by Peter that we appreciated what was happening, and by then it was too late."

Slowly, he got up and walked over to us, attempting to relieve some of the tension.

"None of us are trying to pressure you into a decision, but Jack has made valid points," Ezra continued. "You turning isn't about Peter, and it shouldn't be. You have a future with us, if you choose it."

He nodded once at me, and then made an imperceptible motion towards Mae. She rose quickly and they left the room, leaving Jack and I alone.

We were supposed to hash things out and come up with some kind of resolution, but I didn't know how. It wasn't until I was yelling at Jack that I even knew it hurt me that he'd ever wanted me to be with Peter.

I'd doubted everything since Ezra had claimed that Jack had fallen in love with me. Because if he truly loved me, then why would he ever want me to be with his brother?

"I've made a lot of mistakes with you," Jack admitted quietly. "But I need a chance to rectify them. If you give me time, I swear I can make it up to you." He looked at me, his wounded blue eyes pleading with me to stay.

I wanted nothing more than to be with him, but would it really be worth it? I'd have to give up my brother, and I'd still be trapped in something painful and inescapable with his brother. We couldn't actually be together, no matter what decision I made.

"If you give me time, I know that between Ezra, Peter, and I, we can find a solution to this." Jack took a step towards me, trying to decide whether or not to touch me, before finally deciding against it. "I promise you. There is a way for it to work."

"That doesn't answer everything," I said. In fact, that didn't really answer anything. It was just a vague promise to solve something someday, but it was still a hard offer to resist.

"Milo's your brother, and he's a bright kid. He's not gonna need you forever," he pointed out gently. "In a few more years, when he starts dating and going to college, he's not even gonna wanna be around you. It's just for right now that he needs you."

"That's probably true." I was about to argue that it didn't change anything, but then I understood what he was getting at. "I'm still really young. I could stay with Milo for another three or four years. I could still turn, and I'd still be younger than you are."

"And we don't have to move for another three years or so," Jack nodded in agreement. "Until then, you can keep living with Milo, and Ezra and I can figure out what we're gonna do about all of this."

"Would that be okay?" I asked, looking up at him.

"Why wouldn't it be?" He shrugged, and he had calmed enough where he could grin at the idea. "It's just a couple years. It means nothing to us."

"You don't care what I say as long as I agree to be with you," I smiled.

"That's probably true."

"What if I decided not to change? And I got all old and wrinkly? Would you still want to be around me then?"

"How wrinkly are we talking about?" Jack teased.

I tried to swat him playfully, but he grabbed my arm and pulled me to him. His arms were strong and reassuring around me, and he rested his hand on my cheek, gently forcing me to look into his eyes. His skin was warming up, but he tried not to notice.

"This will work out. Somehow," he promised.

After talking it all over with Mae and Ezra, they agreed with my decision. Time was inconsequential to them, and Mae wanted me to have more time to consider everything.

They also agreed that for both Jack's sake and mine, it would be better if I stayed at home until we got things straightened out in the whole Peter arena. Mae had filled Ezra in on the kiss, and he chastised us for such risky behavior. Peter was a much stronger vampire than Jack, and a rather large threat to both of us.

When I walked in the door with the massive duffle bag slung over my shoulder, Milo was sitting at the computer. As soon as he saw me, his entire face lit up and he rushed over to me, throwing his arms tightly around me and almost knocking me over.

"You're back!" he squealed.

"Sure am." I pried him off, smiling at his exuberance. "Do you think Mom'll mind?"

"I don't know why she would!" Milo looked like he was going to explode. He had truly believed that I wasn't coming back, and for awhile, so had I. "She's at work right now, but I'm sure she won't care."

"I hope not." I knew I had some penance to do with her, and I wasn't looking forward to that. Or getting up for school the next morning, especially since I had spent the last few nights on a vampire sleeping schedule.

"Why did you come back?"

"I figured that somebody had to be here to help take care of you." I reached out and ruffled his hair, and he pulled away, just like I thought he would.

"I'm not a little kid." He smoothed out his hair, but I hadn't even really messed it up. "And besides that, I spend more time taking care of you than you do me."

"That is true," I smiled.

Milo had never really needed anyone to do anything for him. He just kinda wanted somebody to be there, and I could at least manage that.

"On the subject of which, I should probably whip us up some supper." He went over to the fridge, talking amicably about the extravagant meal he had planned for us tonight. Leaning against the kitchen counter, watching him as he worked, I knew that I made the right choice to stay with him.

When I went to school the next day, Jane looked pleased to see me. I'd been standing at my locker, juggling my books, when she walked past me, smiling in her overly seductive way, and murmured, "Good to have you back, Alice."

Admittedly, it'd only been three days since I'd last been to school, but it had been much longer than that since I hung out with her, and I'd barely been active in my own life. At school and at home, I'd been a zombie.

There was no separation in the two lives, though. They were all part of me and what I was doing. I went to high school, hung out with my brother, gossiped with Jane, and in my free time, I hung out with vampires.

Nothing about me had really changed, and even as mind boggling as the events of the last month had been, I was still just plain old Alice Bonham, and that's the way it was going to stay. For a few more years at least.

So when Jane walked past me, I got my books together and bolted after her. She must've really missed me, because she actually stopped to wait for me when I called her name. After a few friendly jabs about being missing in action lately, I filled her in as best I could about what had been happening my life lately, conveniently leaving out the stuff about vampires.

At home, I let Milo help me with the Calculus homework, which really seemed unnecessary. I would make it my life's mission to never, ever find a use for that particular information. Milo made something delicious with salmon for supper and enlightened me on his progress (or the lack thereof) with his new crush, Troy.

All in all, my life felt like it had hit some kind of stride, and maybe I really could get comfortable with all of this.

Jack text messaged me, saying he'd be over in twenty minutes to pick me up. I got ready, and Milo warned me that I had to be up early for school, and I promised I'd be back before one. That still seemed too late for him, and six hours of sleep did not sound like enough to me, but I had to find a balance.

While outside waiting for Jack to pick me up, something startled me. I was *waiting* for Jack. No matter how fast I rushed through getting ready, he was invariably waiting for me. But I had been waiting for so long, that I'd actually gotten a little chill and had to pull my sweater around me.

I dug out my phone to text him just as a silver Audi slid up in front of me, and my heart twirled nervously.

Even through the dark glass of the car window, I saw Peter's green eyes burning at me. That incessant pull that had slowly faded the last few days returned with a vengeance.

My body started to shake, but not because I was cold. My heart started beating in the way that drove Jack mad, and I wondered if Peter felt the same way. I opened the car door and got inside, preparing myself to find out.

- 22 -

Instead of saying anything to me, Peter squealed away from the curb, keeping his eyes locked on the road in front of us. His jaw tensed, and he gripped the wheel tightly.

The car was completely full of the tantalizing scent of him, and my mouth actually started to salivate. We had never been in such close quarters before, and it felt like a bad idea.

Even as close as I was to him, my heart tugged on me to move closer, to reach out and brush my hand against his flawless skin, so I clasped my hands together.

"I just got back," Peter said at length.

The silence felt thick and overwhelming, but I couldn't think of anything to fill it with. My head swam. I felt the hunger for him, burning and frantic, like a rush of adrenaline, only much more intoxicating. By the time we'd get to his house, I'd be delirious with him.

"We need to talk," Peter murmured huskily, allowing his haunting gaze to settle on me for a moment.

"I know."

In my mind, I'd been imagining the conversation with him over and over again. Although since I'd kissed Jack, I'd been envisioning it with me rejecting him, instead of persuading him to be with me.

Once I was with him, filled with his lust, I couldn't imagine not being with Peter. Every part of me screamed that I really had been made for him, no matter what my heart said when he wasn't around.

Despite his proclamation that we needed to talk, he said nothing for the remainder of the car ride.

I couldn't take my eyes off him, and I barely noticed his lack of attention towards me. The days away from him had made me forget how absolutely breathtaking he was.

When we got to his house, the tiniest part of me that wasn't completely enamored with him felt trepidation at seeing Jack. I had no idea how he would react, but fortunately, he wasn't around. I imagined that he was in the house somewhere, but since Peter eclipsed everything for me, I couldn't feel him anxiously hiding nearby.

Mae and Ezra were in the living room, but I barely noticed the tentative way they eyed us up as we walked up the stairs to his room. Peter still hadn't said anything to me, but I followed one step behind him, as if he led me on a string.

"I don't know what they've been telling you while I was gone," Peter told me finally. I had sat down on the edge of his bed, and he stood on the other side of his room, his arms crossed firmly over his chest and refusing to look at me. "But this cannot work."

"What?"

I tried to play innocent, but there was already a welling despair inside me. It seemed ridiculous since I had survived all this time without him. There had been a constant dull ache, but it was nothing that I couldn't live with.

But when I was with him, the thought of being without him felt unbearable.

"It's not the same as it was before," he explained quietly. "The way I feel about you, it's not right. My body insists that it's you, but the rest of me..." He shook his head. "I don't think I should be around you anymore."

"Are you banning me from the house?" I had just come to terms with what was happening, and he was going to take everything away from me.

"I think that this is an impossible situation." He looked over at me, his eyes betraying the hurt and want he had for me. "I can't be with you, and Jack can't be with you. He's tried to hide his feelings about you from me, but I know he feels something for you. Neither of us can be with you, so having you around would be torture."

"That isn't fair!" I jumped to my feet, and already hot tears sliced down my cheeks. He had a finality to his voice that devastated me. "Do they all agree with you? They can't! Ezra-"

"They support my decision," Peter cut me off decisively. "All of them are very fond of you, but it can't work. And since you are 'mine,' it's up to me what we do with you."

"'What you do with me?'" I sobbed. "This is my life! Why do you get to decide what is done with me?"

"Your life is my life. That's how this works."

"Then isn't your life mine?" I clenched my fists, trying desperately to find some ground to stand on.

"That's not how this works," Peter shook his head. "You are human. You have no standing over us."

"So you're all just …"

The room was spinning, and I rested my hand on the bed to keep from collapsing. He was going to take everything from me. The insistent way my body begged for him, the way my heart longed for Jack, the comfort I gained from Mae and Ezra, and the glorious future I had just mapped out for myself.

With his simple, cold words, he was ripping everything away. The ground felt like it was giving way from underneath me, and I had to swallow hard to keep from vomiting.

"Alice, we never meant to hurt you." He sounded sad, but I could barely see him through my own tears.

Part of me wanted to run through house searching for Jack. I knew he would fight for me, make them change their minds, but I felt too weak. More than that, if Peter didn't want me, it didn't even seem worth fighting for.

"You're killing me," I mumbled.

Then it dawned on me. It felt like he was literally killing me. Every part of me, physical and otherwise, was in pain. But I knew that inside him there was a primal hunger for me. I saw how fierce it had been in Jack's eyes, and it had to be stronger in Peter.

"Peter, why don't you just bite me?" I asked breathlessly.

"No," Peter responded hoarsely. "That's a horrible idea."

"No, Peter! Listen!" I walked over to him, willing my heart to beat harder and faster, so the sound would overwhelm him. "I know you want to! You can just bite me, and this will all be over with. I'll be out of your lives forever, and I won't even care. And what do I even matter to you? I'm just another stupid weak human, and you've killed them before."

"I'm not going to kill you." He tried to sound disgusted, but the hunger was at the back of his throat. When he looked away from me, I grabbed his arm and forced him to look down at me.

"Please," I pleaded.

He still resisted the idea, so I remembered what had sent Jack over the edge. I bit my lip, hard, and before I could even tell it was bleeding, his eyes had widened. For him, my scent and taste were irresistible.

"You really want this?" Peter murmured huskily. His eyes looked conflicted, both sad and ravenous. "Do you even understand what you're asking?"

"I know that I can't live the rest of my life without you."

If my mind wasn't an absolute mess from its intoxication over Peter, I might have been able to handle things better. Even if my body hadn't been insisting that I was incapable of surviving without Peter, it would still have been devastating.

I truly planned to spend forever with Jack. It'd be impossible to go to school, to college, to go about my tedious little life and spend every day getting older, sicker, dying, and trying to forget them. I couldn't do it, and I didn't even want to try. It hurt far too much.

"Forgive me," Peter whispered.

Before I could say anything more, I felt his lips pressed hotly on my neck, and then this sharp pain shot into me, like the prick of a needle. It was quickly replaced by this wonderful, warm pleasure spreading through me. It felt so intensely marvelous that I couldn't even imagine ever having felt pain.

My body trembled and went limp in his arms, and I heard myself moaning. Ecstasy rippled through me, and I wanted this moment to last forever.

Faintly, I became aware of how weak I felt. At first, it had just been because the pleasure had struck me so forcefully, and even though it still felt amazing, I could feel my life draining away.

Some part of me knew I was dying, but there was nothing frightening or bad about it. I felt oddly at peace, and I let myself succumb to the drowsy, perfection that flooded over me.

My thoughts were dissolving. There were incoherent images of the sun shining over the tops of the building, and Peter's green eyes, and Jack's laughter. I thought of my brother, and I hoped he understood.

Then there was nothing except the way I felt, buried underneath a warm blanket. My heart had slowed considerably, and my lungs felt empty.

The sharp pain of separation hit me suddenly, along with an intense chill. My mind felt strangely alert, but I didn't even have the strength to open my eyelids.

I could hear the commotion going on around me. Peter wasn't holding me anymore, but I couldn't tell where I was. I just knew that his arms weren't around me and his mouth wasn't pressed to my neck. He had stopped too soon, and I was still alive.

There were banging noises and the sounds of rustling feet. Voices were shouting, and it took a minute for me to able to focus in on them clearly.

Jack was shouting at Peter, calling him all sorts of hateful names, and Peter was saying very little in his own defense. Then Ezra's voice boomed in, and the movement stopped. He had broken up the fight.

"He tried to kill her!" Jack cried, and I could hear the terrified desperation in his voice.

"But she's not dead," Ezra told him soothingly. I felt his strong hands touching my face, feeling my pulse and inspecting the damage. I wanted to yell at them, to tell them to leave me here to die, but I barely even had the strength to breathe, let alone speak. "She's lost a lot of blood."

"She wanted me to do it," Peter muttered, and this was followed by a loud smacking sound.

"Jack! Peter!" Ezra roared. "If you want to save her life, then you have to listen to me!"

"I don't know if I want to save her life," Peter told them quietly.

Ezra let go of my face so he could rush over to separate the fight. I could hear their bodies slamming against each other, and Jack growling viciously.

"Peter, step out," Ezra commanded. "And tell Mae that we need type O negative. We should have some in the cooler downstairs."

"She's going to be alright?" Jack whimpered.

"Peter's right...." I managed breathlessly.

Jack crouched beside me, and I could feel how devastated and powerless he felt. He started saying something to me but forcing myself to speak had used up at the last of my energy. Everything around me fell black and silent.

Slowly and somewhat reluctantly, I felt myself rising to the surface. I blinked several times, letting my eyes adjust to the dim light of the bedroom. I had rather expected to open my eyes and find myself in purgatory.

Instead, I was in the room in the turret, the bedroom that had been mine. A weird weakness washed over me, as if I was lying underneath a weighted blanket, and I still had residuals of the intense pleasure from when Peter had bit me.

I also felt relieved and apprehensive, but I couldn't understand why. They seemed out of place with everything that had happened, but then I stirred a little and found the source of the emotions.

"Hey," Jack whispered. He'd been sitting in a chair in the corner of the room, but when he saw me waking up, he came over and climbed on the bed next to me. "How are you feeling?"

"Really, really tired," I said groggily, and when he smiled, I saw there were tears in his eyes.

He brushed the hair from my eyes, and his fingers traced down the side of my face, past my jaw line, and lingered on the trace of the bite Peter had left on my throat. His expression hardened painfully, so I swallowed and looked away.

"Am I gonna have to go?" I asked.

"You can stay as long as you want." He moved his hand from my neck, resting it on the covers over my stomach.

"Peter said that I wouldn't be allowed to see any of you anymore," I told him thickly. A deep pain welled in my chest at the thought of it, and even without Peter here fogging up my mind, suicide didn't seem like that bad of an idea.

"No. That's not going to happen," Jack said firmly. "I had agreed to it temporarily, until we could get things sorted out better. Peter was convinced that he couldn't be around you, and apparently, that wasn't far from the truth." Just mentioning Peter made his voice fill with a deep anger, and I felt a jealous protectiveness radiate from him. "After what happened, we decided that was a horrible decision. So Peter's gone."

"What do you mean he's gone?" I looked at him plaintively, and Jack tried to hide that it hurt him that I was even asking about Peter.

"He's going to go out on his own for awhile. He's done it before." Jack shrugged, like it wasn't anything for me to concern myself with. "We all just think it would be better for him not to be around you, at least not while you're still human."

"So he just won't see you guys for three or four years?" I was tearing their family apart, and that did little to make me feel better. Admittedly, I wanted to be around Jack and his family more than I wanted to be alive, but not at the cost of ruining their lives.

"No, he won't see you for three or four years," he corrected me. "And maybe me too. But trust me, I don't really have any urge to see him."

"It's not his fault," I insisted quietly. Jack scoffed and looked away from me. "It's really not. I asked him to do it."

"He knew better." He shook his head seriously. "He knows how much…" Just the thought of me dying agonized him. "If you had died,

I would've killed him. It would've completely destroyed everything we had here, and he knew that."

"You can't kill him over me," I said. "I don't want to be the cause of your family's destruction."

"Well, then don't do anything stupid like getting yourself killed." He had meant to sound joking, but it came out more as if he was pleading with me. "It's too late, Alice. You already mean too much to us. Dying doesn't change that."

"How am I still alive?" I attempted to change the subject.

"Ezra gave you a blood transfusion with the blood bags we have," he explained casually.

"He can do that?" I felt wide eyed. Blood transfusions probably weren't the most difficult of procedures, but still, he'd saved my life.

"He can do anything." Brushing it off, he smiled at me. "When you're around for three-hundred years and you're life revolves around blood, you pick up a thing or two about it."

"So what happens now?"

"You need to get some rest, because the blood loss makes you tired and weak. And then I'll take you home in the morning, so you can go to school." His blue eyes looked softly at me.

For the first time, I could really feel how much he loved me. It was like a warm, safe blanket wrapped around me, and I tried to ignore the aching pain in my chest for Peter.

"Thank you," I whispered.

"There's nothing to thank me for."

Settling more into the bed, he reached out and pulled me over to him. Wrapping his arms securely around me, I rested my head on his chest and listened to the slow, faint sound of his heart beat.

I felt totally and completely safe with him, and I wanted to stay that way forever.

Nothing between us had really been solved. For now, our best solution was simply to send Peter away, but who knew how long Peter would really be gone for?

Until things were in place, I would just have to go about living my life as normally as possible. Going to school because it made my mother and Milo happy and hanging out with Jane so I didn't become too dependent on Jack for my happiness (even though I had a feeling that it was already too late for that). While I still had the chance, I would spend as much time as I could with Milo.

But really, it was only a matter of time before everything changed. I snuggled deeper into Jack's arms and tried not to worry about any of that now.

Read an excerpt from the second installment in the *My Blood Approves* series:

Fate – available now:

Summer nights were too short. Vampires spent more time indoors in the summer, but heat didn't agree with them anyway.

Jack lived in a beautiful house on the lake. It would be a rather conventional square house if not for the balconies and the turret that connected the house to the garage. As many times as I had been here, it never really stopped being intimidating.

We spent a great deal of the summer in the backyard, either lounging on the stone patio or swimming in the lake or taking out the Jet-Ski's. Milo and I spent so much time on the water that Mae bought us several swimsuits to keep at the house.

I changed into my suit, keeping the towel wrapped around me when I came out of the bathroom, and Milo had already changed into his swim trunks. He sat at the island in the kitchen, munching on some grapes, and helping Mae.

Mae had been the eldest when she turned, at twenty-eight. Her skin was flawless white porcelain, and her caramel waves of hair had been pulled into a loose bun. Wearing only her bathing suit and an apron, her warm, honey-colored eyes danced as Milo talked to her.

As a vampire, she didn't eat, and since Milo was an excellent cook, he became her sous chef, helping her prepare all the meals she made for our benefit. I would've protested all the extra work and expense Mae put into it, but it was obvious that she relished this sorta thing.

"Where's Ezra?" I asked, walking over to the island and stealing a grape. Mae was making some kind of fruit dip with cream cheese and yogurt, and slicing up apples, pears, and strawberries.

"He's taking a nap," Mae informed me in her warm, British accent. "He's a little jet lagged from the trip."

Like the other two boys, Ezra was incredibly attractive. His eyes were deep mahogany and infinitely warm. His skin was the same tanned color as Jack and Peter's, and his sandy hair had soft blond streaks through it.

The most powerful thing about Ezra was his voice. It was low and resonated through everything. He had a faded accent that came from being born in England, but he hadn't lived in Europe in over two-hundred years.

Through the glass French doors off the dining room, I saw Jack rollicking about with his Great Pyrenees, Matilda. The deck lights revealed the taut muscles of his chest and back as he rolled around with her. The stones of the patio should've left him battered and bruised, but he'd have nothing to show from it.

"Alice, do you wanna try it?" Mae asked, pulling my gaze away from Jack. She held out an apple slice covered in dip, but I shook my head.

"I'm getting pretty chilly. I think I'm gonna head outside."

"I'll be out in a minute," Milo said through the mouthful of the fruit he'd sampled.

"Okay," I nodded and headed out the French doors into the night.

Jack ventured off the patio in his pursuit of Matilda, but I saw easily in the light of the full moon. It was much warmer outside than it had been in the house, but I kept the towel wrapped around me. I walked down the patio onto the small lawn that separated the house from the lake.

Matilda caught sight of me and bounded towards me. She'd knock me over, since she was used to vampires who could handle her lunging at them, but Jack overtook her and playfully tackled her. Then he stood up, brushing the grass from his swim trunks, and grinned at me.

"Are you gonna go swimming with the towel too?" Jack teased.

"Maybe." I pulled the towel more tightly around me, and he laughed.

Matilda sniffed me heartily before concluding that it was only me, and then sauntered off, wagging her tail slowly behind her.

A mischievous glint caught Jack's eye, and after spending a summer getting thrown in the lake, I knew exactly what it meant. Dropping my towel, I turned and ran towards the dock. He trailed a few steps behind me, even though he could easily sprint past me. The sport was in the chase for him.

I almost made it to the edge of the dock when I felt his strong arms looping around my waist. I squealed and let him twirl me around once before he released me, sending me soaring into the air and landing in the lake with a loud splash.

Jack took a running jump and leapt out, flying over me and splashing way out in the lake. He howled excitedly, as if he hadn't made that same jump a million times.

"Jack!" Mae leaned out the French doors and shouted out at him. "You've got to keep it down so the neighbors don't call the police again." It was after midnight on a Wednesday, and the neighbors weren't big fans of the noise.

"Yeah, Alice," Jack said.

"Oh, whatever," I rolled my eyes. "As if I'm even half as loud as you are."

Jack laughed, taking long strokes out farther into the black water. He swam slow circles around me, but I was content to float on my back, staring up at the full moon and the stars shining.

I had never really had the courage to swim too far from the shore when the water was so dark. I always had these horrible visions of being eaten by some unseen monster coming up from the depths of the lake.

Milo joined us in the lake a bit later. Mae stayed inside to continue chopping fruit. She always went overboard trying to feed us. We were just two people, but she cooked like we were an army. It only made it more obvious when they didn't eat anything, but Milo had only made a few comments about it.

Surprisingly, he hadn't really caught on that they weren't human. Jack had been more discreet about his paranormal abilities, but Milo was a smart kid. I thought that he suspected something but let it go, because they didn't seem dangerous and they made me happy.

"It's a really beautiful night out," Milo said. He floated on his back, admiring the night like I was.

"It's been a fantastic summer."

"I can't believe it's almost over," Milo sighed.

"Don't remind me!" I cringed.

"It won't be so bad."

School was only three short weeks away. Milo tried to convince me that it had little effect on my life, but it changed everything. There'd be no more all-nighters with Jack, and soon everything would get cold and snowy, and Milo would make me do homework.

Something grabbed me and pulled me under. I tried to scream but water buried me. I pictured some evil sea creature coming to eat my soul. Clawing my way to the surface, I grabbed onto something strong and soft and pulled myself up.

As soon as I reached for him, Jack pulled me up out of the water and let me cling on to him. Over my own frightened gasps, I heard him laughing softly, and I realized he'd been the one that grabbed my ankle. After a summer of similar antics, I should've caught on that Jack thought it was funny scaring the crap out of me.

I should've slapped him or told him he was a jerk, but the feel of his arms distracted me. His chest pressed up against mine, and he had to feel the frantic beating of my heart that drove him crazy.

I looked up in his soft blue eyes, and I felt breathless for a whole new reason. His laughter died down, and his smile faltered as his body temperature started to rise, smoldering against my skin.

Ordinarily, he would've pushed me away by now, but he let me linger in his arms. My thoughts went back to that amazing kiss, and I tilted in towards him, hoping he'd let go just long enough for one innocent kiss.

"Hey! Look! A shooting star!" Milo shouted.

It was just enough for Jack to realize what was happening, so he pushed me back and swam away. Jack did everything he could to keep from letting things get out of hand, and sometimes that meant that he'd physically push me away. It was getting harder to shrug off, though.

Although I hadn't asked about it, his temperature only seemed to rise when things between us got physical. During the crazy passionate kiss, his skin had felt like it was on fire.

"Did you see it?" Milo asked.

I meant to shoot him an angry glare for disrupting my rare moment with Jack, but then I saw Milo just staring blissfully at the sky. He hadn't been paying attention to anything but the stars, so he hadn't known that he'd interrupted.

"Nah, sorry, I missed it," I said

"There'll probably be another one," Milo assured me, and I probably sounded very heavy with regret. Sure, I do love a good shooting star, but kisses with Jack were even a rarer commodity.

"I hope so."

I treaded water, and Jack moved on to harassing Matilda. He'd gotten very good at finding ways to ignore me. Poor Matilda stood at the end of the dock, barking her refusal to jump in. Milo tired of his stargaze so he went over to join Jack in cajoling the dog in the water.

Being in the water suddenly didn't feel like much fun. The adrenaline from the near sea monster death, followed by the near kiss, left my body feeling achy and tired. I knew Jack would do his best to steer clear of me for awhile, and even if I understood the routine, it didn't feel good.

"I think I'm gonna head back inside and see if Mae needs a hand," I said to no one in particular, which was just as well. Matilda was far more captivating than I was.

By the time I made it to the shore, I heard the loud splash and their shouts of triumph. Matilda finally jumped in the water. If only my resolution with Jack could be that simple.

Wrapping the towel around me, I stepped in through the French doors. My skin froze instantly, thanks to the artic draft from the air conditioner. Amy Winehouse blasted out of the stereo, Mae's one new guilty pleasure. Jack was always trying to get her to listen to new music, and so far the only things that took were Winehouse and Norah Jones.

Mae danced around the kitchen, singing into a spatula, and despite my aggravation over the Jack situation, I couldn't help but laugh.

"Oh my gosh!" Mae put her hand over her heart and her golden eyes flashed with embarrassment. "You scared me!"

"Couldn't you hear me come in?" I asked as she turned down the stereo. "Aren't you guys supposed to have super hearing or something?"

"Well, yes, when we're paying attention," Mae smiled sheepishly at me. The fruit snack looked complete and nicely arranged on the island, and she was just cleaning up when I interrupted.

"Do you need a hand?" I offered.